1 Bat

No. 2 P_____,

88 Keys,

&

Liberace:

Musical Recollections by Bo Ayars

My years with "Mr. Showmanship,"

"The King," and others

who made Vegas, Vegas

Bo Ayars

Published by BookLocker.com, Inc., Bradenton, Florida.

Printed on acid-free paper.

BookLocker.com, Inc.
2016

First Edition

Cover design: Joni DeRouchie

Book layout: Mark Merrill

Editor & Back cover: Elie Charpentier

Acknowledgments

You're strolling down a street, heading somewhere, but not sure where. That's when you need directions, help, and support. And that's what this book has been to me, a stroll down the path of my life, seventy-five years so far, during which time I've received much-needed support from my parents; my sister, Penny; my two sons, JJ and Evan; and my wife, Barbara.

Listen, if you're not happy with this book, you can blame her. She's the one who started it by saying, "I'm so tired of hearing these same stories over and over. Why don't you just write a book?"

And here it is.

I was introduced to Mark Merrill, who painstakingly recorded all of my words, sitting with me at a bench in Columbia Park, organizing, encouraging, and suggesting.

Then I met Elie Charpentier, my editor, who fixed commas, spellings, and, in her late-night madness, helped craft the book into, well, a book.

Thank you to my friends here in Portland: Dave Duthie, my boat partner; Warren Black, who helped me keep my focus; Tony Starlight and Ms. Starlight for their constant encouragement and friendship; all the musicians with whom I've gigged; and the many fans and friends of Liberace, some of whom, like Hildegarde Lindstrom, I've known since my first days with Lee.

And many thanks to the Liberace Foundation for the Creative and Performing Arts, which has helped keep the name of this legendary performer in the public eye. Liberace was, indeed, one-of-a-kind, and I thank him for thirteen years of musical fun, travel, and learning what a true showman is.

A MEMENTO

Table of Contents

Prelude:

An Introductory Piece of Music, Especially for the Piano

It's late January 1973 in a large arena in Baton Rouge, Louisiana. The audience of 15,000 has calmed down a bit; the spotlights are aimed at the entrance to one of the main aisles in this huge coliseum. And there I am, standing at the conductor's podium, baton in hand, ready to conduct my very first full-length Liberace show. I had rehearsed the scores several times back in November at the Nugget Casino in Sparks, Nevada, breaking in as Lee's conductor after having replaced his conductor of twenty-six years, Gordon Robinson. Each night at the Nugget, I had conducted a little bit more of Lee's show, but I had never run it all the way through. So, this was it, my big night!

Thankfully, the rehearsal with the eighteen-piece band earlier in the day had gone fairly well—but now it was the moment of truth. This Baton Rouge show included a young Australian singer, Jamie Redfern; an eleven-year-old juggler, Albert Lucas; and several challenging classical and popular selections played by the entertainment icon himself, Liberace. It was now up to me to steer the musicians through all of it—a challenge and an important moment for me—one I wouldn't forget.

I realize, now, that I'd been aiming at this particular moment from the day I first tried playing my next-door-neighbor's piano. *That* moment, I honestly don't remember, but it was the beginning of my future life.

Mine is a musical story that begins in Bakersfield, California, and will finish, well, who knows where. It is a story that includes ventriloquists, jugglers, and banjo players, as well as my work with some of the biggest names in show business, including thirteen years as musical director for a man whom I consider to be the greatest showman of all time: Liberace.

It's also *my* musical story and covers time spent and music made everywhere, from Harvey Auditorium in Bakersfield, California, to the famed Mozarteum Conservatory in Salzburg, Austria, back to Radio City Music Hall in New York, and to the glittering casino showrooms of Las Vegas—with literally thousands of stops in between. I hope you enjoy reading it half as much as I enjoyed—and still am enjoying—living it.

Movement:

A Principal Division of a Longer Musical Work

The First Movement:

My Early Years

> Listen my children and you shall hear
> Of the midnight ride of Paul Revere,
> On the eighteenth of April, in Seventy-
> five;
> Hardly a man is now alive
> Who remembers that famous day and
> year.
> —H. W. Longfellow

> My father would recite Longfellow's
> lines once a year,
> since I was born on April 18, 1941.
> —Bo Ayars

1.

The Call

My dream job started with a phone call from Seymour Heller, Liberace's business manager. It was the call that changed my life. And I remember it as if it were yesterday: I was sitting in a woven-reed, aluminum-framed chair in the living room of my apartment on the Las Vegas Country Club golf course.

"Lee says he likes you," Seymour began. Lee's real, Americanized name was Walter Valentino Liberace, but he insisted his friends call him Lee.

"I think we get along," I replied. Seymour was very well known as a manager and agent, having represented some of the biggest musical names in show business, including Guy Lombardo, Tommy Dorsey, and Glenn Miller.

"Gordon is going to retire. You probably already knew that."

Not just I, but everyone, knew that Gordon Robinson, Liberace's conductor of twenty-six years, was stepping down. News like that traveled fast in the Entertainment Capital of the World.

"Yes, that's what I understand," I said, trying to sound relaxed—indifferent, even.

"Lee thinks you're the guy to replace him, but we need to be certain. Can you make it up to Sparks? We wanna be sure you're a fit. Maybe conduct a few shows, see how it works out? He wants to make sure the two of you work well together, and he wants you to get to know the show," he said.

Musically, I knew I was ready to be in charge of an orchestra that would back up someone like Liberace—*Mr. Showmanship.*

"Sure, I can do that."

I couldn't tell from Seymour's words what he thought of me becoming the new music director for his biggest client, but I thought I detected a little sigh of relief.

"Oh," he said as an afterthought, "and I'll send you the financial details."

Money. I didn't care about the money. I just wanted the job. And now, I realized the job was mine—well, almost mine. I never had cared too much about money, but now I realized I should be a little practical and not give everything away. So I said,

"Maybe you could give me an idea now."

Seymour responded with a figure. I don't exactly remember, but it was about the same as what I was already making. I knew I was worth more. I'd been on the Las Vegas scene long enough to not only have worked with—but to have held my own with—Elvis Presley, Barbra Streisand, Robert Goulet, Connie Stevens, Diahann Carroll, Jim Nabors, and others. I knew how to use my hands to lead a group of musicians. I knew how to manage a rehearsal and how to quickly solve a multitude of musical problems. Yeah, I was worth more.

"Seymour, I'll need more than that," I said. I think my whole body shut down for about five seconds, waiting for his answer.

"Well, I can give some, but not a lot. How about twelve hundred a week?" he said.

I didn't reply. I sat there thinking that Joe Guercio, my mentor, was the greatest career maker in Vegas for a reason, and that Seymour knew it. I wouldn't come cheap. And I waited. After about ten seconds of silence, Seymour said,

"Bo, hang on, I'll be right back." And the line went dead. All I could think was that I'd blown it, my dream job, all because of money. Then, suddenly, he came back on the line.

"OK, we can't go any higher, but we can do first-class airfare everywhere you go. There's a lot of travel involved, as you know, and Lee will probably want to go over some of the details of the shows while we're traveling."

Seymour had hit my soft spot. I've never been a small guy, so the wider, first-class seats would be a godsend, given all the time I'd be flying with Liberace. I figured that any additional salary concerns could be addressed later.

"That sounds good to me," I said, finally able to breathe normally.

I now realize that, although I was musically ready for the job, emotionally, I wasn't. In the past, handling my emotions had been fairly easy. I had simply put a lid on them; had ignored them—and the emotions of others—while focusing on my work. Now, as I noticed that people listened to me more intently—not necessarily because of what I was saying, but because of my lofty position—the prestige of being Lee's conductor quickly took over and fueled even more my overwhelming need to be in control, to be the center of attention. I found myself walking a little taller, speaking more authoritatively, and ordering things be done instead of asking, because I knew that what I said was now more important because of my job. *Didn't people know who I was?* I was special. And, ever since I can remember, I've always believed I was special—different—but in a good way. Unique. And I think it all started with how I came into this world.

2.

My Earliest Years

About four months after my birth in Glendale, California, I was adopted by Bob and Becky Ayars. Soon afterwards, we moved to Bakersfield, California, the city in which we remained until I was eleven years old. The story my mother told me whenever I needed "strokes" began when I was probably four years old.

"Tell me again how I was adopted," I would say.

"Well, we wanted children, but we couldn't have any. A friend told us of a special home with lots of children."

"And?" I'd ask.

"She took us there and showed us a room full of babies. They were all crying, except one. That one was laughing, and we said, 'That's the one we like best.' In fact, you looked so cute that I took a bite out of your ear." I would grin, quickly put my hand up to my left ear and touch the small indentation in my earlobe. I still do that because I still love that story.

When I was somewhat older, I learned the part of the story that didn't make me feel so special. In 1941, "out of wedlock" meant an entirely different thing than it does today; there was a stigma attached to not only the mother, but to the child, as well. My parents explained the circumstances of my adoption to me in detail: my birth mother gave me up right away, only to later change her mind and try to find me, which was not allowed. This led to me being placed in several different foster homes, and it was from one of these homes that I was adopted.

Did this shifting from foster home to foster home at a very early age affect me? I'm not sure. I've read that in some cases, frequent moving amongst foster homes may negatively affect a child, but, not being into analyzing my mind, I honestly don't know if it did. What I do know is, I've never thought of my parents as being anything other than my parents. They loved me, nurtured me and supported me. What more could I ask?

Bakersfield is a city located near the southern tip of California's San Joaquin Valley, about halfway between Los Angeles and Fresno. In the 1940s, it was still a small farming and oil town, and at the time of my birth it numbered no more than 136,000 residents, less than a fifth of its current size. I think the main thing people knew about Bakersfield back then was that it was hotter than Hades most of the time.

Our house was a smallish, two-bedroom, one-story ranch with a few "Spanish" touches—a red tile roof and lots of arches—to which my dad added an extra bedroom, which gave me my own space after my sister's adoption. We were, I guess, a typical family for the time: Dad went to work, Mom stayed home, and we kids walked the few short blocks to school. There were several other families with children on the block, and we always enjoyed playing together. The summers were quite hot, over 100 degrees most days. The winters were cool, not cold. And we had a local ice cream store, Dewar's, a favorite place that is still in business. I learned to swim at Beale Park for five cents a lesson. Pet-wise, we had a wide variety: two large ducks that had started out as cute little ducklings, given to us as an Easter present; several small birds that had fallen out of their nests in the red tile roof; and Honey, a Cocker/Collie mix, my first dog. Most of the small birds survived only overnight. We gave away the large ducks, which turned out to be geese. Honey, however, was with us for several years; a great one-and-only dog.

For people seeking a good time, Bakersfield Inn and The Saddle and Sirloin Restaurant were the hot tickets then. And my parents founded a dance club that, to the best of my knowledge, is still active in the area. They took me to Harvey Auditorium, the local symphony hall, where I remember seeing the famous Broadway star and screen actress Anna Maria Alberghetti in concert. I don't remember all the times we went, but I always loved going there to hear music. According to my parents, I would sit in the balcony and wave my arms as if I were conducting the performance. So I guess it was only a matter of time before I discovered the piano and my gift for music.

It was a short time, actually. I began playing when I was four as a result of our neighbor's spinet piano. According to my mother, I could often be found at their house plunking away on it, something they patiently tolerated from their four-year-old neighbor. After a few months, though, my parents were shamed into buying a piano for me—a Cable-Nelson baby grand. I started piano lessons with a neighborhood teacher who, after a few sessions, told my parents I should be studying with someone more advanced. So Mom started to look for other piano teachers for her son, the four-year-old budding musician.

That's how I became the pupil of Ms. Shavers. Looking back, I realize that she was not only the first person to interest me in music theory, but she was also the one who discovered my gift of perfect pitch, something I had never heard of. Up until then, I'd thought little, if at all, about my musical ability; it was simply something I could do that others could not.

"Play a note, any note," I'd say to Mom. She would, and, while she made sure I wasn't watching her hands, I'd tell her exactly what note she was playing. As neat as that sounds, perfect pitch is, for many musicians, a total distraction and a definite liability. Hearing a flute play what is supposed to be a B♭, and knowing that the note being played is actually a little sharp or flat—and, therefore, out of tune—is a royal pain in the musical butt. In college choir rehearsals, Bob Fountain, our conductor, would often say, "Let's change the key of this piece and make it a whole step higher." This would always be followed by audible groans from the eight or ten singers with perfect pitch.

I can't speak for others who have this affliction—er, gift—but for me, it's like this: when I see a note on a piece of sheet music, or even when I see a chord symbol, that note or chord sounds in my brain. Yes, I can actually hear it, usually as the sound of a piano, my main instrument. Sometimes, if there are a bunch of instruments in the score, it'll get confusing, so I'll just close my eyes and hear, for instance, the oboe's tuning note, A, in my head. Or, I'll picture a piano and focus on middle C and hear it in my head. Now, this might sound like fun, but if you're trying to transpose a piece into a different key, well, not so much. To do that, I literally have to plod along, note by note, chord by chord, telling myself, "No, it's not an A, but a G; no, it's not a B♭7 chord, it's an A♭7 chord." Ugh! I guess it would be like reading a book, and every time you see the word "the," you have to say or read the word "color." It makes no sense, I know, but that's the frustration I go through when trying to read a piece of music in a different key. But even though perfect pitch can be a major problem for musicians, at a young age I found that having it helped me gather the attention I needed. I was different, unique, special—and that was fine by me.

Nor was I glued to the piano. Practicing wasn't my favorite thing, but I did enjoy the recognition I received when I played for others. Even though Ms. Shavers didn't schedule many recitals, she did have me write simple piano pieces—nothing elaborate, mostly single melody lines with some chords. She belonged to a state organization that held yearly "tests" for many of their teachers' students. The students were measured on their ability to perform, as well as on their general knowledge of music, including melody, harmony, rhythm, etc. I'm sure my small compositions added to my score, and when I did well in those yearly examinations, Mom and I would stop at the aforementioned Dewar's ice cream store on the way home, and she would treat me to a hot fudge sundae. I always tried to avoid a low score, and I had the weight to prove it.

It's probably a matter of fact that Ms. Shavers had as much to do with my musical success as anyone. Through the process of writing those single melody lines and putting down those chords, I learned all about basic music theory—the reason music sounds like it does—which provided the foundation of what would become my professional life. It was this professional life that finally, and unconsciously, taught me the bottom line: not only did music come easily to me, it also brought me that extra attention I so desperately craved, which made me feel even more wanted. I also soon discovered that music made me feel different, a standout in the crowd, superior to others—or so I thought. In this musical environment, I thrived. It satisfied my need for acceptance from an audience I could control, thus assuring me of the most important thing: I would be appreciated.

BOBBY AYARS - AGE 3

BOBBY AYARS - AGE 6-8 MONTHS

BOBBY & PENNY AYARS
WITH A FRIEND

3.

Houston

My mother's claim to have never been east of Riverside, California, suddenly changed in April of 1952, when my dad's job was transferred to Houston. After packing and saying goodbye to our possessions in the moving van, including our trusty Cable-Nelson piano, we began the drive to our new home in Texas. I remember my mom organizing a large group of paper sacks, each one marked with a time, and some marked with a date. They each contained a small toy or game, something to keep my eight-year-old sister and me amused during the long ride. We went through all of them in the first three hours of our trip across the desert. Well, she tried.

Our first stop was Las Vegas, where, after a quick dip in the hotel pool, my sister and I were treated to a Vegas show at The Thunderbird Casino, featuring comedian Rose Marie. I remember seeing her in a spotlight and not understanding why everyone was laughing at things I didn't comprehend. I guess my sister Penny and I were a bit underage for this type of show. The next morning happened to be my eleventh birthday, and we visited Boulder Dam and saw Lake Mead—a great present. Then we began the really long drive to Houston in our aging, dark blue, 1948 Buick Roadmaster Straight-8 sedan, our one and only car for many years.

It took us several days and, after a final 800-mile, non-stop run from Tucumcari, New Mexico, we arrived at our motel on Buffalo Drive about 1:00 a.m. We stayed there about a week, then moved into an apartment complex while Dad settled into his new position at the Marathon Oil Company. The complex had a swimming pool, which was closed until the first day of May. Obviously, the pool's opening day quickly became as anticipated as Christmas in hot, muggy Houston. We were just a few blocks from NBC—not the TV network, but the National Biscuit Company's new plant in Southeast Houston. The smell of all those cookies baking in the afternoon was almost more than we could stand.

Our first house in Houston, 4231 Markham Street, was just south of Westheimer Road, west of downtown. At that time, it was about as far west as one could live while still being in Houston. It was close to Post Oak Road (now Boulevard), the invisible western boundary to the city. If you continued west on Westheimer, you'd pass a few large homesteads, some small farms, and then disappear into no man's land. At first, our house had no air conditioning; that appliance hadn't yet been perfected in the early '50s. In the summers, we opened all the windows, turned on the central fan and, mostly, just didn't move. This uncomfortable problem was solved when we finally got A/C. The unit consisted of a large, enclosed fan right next to the house and a very large wooden cooling tower behind the garage. You can still see some of these cooling towers on older buildings. The tower was about three by five feet at its base and at least seven feet high. Water was pumped to the top of the tower, where it would spray down to the bottom, cooling in the process. Then it was pumped to the coils in the fan box next to the house, and the fan would blow the cooled air into the house. My favorite chore during the summer was to clean the cooling tower: I'd remove a few of its wood slats and climb in, wearing my bathing suit, then take a stiff brush and clean the algae from the slats while the cool water poured down on me. It was my own private waterfall. During really hot spells, ours was probably the cleanest cooling tower in town!

The move to Houston was more than just a geographical move. It necessitated what some would call a transition in perspective. For me, it was definitely a wake-up call. My sixth-grade class taught me manners, southern style. Being the new kid in class was difficult, so when the teacher called on me around the third day of class, I started to feel better again. Problem was, I didn't understand the question.

"What?" I asked.

The boy next to me hit my arm and said, "Don't say 'what.' Say 'Ma'am,' stupid! You say 'Ma'am,' not 'what!'"

I learned my first lesson in southern etiquette that day in school, and it was reinforced by my parents at home. I was continually told to

"Always stand up when a woman or older person enters the room."

"Always let the woman walk in front of you and hold the door for her."

"Always help a woman with her chair when she sits at the table."

"Always help a woman on and off with her coat."

These basic rules of social behavior have stuck with me, though I'm sure in today's independent society, they're thought of as silly and outdated. Well, not to me. I think they still matter.

Another important cultural lesson I learned in Houston has to do with segregation. In the '50s, Houston was segregated, something I really didn't understand. Even though my parents were very liberal, they never really discussed this situation with my sister or me. And so I began to accept whatever I was told by the kids at school. Moreover, unbeknownst to me, I was also absorbing some of the feelings about segregation from my environment: blacks were different from us. *Why,* was never really explained. But in 1950s Houston, black people rode in the back of the bus, used separate drinking fountains and restrooms and lived in their own part of town.

And then came a revelation. Watching a new house being built across the street, I saw one of the workmen, a black man, take out a pad of paper and a pencil and begin to write. For some reason, witnessing that particular act—insignificant as it may seem—changed me. Being submerged in the culture of the city at that time, I had never thought about whether blacks, or "Negroes," could or couldn't write. Seeing such a simple thing as a black man writing made me realize that, despite what I'd picked up unconsciously from the segregated environment, black people were, after all, the same as us. I began to notice how the "Negroes" were treated, and I silently resented it, realizing that it was wrong. Looking back, it is frightening how segregation as a way of life could so easily dull a young person's awareness of right and wrong, to the point that anything *other* than segregation would seem wrong. It's not surprising that I later chose entertainment as a career, an environment rich in cultural diversity. And I attended Oberlin College, the first college to admit African Americans as a matter of official policy, and the first college to admit women.

I'm proud of that institution for many reasons, those two not least among them.

Settling into Houston also meant getting back into a music routine, something my parents, thankfully, took very seriously in spite of their own limited musical knowledge. Lots of people think a musical offspring is the product of musical parents. Of course, being adopted, I can't really comment, but both of my parents enjoyed music. As for my dad, I will say that music was something he enjoyed more as a listener than as a performer. Actually, he was largely tone deaf when it came to singing, meaning that he could sing a melody, but it . . . well, let's just say that he was a hummer. When he'd do odd jobs around the house, he'd hum snatches of songs, never the full song or lyrics, just a couple of notes of the melody. But these snatches stuck with me. Years later, someone asked if I knew the song "Indian Summer." I said I didn't and asked them to hum a few bars. It turned out to be one of the songs my dad had hummed, and I played it as if I had known it all along.

My mom, on the other hand, had taken piano lessons in college, yet around us, only played one of the pieces she knew (by Schubert or Grieg, I think), and then only about twelve bars. She told me that once, for a recital, she had memorized her particular piece by visualizing all the pages of music in her mind and had practiced "turning the page" as she played it. In the recital, however, when her mind got to the bottom of the first page, " . . . I just could not turn the page. So, I stopped and went back to the top of the page and played it again. But when I came to the bottom of the page, I still could not turn the page. I actually did this several times, finally gave up, stood, bowed and walked off stage." That's probably why my mom was always reluctant to perform for anyone.

And then there was me and my ego. As I said, I am grateful that my mom and dad were very supportive of their young son's musical ability. This is not to say they were always diplomatic. I remember Mom sharing a story with some of her friends over tea one day:

"When we found out that Bobby had so much musical ability, we got a book on gifted children."

"How exciting!" they all said. "And what did you learn?"

"I read it and discovered that Bobby is really not so much gifted. He's just musical." Thanks, Mom.

Speaking of my name, by the way, I'm actually a junior, having the same name as my dad: Robert. When I got too big to be called "Bobby," my mom started calling me Bob. But, my dad would answer. So, my mom chose another name. She was good at coming up with unusual and funny names, and often called me McGillicutty, Johnson, or, sometimes, just, "Hey, you . . . " She remembered a 1940s saying about "Bocephus, the Dog-Faced Boy." I recently looked it up and found that it was actually the name that Rod Brasfield, a ventriloquist on the Grand Ole Opry, had given his dummy. After a few months of calling me "Bocephus," she shortened it to "Bo," thank goodness. But having an unusual name is something I learned to appreciate. I was much more easily remembered as "Bo" rather than as "Bob," the pianist. As far as the Dog-Faced tag goes, well, I won't go there. Actually, until I moved back to the L.A. area in '65, I was known as Bob, or, in college, as Mr. Ayars. It was only at home that I was called Bo.

"Bo's" musical education didn't end with the piano. I had been given a clarinet several years before as part of the Bakersfield schools' music program. At home, I squeaked and tweeted, practicing on that one-piece, silver student model until my parents decided the sound might improve with a better instrument. So they bought me a used, black ebony Bundy clarinet for eighty dollars. I liked it because it didn't look like a student model. I'd polish the silver keys, swab out each section and practice putting the reed on just right. All of this, unfortunately, didn't improve my playing very much. I do remember, though, sitting in my room in Terre Haute and playing into an empty metal wastepaper basket, trying to duplicate the melodies of some of my big band recordings. I wasn't that good, but I did enjoy it.

Looking back, I imagine that playing the piano by ear, having perfect pitch, and picking up the clarinet—all before I was eight—must have been pretty heady stuff for me, and I became hooked on it. Later in life, I'd use these musical skills to impress people, to show off for girls. My music garnered attention, and as I said before, I was willing to go to any lengths to get that acceptance and avoid being forgotten.

An example of this need, of this fear of not being accepted, is the story of how I got to be "school pianist" at William Penn Elementary School in Bakersfield. It seemed that everyone was running for some neat-sounding office, and, even though I was known in school, I didn't feel I had a chance of ever being elected school president, vice-president, secretary, hall monitor, or even playground monitor. So, I decided to set my sights higher in order to ensure my election.

My plan was simple: I would create the position of school pianist, knowing that I would win. After all, I was the only horse in a one-horse race. I told my parents that I was running for school pianist, confident that they would consider it a real position that I had been asked to fill. And, sure enough, neither one questioned if there really were such a position. At school, the teachers let me go ahead and create the office since I was so gifted and special. My dad, the engineer, began designing square pieces of paper with a hand-drawn piano and the phrase "Vote for Ayars for School Pianist." My mother told the neighbor ladies all about my winning the election. I, of course, was thrilled with my victory and enjoyed all the added validation. My sister, Penny, jealous of her older brother's "accomplishment," rebelled with a tantrum that prompted my mother's standard response to such situations: "Sweetness and light," she would say. "Remember, sweetness and light."

The message was clear: don't show any feelings that are unpleasant or negative; keep your emotions inside and smile; and maintain a pleasant demeanor whenever possible, no matter the situation. That philosophy reminds me of the black-and-white, unemotional rendering of the characters in the beginning of the movie *Pleasantville,* or of how perfect and happy everyone was in *The Partridge Family*—no negative emotions, ever. It was a message I would remember—a message that would come to define me.

It was very hot in Houston, worse than in Bakersfield, clammy and sticky, making your shirt stick to your skin. You were actually about as wet standing outside as you were standing in the shower. Though many large stores had air conditioning, most of the older residences didn't. One such residence was that of my very fine piano teacher, whose name, unfortunately, escapes me. I remember many hot (temperature-wise) piano recitals at her home, an older house in the upscale Rice University district. During these Saturday or Sunday afternoon recitals, I'd sit in the sun porch next to the living room while waiting to play and fan myself with a program to try to keep cool. I don't remember being nervous sitting there, just excited. And when it was my turn to perform, I would walk into the living room (now full of other students' family members), sit at the Steinway and play my piece, usually a Bach Invention or a Schumann piano work. All I could hear, besides the piano, were several small electric fans, all turned to "HIGH" to help cool the house. That sound is one of my keenest recollections of Houston.

Musically, I remember those fans because of their pitch. I didn't know it at the time, but most of them had a 110-volt, 60-hertz electric motor that produced a hum near a low B♭ (B-flat) in pitch. (Leave it to me to know.) With all those B-flats sounding, it was difficult to play my selected piece, a concerto in A Major by Mozart, written one half step below that steady drone of fans. See? Perfect pitch, rearing its ugly head again . . .

I continued my piano lessons in Houston, learning to accompany other young musicians and writing more little piano pieces. At one recital, I was to play several pieces by

Bach, Mozart, and Schumann, as well as a few of my own small compositions. The recital hall was above the Steinway piano store on Main Street. It was a nice auditorium with a large stage, curtains, etc. I had practiced all my pieces, including the original compositions. Right before I was to play, however, my teacher suggested that I introduce each of my original pieces with a little speech, a few words about the selections, which was something I had never done before. I had no idea what to say. The original piece was called "Moods," with each short piece showing different emotions: happiness, sadness, melancholy, etc. So when it came time to play the pieces, I stood by the piano, looked at the audience and . . . completely froze. I tried to think of something to say, but nothing came out of my mouth. Nothing. After what seemed like a thousand years, I turned, mortified, and walked off stage, sort of like my mom had done when she hadn't been able to turn the page in her mind.

To think that I, the boy wonder—so in need of appreciation and attention—had failed so miserably, still amazes me. But the failure totally motivated me to avoid making a mistake like that again. And, actually, that motivation really helped me later on. Many times when I was under stress as an orchestra conductor, cruise director, or booking manager, I'd have to come up with some remedy or response to an awkward situation. I became known as someone who didn't buckle under pressure, someone who stayed calm and collected while finding the solution to a problem. Little did people know, I was whispering "sweetness and light" under my breath the whole time.

4.

Terre Haute

I remember Houston's Lanier Junior High School quite well. It was the first time I traveled some distance from home, and that made me feel more adult. My dad would drop me off at school on his way to work, and instead of staying in my assigned room as I'd done in elementary school, I would walk to each of my classrooms, a first. Lanier, being an older school, had no A/C. Instead, in the hotter months when the temperature and humidity were close to ninety degrees and ninety percent, each classroom would turn on huge fans that were set on large stands. All those roaring fans made it difficult to hear the teacher, but nobody dared turn them off.

I played my eighty-dollar clarinet in the Lanier band and was selected to participate in the all-city band. This was my first time playing clarinet for people other than my parents and classmates. In the all-city band, if you were good, you made first or second chair. I was considered just OK, so I was put into the third clarinet section.

"Third clarinet?" I thought. "I'm better than third clarinet."

But I wasn't. There were many kids who were better than me, and, unhappily, I found myself seated next to one of them during the band's first rehearsal, a girl with long, blond hair who played a professional clarinet. I read through my part, trying not to make any mistakes, but I know there were quite a few. I bravely played on, skipping over sections that I hadn't seen or that were too difficult for me to play. My music stand partner, however, performed our part flawlessly, and after the rehearsal I discovered that she had been practicing the piece for several weeks. I realized then that I was really a pianist who, now and then, played clarinet.

I also realized that I needed to practice if I were going to improve. And this applied to not just the clarinet; sooner or later I would run into someone who would outplay me on the piano, too. This, I suppose, was the first time I had to come to terms with the fact that, despite what my family and friends and I thought, I wasn't the best. I wasn't the top, or even amongst the top, musically. I think it was then that my need for acceptance and appreciation turned into a need to control. When I was the most talented person in the room, the center of attention, I felt safe. But now, I was vulnerable to those who were better, to those who understood the importance of commitment and practice. Talent was important, but it wasn't enough. I felt lost, empty, and alone. I needed a plan.

And again, my fear of rejection was the other side of the coin: I felt compelled to fit in. I didn't want to be ignorant or unknowing of any situation, as this would prompt my feeling of inferiority. It's a battle I've waged all my life: not wanting to appear unaware of anything that might be expected of me, no matter how trivial. "If you appear stupid, you'll be thought of as stupid." And even though I've performed in front of many people, I'm still terrified of making any mistakes. Music gets me attention, but, if I fail at it, I'll be rejected. That's been my story.

On the lighter side of this conundrum is what I call the "Spam Era." When I first attended Lanier Junior High in Houston, I asked my mother to make my lunch, which she faithfully did every day. A staple at our house was Spam, usually in sandwiches. Mom must've thought that eating these homemade goodies at school made me feel more, well, more comfortable. Actually, the reason for my request was simple: I didn't want to be seen as inexperienced, or even stupid, for not knowing the school cafeteria routine. Did I pick up the tray or did someone hand it to me? Did I take the silverware out of the holders before getting my water glass? Did I ask for the food in front of me or did I just take it? How much should I take? Would I be seen as rude if I took too much? There was so much to know, and I didn't want to seem unknowing. As a result, for two years my school lunch consisted of nothing but homemade Spam sandwiches.

It seemed as if all rules had been created to make me look inadequate and out of place. I know this feeling is common for early teens, but few go on to build careers around it. I grew to want only positive attention, no matter how I got it. I played piano, told jokes and basically schmoozed in order to get people to like me. I would do anything to avoid the opposite response. And from my earliest recollection to the present, I've always been hesitant to go someplace new, where I don't know "the routine." Even today, I still return to the same restaurants, the same stores, the same vacation spots—the same everything, every time.

A few weeks into the school year at Lanier, I was asked to join a small, informal dance band formed by Bill Day, a young drummer in the school band. The name of the group was Bill Day and His Musical Knights. It was a five-piece band: Mike Hattwick on trumpet, Johnny Pickett on trombone, a girl named Gail on piano, Bill on drums, and yours truly on that eighty-dollar clarinet. We practiced about once a week at Bill's home in a room above his garage. Our repertoire consisted of small, six-piece combo charts that Bill had purchased, titles like "Tuxedo Junction," "String of Pearls," and "Stardust," my dad's favorite. Bill's dad was in the medical profession, and we were sometimes asked to play for small dinner functions. I would put on my coat and bow tie, stand up for my clarinet solo, be fed, and then receive ten dollars for my work. At age thirteen, I was a professional musician. I had arrived!

Our band was also featured in our school's annual spring music concert. As usual, I stood up for my clarinet solo, trying to remember how Benny Goodman looked when he soloed. I thought I did pretty well. Afterward, my mom said that my dad was clutching his fists all throughout my solo, hoping beyond hope that I wouldn't squeak. And, lo, there were no squeaks that night. Many years later I was reacquainted with our trumpet player, Mike Hattwick—now Dr. Hattwick—in McLean, Virginia. My ex-wife Elaine had made the discovery during an office visit. I find that as I grow older, this kind of rediscovery happens more frequently, giving proof to the old axiom that "as you grow older, the world shrinks . . . "

It was also in Houston that I had my first date. It was with Kay Anderson, my dad's boss's daughter. My dad drove. We picked Kay up, went to a movie, and then the three of us went to a local malt shop where my dad discreetly sat at a distant table while Kay and I sat together, talking about the movie and school stuff. As it turned out, the Anderson family was transferred to Terre Haute, Indiana, about a year before we were. It was nice to know someone when we arrived in that new town.

When my dad told us he was being transferred again, this time up to Terre Haute, Indiana, I was excited. I had always wanted to live somewhere where it snowed. There was no chance of that in Bakersfield, and Houston got a good covering of frost a couple times a year, but no real snow. The possibility of living in snow country pushed the problem of being the new kid in town right out of my mind. My dad's thinking went the other way. He'd made a couple trips to Terre Haute and had found it to be as hot and muggy in the summer as Houston. With this in mind, he found a great deal on four large air conditioners in a Houston appliance store. I think his idea was that if they couldn't be installed in our new home in Terre Haute, he could always sell them. For me, the move meant that I'd be leaving neighborhood friends as well as the small combo band. Yes, I felt sad, but I was really looking forward to the new environment, too.

We drove to Terre Haute in the early summer of '53, a car trip made longer by the lack of interstate highways. Our route took us through a portion of Louisiana, Mississippi, Tennessee, and Kentucky, then up to Terre Haute, on the banks of the Wabash River. I remember driving through many small towns, some with traffic signals, and most with people hanging out outside because of the heat, which caused my dad to talk about our new air-conditioning units. I kept thinking that it would be nice to have one of those in our hot and muggy car. One thing my mom noticed was that in most of the small towns we drove through, the nicest houses were always funeral homes. I don't know why I remember that, but I think it's still true.

When we got to Terre Haute, we stayed for about a week at one of the two large downtown hotels, the Deming. I loved it because they had an all-you-can-eat buffet on Thursdays at lunchtime. The hotel was just a few blocks from my dad's office, and my dad asked a few of his coworkers to meet the family. One particular Thursday, I met Loyal Trumbull, the son of one of my dad's associates. The two of us inspected the buffet's specialty, a huge pile of shrimp, something for which I had developed a taste in Houston. As soon as we returned to our table, Loyal and I dove in and devoured a huge amount of shrimp and cocktail sauce. So much so, we figured, that the buffet price of $4.95 went up to $5.95 by the following Thursday when we returned. Loyal was my first Terre Haute friend and helped me to adjust to the new town.

Anxious for us to live somewhere other than a hotel, my dad rented a nice house at 255 Monterey Drive, not far from my temporary new school, Woodrow Wilson Junior High. The house didn't have room for our piano, but that was taken care of a few months later, just after Christmas, when we moved into our larger, permanent home at 2730 Wilson Street. This section of town was, at the time, not officially in Terre Haute, and so my sister and I attended Thornton, a smaller county school that taught kindergarten through ninth grade. I really loved this little school. It had a great music program, the beginning of the "feeder" system of enhancing music education at all levels. The idea was for children to start playing and learning music at an early age. Then, as they advanced in grade, their musical education would inform and support each new level of musicianship. Bottom line: you're never too young to learn about music.

At Thornton I also met my first real girlfriend, Hillary Hollis, though I'm not sure we thought of each other that way. We would hold hands and walk around the school's outdoor track. That's what going steady meant, back in the day. Hillary was a gifted violist, and we attended the same Presbyterian church downtown. There, in the choir, we'd sit next to each other and hold hands under our robes. Ah, youth.

Our well-worn Cable-Nelson piano was set out on the enclosed sun porch at our new home on Wilson Street. My parents checked around for piano teachers and found a very special one, Ms. Anna Hulman, the great aunt of Tony Hulman, the head man at the famous Indianapolis 500 race. She lived with her sister in a very old home on South Sixth Street. It even smelled old. Ms. Hulman was quite elderly when

I took lessons from her. She was very pleasant and knew how to draw music from her students. I vividly remember her explanation when I asked how the human arm works. In fact, she seemed almost too delighted with the question as she paused, rose and returned with what looked like a tie box.

"Now, Bob, this was a gift from a dear, dear friend of mine. A doctor," she began. Then she slowly opened the box. I peered as closely as I could, seeing nothing, as her old grandfather clock tick-tocked in the background.

"Since he was a doctor, he had a keen interest in how the body works."

She continued to open the lid, slowly, inch by inch. I leaned forward, looking, but still found nothing.

"After his death, I learned he had willed this to me because I didn't understand how fingers work as much as he hoped I would."

She opened the box all the way, and there it was, finally, the skeleton of a human forearm and hand. I was stunned.

"Uh . . . is that . . . " I finally stammered.

"It was amputated after his death, of course. Wasn't that nice of him?" She smiled. "He wanted me to be able to show students how fingers work on the piano keys."

"Is that . . . "

Her cat leaped up on the bench behind me, and I must have jumped six inches.

"Real?"

"Of course it's real . . . but not the rubber bands, of course. The human arm has actual muscles. Pull on one of them, Bob, to see how it works."

"Uh . . . "

"Notice how the rubber bands are attached to the finger bones, how they run up the arm. Those are to show how the muscles and ligaments work."

Her peculiarities notwithstanding, I did enjoy my lessons with the eighty-year-old Ms. Hulman in that very old-smelling house. Today, there's a scholarship in her name at Indiana State University.

Not long after we moved to Terre Haute, I met Liberace for the first time. My second cousin, George Arnold, was an ice skater and a friend of Lee's, having done shows with him in the L.A. area, and they were on their way to New York City, where Lee had an upcoming engagement. At that time (the summer of '54) flying cross-country was rare—there were no jets. It was either train, bus, or car. So, they were driving George's Triumph sports car, a TR3, from California to New York, and stopping on the way to see George's favorite cousin—my mother—and her family in Indiana. George and my mother had always been close, he often calling her "sister." They were both extroverts, and got along well.

When they arrived, cousin George introduced Liberace as a well-known pianist who was going to go far in the entertainment world. My mother, being very proud of her thirteen-year-old musician son, insisted I play for him. I chose a Bach Invention and a couple of original songs I'd written. Lee seemed impressed and told me to "keep practicing." And that was my introduction to Liberace. I brought up this first meeting many years later:

"You're kidding! That was you? Well, don't tell anyone," he said with his famous wink, "I wouldn't want people to think I'm older than I am!"

Terre Haute had one local TV channel, WTHI, and in the mid-'50s, one of the main on-camera personalities was Jerry Van Dyke, Dick Van Dyke's brother. He was used as the humorous co-anchor and did on-air commercials for local vendors and products. There was an organist, Nancee South, also a local woman, who had won the Arthur Godfrey Talent Show and had appeared with several musical celebrities of the day. As I remember, she was "it" when it came to live music in Terre Haute.

The Wiley High School choir, of which I was a member, did the standard version of "'Twas The Night Before Christmas," by Fred Waring. Someone had the idea that we should perform it live on local TV at WTHI, Channel 10. So, there I am, playing Santa, blind as can be without my glasses (not the right look for a Santa), and I meet Nancee South. Actually, we just shook hands, so it wasn't much of a meeting, but she seemed pleasant.

I got my first taste of a real music job when I was asked to play piano for Jerry Woodward, a local trumpet player from a different high school. His forte on trumpet was a song called "Sugar Blues," a trumpet virtuoso piece that called for a "wah-wah" effect with a handheld cup mute. My first series of gigs with his band was in a VFW hall in Brazil, Indiana, a very small town about fifteen miles east of Terre Haute. The band consisted of Jerry on trumpet, a drummer (who was much older than the two of us), and me on piano. That was it. To me, it sounded empty, so I was planning to fill in as much as I could. Anyway, the very first song we did was "Stardust," the favorite of my dad's that I often played at home. When we finished our first time through the piece, Jerry put down his horn and told me to take a solo. So, I soloed by playing "Stardust" accompanied by drums. The few couples on the floor kept dancing during my solo, so at least I was keeping some kind of a beat.

The rest of the five-hour job was the same. We'd play a song all the way through, then I'd take a solo. The faster the song, the more challenging it was to play, as I tried to fill in all the missing parts I was hearing in my mind: a bass, a guitar, some horns, strings, etc. Initially, the thought of doing this was particularly intimidating. As the night progressed, however, the feeling of power, of control, was intoxicating. I worked with this band on several Saturday nights, which prompted my parents to make a rule: yes, I could play late jobs on Saturday nights, and yes, I would definitely attend church the next morning, regardless of how late I had come home.

Speaking of church, I took pipe organ lessons from our local church organist. I didn't want to be an organist, but I enjoyed learning about the pipe organ and what it could sound like. It's a tricky instrument, and not easily mastered, but I loved the big sounds I could get from that Möller organ with its real, thirty-two-foot-long pipes. I did have trouble, though, when playing some Bach organ pieces, trying to coordinate my hands and feet. Especially my feet. I wore a size 12 D shoe, much too wide for the narrow organ pedals, so I'd take my shoes off and play the pedals with my almost-bare feet.

On the Saturday night before Easter, I got a call about 7:00 p.m. from my organ teacher. It seemed that he had severely burned his hands while dyeing Easter eggs and, "Could you possibly play for me in both services?" I suppose most people would have been a bit frightened about taking on the responsibility, but I wasn't. For some reason, I saw it as a challenge.

The next morning, my parents and I drove to church about an hour before the services were to begin. I met with the soloist and practiced her songs on the piano in the church basement. Then, I put on my choir robe and headed to the sanctuary, a large, open area with the organ directly behind the pulpit, positioned so that the organist's back faces the congregation.

I sat on the organ bench and took off my size 12 D shoes. After putting markers in my hymnal for the service's various hymns and short musical sections, I waited for a signal from the pastor and started playing. I honestly don't remember much about how or what I played. My only memory is of my mother, grabbing me by the arm down in the church basement afterwards.

"Why did you take off your shoes?" she cried.

I explained about my large shoe problem.

"But your white socks! You were wearing your white socks in church! Everyone saw them when you put your feet back on the organ bench. Everyone! I'm just glad you didn't have a hole in them." So much for a pat on the back and a "job well done."

During my days at Wiley High School, I played piano for several different dance bands who performed in the Terre Haute area. Sometimes, it was with a talented alto sax player who emulated Paul Desmond of the Dave Brubeck Quartet. Other times, it was with a drummer, Boone Dunbar, from Brazil, Indiana. His specialty was playing drums while singing great blues songs in a gravely voice. He was also a delightful gateway to the jargon of the current jazz players, using such musical words as "cool," "swingin'," "crazy," and the ever-popular, "yeaaah." I played several gigs with him and always enjoyed the easy way he played and sang. I also learned lots of new songs in the blues genre. It was my first time working with a true professional. Just after I played with him, he was asked to join Lionel Hampton's band for a tour of the Midwest. Boone is very well remembered in the Brazil/Terre Haute area.

Most of the music jobs were dance jobs—no shows or background music—just plain dancing. We played proms, wedding receptions, and different school sock hops. The bands usually consisted of a trio: a drummer, an upright bass player, and me on piano with, depending on the event, a horn or two. Most of the pianos I played were in bad condition. Many of them were total wrecks in need of a lot more improvement than the quick tuning I could offer. I found several empty Budweiser beer cans in one large upright. On another one, someone had taped the out-of-tune strings with some duct tape to keep them from ringing. In another, a pencil eraser was wedged between the strings to silence a bad string. Years later, Liberace told me to "beware of thin chefs and painted pianos." I've played more than my share of painted pianos.

Musically, I was a big fish in a little pond. I enjoyed being asked to do all the various musical events, including playing at the high school's all-night senior party. I did that when I was still a sophomore, and felt very honored to be allowed to stay up all night and be paid for it. The next year, when I was a junior, I wasn't asked to play that year's all-night party, but some of the seniors asked me to come to the event and sit in. I took that as an invitation. But, according to my dad, it wasn't a true job, and " . . . no, you can't go." Boy, did I want to go to that all-night party! I went to bed early, lay there for several hours and, at about 1:30 a.m., snuck downstairs and out the back door, shutting it quietly. I then opened the garage door without making a peep, put the big DeSoto in neutral and slowly, quietly, pushed it down the driveway and into the street. I kept pushing until I thought I was far enough away from the house, then got in, started the engine and drove to the party. I had a great time sitting in with the hired band until the

Cinderella hour arrived. At about 4:30 a.m., I left the party, drove to half a block from home, turned off the engine and, again, pushed the DeSoto back up the driveway and into the garage. Things were going very well. Then, still not making a sound, I closed the garage door, went to the back door, slowly opened it and found my dad, standing there, arms folded. "Have a good time at the party?" he asked. How did he know!? I had been so quiet—not a sound, nothing. Then later, when I had two boys of my own, I discovered his secret: just put yourself in your kids' shoes and ask yourself, "What would I have done at that age?"

I also played a fair number of dance jobs with some of the guys from the Wiley High School Marching Band. One of the drummers, Larry Shaffer, and I became friends, often trying to jam to some of the more progressive jazz songs of the day by Dave Brubeck, André Previn, Dizzy Gillespie, and Stan Kenton. This was the mid-'50s, and to us, true musicians didn't touch rock and roll. Well, some of us may have tapped our feet to a few Elvis songs or may have secretly wanted to hear the Penguins' "Earth Angel" pop ballad when we were out dancing with our someone special, but songs like "Take Five" and "Giant Steps" were our favorites. Often, while driving back to Terre Haute from a Saturday night gig in a not-too-distant town, we'd try to pick up Dick Martin's music show, "Moon

Glow with Martin," from WWL, the large (at the time), 50,000-watt radio station in New Orleans, Louisiana. The station would keep drifting, and we'd scramble to find a clearer place on the dial. There was nothing better than finishing a job in Green Castle, Indiana, hitting the local all-night diner, and listening to cool jazz while driving between darkened Indiana cornfields.

My final accomplishment in Terre Haute was composing the processional for our graduating class. It was a simple march, but I think the idea that a local boy had actually composed it seemed to impress people. I used this march as one of my audition compositions for Oberlin Conservatory of Music. I can't believe they thought my amateur scribblings were any good.

During my high school years, I got good grades and a goodly amount of attention for my music. I rarely got into trouble. Actually, I was afraid to try anything I didn't know about or understand. Studies, band, orchestra, various choral groups—all kept me busy with things our culture deemed acceptable for young people to do. No drinking, no drugs, no sex. I had an area of expertise—music—and I was motivated to pursue it. Besides, music got me the attention I wanted. I saw that my sister's rebelliousness usually got her into more trouble, so I withheld my feelings and used my mask of "sweetness and light" to avoid being punished (rejected) for being bad. Music also made me feel appreciated. And, boy, was that important!

Speaking of drugs, the most serious drug abuse opportunities faced by our generation in Terre Haute were cigarettes and alcohol. Oh, I'm sure there were other forms of "high," but I was ignorant of them. I felt very embarrassed when my mother discovered a pack of smokes in the back of my closet. Like most every kid, I started smoking because of peer pressure, plain and simple. But I really didn't like the taste of beer or wine or hard liquor, no matter how uncool I looked. One of our high school scandals happened the night one of our star senior football players got drunk on beer and knocked over a tombstone in a local cemetery. Another was when a sophomore girl got pregnant. Regarding the pregnancy, my mother was involved with a national organization that helped young girls who were "in trouble." There was a large home in town where girls would stay until they delivered their babies. My mother always spoke sadly about these girls. Maybe, unconsciously, I related their plight to my birth mother back in Los Angeles.

If I had to sum up my years as a teenager, I think it can reasonably be said that, as long as I was in control, I was happy. I made it through those years with fairly good grades, a few good friends, and, of course, my music, that all-important key to my happiness and success, or so I thought. Now, it was time for the next hurdle.

COUSIN GEORGE ARNOLD ON THE LEFT

"THE SAINTS" 1958 JAZZ BAND - BO IS 4TH FROM THE LEFT

BOB AYARS AS THE POLICE CAPTAIN, WITH MUSTACHE
"PIRATES OF PENZANCE" - WILEY HIGH SCHOOL

5. Oberlin

My parents and I shared the unspoken assumption that I would attend a "musical" college. I never considered myself anything but a musician—not a fireman, pilot, doctor, or lawyer for me. It really wasn't a hard choice. Very simply, it was clear to everyone that music was what I did best. In hindsight, I'm glad I followed the musical path. For me, it's good to be a musician.

About thirty-five percent of my Wiley High School class of one hundred were going right into jobs, getting married, or joining the military. My college-bound friends were applying to IU (Indiana University), Purdue University, and Indiana State University, named Indiana State Teacher's College back then. A very few others were heading to some of the Ivy League schools. For me, the question was which college or university I should attend to learn more about music.

There were certainly enough options in the Midwest. In the spring of my junior year, with my parents' help, I narrowed the search to three schools: Northwestern, just north of Chicago; DePauw in Greencastle, Indiana; and Oberlin Conservatory of Music just south of Cleveland, Ohio. I wanted a place that wasn't a huge school like IU. Northwestern was big, yes, but it had a great music program. DePauw was a small college in a small town, as was Oberlin. But Oberlin had two important things going for it: it was very highly thought of, and it offered a third-year study abroad program in Salzburg, Austria. In retrospect, I really was naïve about what to look for in a college or university. They all had good teachers and nice facilities, but I was totally ignorant about even the kind of musician I wanted to become. All I knew was that I played piano very well and received lots of attention for it.

My parents and I spent a couple of weekends visiting DePauw and Oberlin. DePauw wasn't far from Terre Haute, and the town's main industry was the college. It had a homey feel, I liked what I saw, but, honestly, I really didn't know what to look for.

The weekend we visited the Oberlin Conservatory of Music, I remember walking around the Conservatory practice building, hearing hundreds of pianists, each playing a different piece, all at the same time. It might have been noise to some, but to me it was energetic, inspirational, and thrilling. Even though we weren't given a true tour of the buildings, I instantly felt connected to the Conservatory. I just sensed that Oberlin could be the place for me in the fall of 1959.

Instead of just visiting Northwestern for a weekend, I applied to be and was accepted as a "cherub" and attended a two-week summer program on the shores of Lake Michigan between my junior and senior year of high school, sort of a pre-college experience—and, boy, was it ever. I took classes in piano and a beginning class on organ, a hold-over from Terre Haute. After a few lessons on the organ, however, my teacher suggested that I stop studying organ and concentrate on the piano. Maybe it was my size 12 D shoes, but I think it was really because I just didn't have the talent or perseverance to continue studying the organ. That was a huge letdown for me: to be told that I wasn't good at music. It was the first of several setbacks I would experience at Northwestern.

The piano lessons were not what I expected, either. My previous piano teachers had given me a limited amount of experience with serious piano works, focusing more on piano technique than on musical repertoire. My fellow cherub piano majors were more advanced; they all had been grounded firmly in the classics, and several had performed concertos with their local symphony orchestras. Yes, I was good at playing by ear, but at Northwestern, I was a small fish in a big pond. I became just another piano player, nothing exceptional—another blow to my ego.

So, I ended up dropping my piano studies—another setback. It wasn't that I totally gave up studying piano; I just couldn't deal with the dawning awareness that I wasn't that good, or as good as I thought I was . . . or should be. But, still wanting to be part of the program in some way, I shifted my focus and signed up for the only other instrument I knew, the clarinet. Northwestern was known (and still is) for having a dynamic band program. That summer, the large symphonic band was populated with serious professors and their students, quite a dedicated group of musicians; but to me, it just looked like fun. Even though I wasn't as competent as they were, I'd be part of something musical. As I recall, each student player was given a brief audition. Evidently, I didn't do well at all, because I was given the fourth clarinet book and fourth chair. To put this into perspective, the clarinet section of the band was divided into four sections, with each section having four clarinet players. So, being last chair in fourth clarinet meant I was sixteenth out of sixteen clarinetists. But that was fine with me. I was a member of the band and was looking forward to playing in such a large group of really good musicians. Oh, and I noticed a very attractive oboist from New Trier High School in the Chicago area. She wore glasses and had a great smile. And she was the first oboist! But I merely gazed at her from the last chair of the clarinet section, nothing more . . .

One afternoon, the band was sight-reading several different pieces, auditioning them as possible new material for the various instrumental professors. The pieces included band transcriptions of works by Romantic symphonic composers:

Beethoven, Strauss, Respighi, Stravinsky, etc. Toward the end of the hour, we switched to playing some marches. Most of these marches ended on the third beat of the measure, a musical idea sometimes called a "stinger." One particular march, however, ended on the very first beat of the bar and didn't employ a stinger ending. Everyone, professors and students alike, played the first beat of the last measure and stopped . . . except me. I played a very high, very out-of-tune note on that "not-to-be-played" second beat: a fourth clarinet "solo" that wasn't written in the score. The silence after my note was deafening, and the glares from the other students, even louder. The professor playing first chair clarinet turned around and gave me THE LOOK. Even the first oboist with the glasses and great smile turned and glared at me. I'd ruined the march, the band, everything. I stared at the music, trying to convey the possibility that my part had been written incorrectly. They didn't buy it. Then I stared at the floor, not knowing what to do or say. Of course, every member of that sixty-piece band knew that *I* was the one who had played that wrong note—no hiding, no excuses, no doting mother to defend me; nothing to do but try to curl up and become invisible, and that didn't work.

For several minutes, I was a wreck, emotionally. I found it very difficult being surrounded by the other students. I honestly had trouble even looking at them, knowing that they all knew they were better than me. And yet, if I were to quit the band, even more people would find out, and I just couldn't deal with so many people looking down on me and my musical inability. Music was my identity; without it, I would be nothing.

I remember going for a cup of coffee at a local diner after that band practice, trying to run away from my feelings of rejection. I kept thinking, first my organ teacher, then my piano teacher, and now, nationally recognized band director John Paynter, and music professors from major colleges, including Oberlin and DePauw, plus my fellow students—all of them knew I was a terrible musician, and that they were much better than me.

After about an hour, I did what I always seemed to do. I hid behind the mask of "sweetness and light" and smiled, not wanting anyone to see how much I was hurting inside. And, either to hide or to deflect my emotional angst for the remainder of my time in the band, I gathered up what courage I had left, went to the band office and officially switched from clarinet to bass clarinet: same fingering, just bigger.

But, just my luck, there was already a very fine bass clarinet player in the band, a fellow cherub, so I spent the first day trying to match my feeble bass clarinet sound to his excellent tone. I ended up not playing at all. Better to be silent than to squeak. But not contributing to the sound of this great concert band was definitely no fun for me. So, after a few days, I switched again, this time to an instrument that no one else was playing: the singularly unique, one-of-a-kind, huge, contra-bass clarinet, and not just the large, wooden E♭, but the

metal Double-B♭, to boot. This instrument was enormous, and it took me ten minutes just to unpack it and put it together. Playing-wise, I spent most of my time doubling the tubas, sort of an *um-pa, um-pa,* but, hey, I was playing in the band, and, being the only contra-bass clarinet player, I was once again unique and, therefore, happy.

When I got back home, I applied to and was accepted to all three institutions. DePauw was nice, but hadn't really grabbed me as a place to expand my musical world. Northwestern had left a bad taste in my mouth—of my own doing, of course—and I just wasn't keen on going back there. So, that left Oberlin Conservatory of Music, and I entered there in the fall of '59.

I knew my dad tried to arrange scholarships through his company, Marathon Oil, but he ended up paying for all of my Oberlin schooling: tuition, room, and board. At the time, it was about ten thousand dollars for four years. He borrowed the money and paid it off year by year, something for which I will always be grateful.

I was excited about this new chapter for me in music. I moved into Noah Hall, one of the freshman dorms, said goodbye to my parents and sister and started to explore my new home. Class-wise, every incoming Conservatory freshman took the same core curriculum of classes, so I knew my schedule: Music History, Music Literature, Music Theory I, Composition (my major), Piano (required of every Conservatory student), Choir (an elective), and PE, either swimming or tennis, a requirement back then. I chose swimming and got my Red Cross Lifeguard Certificate.

My first few days at Oberlin were eye-opening—and ear-opening—to say the least. Music, its sounds and sights, surrounded me: music teachers, music students, student recitals, jam sessions in the practice rooms, afternoon bull sessions in the student lounge at the Conservatory—all of these filled up the hours in my day. In those first few weeks, I found that if I wasn't practicing for my piano lesson or trying to compose the next great symphony, I was attending classes or singing in different choirs or practicing life-saving in the pool. The majority of my time was spent with music—learning more about it, practicing it, listening to it. And to me, it was just plain fun.

The main social areas for students were the various eating halls. I was assigned to Dascomb, a freshman girls' dorm. While some of the other dining halls were in converted older houses, Dascomb was one of the newer dorms, modern and up to date. After the eating area, my favorite place to be was the lobby, where they had a piano. When the students discovered that I played pop music, the lobby became sort of a piano bar every evening after dinner. I enjoyed playing, performing requests, and, of course, showing off.

I met and hung out with a couple of freshmen who were in the College of Liberal Arts. They were great followers of then-famous musical satirist Tom Lehrer and asked me to accompany them when they sang some of their own silly songs about the more humorous aspects of Oberlin life. We became semi-popular and were often asked to perform small, after-dinner shows in some of the other dining halls. One of their songs was about Jell-O, one of the "staples" at Oberlin:

The class of '27 had vanilla,

It was boiled and poached and stewed and steamed and fried,

Each serving was topped with a pink marashmilla',

That looked like it had settled there and died.

It wasn't Broadway, but it was fun.

At Oberlin, every Conservatory student was required to take piano lessons to have some facility with the piano, regardless of their instrument: singers, trombone players, everyone. (In our class, there were some brass players who actually had never touched a piano.) This requirement meant that every Conservatory student would need to use a practice piano at some time.

Therefore, the first and most important challenge for a new Conservatory student was to find a piano upon which to practice and/or compose. The problem was, the numbers didn't add up. There were almost four hundred Conservatory students and about two hundred pianos. None of the pianos in this big practice and teaching facility were of the same quality, size, or condition. The lowest level pianos—the pianos on their last "notes"; the pianos that had been taken apart, examined, and mostly put back together; the cadavers of the piano kingdom—were used by the piano-tuning students. These pianos lacked tone, made squeaky noises when their pedals were depressed and, in many cases, lacked ivory or plastic coverings on many of their keys. I usually got one of these pianos.

I was advised about many of the unwritten Conservatory rules and regulations by my college-assigned "big brother," a sophomore piano major named Stanley Cowell, who is now a noted jazz pianist and music professor at Rutgers University. During my Oberlin orientation, Stan did his best to explain some of the "facts of life" of a Conservatory student: what the Conservatory classes and professors were like, the pros and cons of getting a bike (the traditional means of transportation around campus), and other nitty-gritty of Oberlin life.

I learned that the main practice building, Warner Hall, opened at 6:00 a.m., the same time that Dascomb Hall, my assigned eating place, opened for breakfast. That was a no-brainer for me. I'd go to breakfast at 6:00, finish about 6:30, and then head for Warner Hall, where at least one of those two hundred pianos would be available and just waiting for my flying fingers and creative brain.

That first morning, I ate a quick breakfast, went to Warner Hall and found every single piano on each of the three floors taken. Well, not necessarily with people, but with a coat, some books, even a bicycle. "So, that's the routine," I thought. "You get here, throw something in a room, and it automatically becomes yours." It didn't seem quite fair, but I was a newbie on campus. There was always a mad rush to get the best practice piano, and the early bird got the best Steinway—but only if he or she "deserved" it. More on that later.

So, for the next several weeks, I got up at 5:30 a.m. and headed for the practice hall with several books: some music history and a blank music manuscript book. At about 5:45, there would be a crowd of about one hundred students waiting for the building to open and, when it did, there was a mad scramble for the practice rooms. People ran up and down the hallways and stairs, hell-bent on securing "their" favorite instrument. That first month, I averaged finding a vacant piano only two days a week, and they were usually the lowest quality. Simple math: there were more students than there were pianos.

Now, a bit about the piano "pecking order." I'm not a piano tuner. It's hard enough trying to play one. But I do understand the things that make a piano sound like a piano, and one of those is the length of the strings. In concert halls, you find the big concert grand pianos, usually 9 feet in length, with some even longer—9.6 feet for the Schimmel and the Bösendorfer. Their tone is amazing: big, bright, and rich. You play a chord at any volume, and it's alive with tone. On some concert grands I've played, it's like driving a Corvette. The more you press down on the keys for more depth and tone, the more potential you realize remains, waiting to be unleashed. It is truly inspiring to play one of these grande dames of the piano world. There are lots of good manufacturers, like Bechstein, Mason & Hamlin, Blüthner, the famous Bösendorfer, Schimmel, newcomer Fazioli, and, of course, Steinway. In Warner Hall, almost every grand piano was a Steinway, and, due to an unwritten rule, these concert grands were "reserved" for senior piano majors. As an incoming freshman, one didn't want to be caught playing or practicing or even *looking* at these special concert grand practice pianos. When I walked by these rooms, I always paused to listen to a potential piano great, hoping to hear or pick up who-knows-what.

There were also certain pianos that were reserved for the rest of the piano majors. These pianos were mostly seven-foot Steinway Model Bs, what we now call "killer Bs." These instruments were, and still are, great pianos with lots of sparkling high notes and rich low tones. There were quite a few more of these Steinways, and again, the unwritten rule was that they were to be used primarily by sophomore, junior, and a few very talented freshman piano majors. The bottom line? If you weren't a piano major practicing for your upcoming recital, you stayed away from the "killer Bs." That was the way it was for every Conservatory student, like it or not.

During my first few weeks, I discovered more and more about this wonderful world of music I'd chosen. First and foremost was the simple fact that, while I may have been the big fish in the Terre Haute pond, here at the Oberlin lake I was surrounded by big fish from all the other ponds. And, like my experience at Northwestern, I found that many students at

Oberlin were much more experienced and talented than I, Bob from Terre Haute, was.

Here's a big fish story that has stayed with me. One afternoon, during the week before classes started, I was checking out Warner Practice Hall and, luckily, found a very small, vacant room with an old, large, upright piano in it. I closed the door, shutting out the mingled sounds of all the other practice rooms, and with my trusty music notepad and pencil, tried to write something "meaningful," something original. After several starts, nothing sounded any good so, to clear my brain, I started playing a little jazz tune I'd heard, just chord changes, really. It felt weird, playing jazz in the middle of Beethoven, Bach, and Mozart. That's when Melody Peterson came bouncing into my practice room.

Of medium height and a bit angular, Melody had long, blonde hair in large curls that were, like her, in constant motion. She was definitely high energy. Optimistic and a little bit pushy, she was all about her own universe: what she wanted to do, and how she wanted to do it. If you weren't on board with what she was saying or doing, then you were pretty much in her way. She was an incoming freshman piano major.

"Hey, you play jazz?" she said, putting her books on top of the large upright.

"Well, yeah, a little," I said, uncertain of what it was I had just played.

"Here," she said, stepping toward the piano, "Let me show you a neat song I just figured out."

It was clear that she was going to take my place at the piano whether I wanted her to or not. The instant she was seated, she began playing a jazz melody with some really challenging jazz chords.

"A Brubeck tune," she said, playing on. "'The Duke,' in honor of Duke Ellington."

I had never heard it before and couldn't get over what a great tune it was, a good melody with great chord changes. I also couldn't help but notice what a fine jazz player Melody was. No, she wasn't just good, she was great; secure and experienced. I tried to listen objectively, hearing all the different harmonies in the song, but I kept thinking about how much better than me she was, and about how much better so many of my fellow students were, and suddenly I felt very small and out of place, just like I had at Northwestern when I'd been surrounded by extremely talented musicians. And Melody was just the first of several discoveries I would make over the next few months. Yes, I had definitely left my small Terre Haute pond.

When she finished, I told her what a great a song it was and how well she'd played it.

"Yeah, well, I heard it earlier today and just had to get it in my fingers."

We chatted a bit more, and then she asked me if I was taking the test that afternoon to get out of Music Theory I.

"It's really boring, I've heard; y'know, just the basic stuff we already know," she said. Her last comment made me feel a little bit better, as if she were putting me in her league, sort of.

"From what I've heard of you through the door, you already know a lot of that stuff. You really ought to take the test to get out of it."

She told me there was a signup sheet outside a professor's room downstairs.

"You really ought to take it, y'know," she said, bounding from the room as abruptly as she'd entered it.

Get out of Theory I? Somehow, it just didn't feel right—trying to skip a college course before even going to one class. Up until then, I had pretty much followed life's rules by (most of the time) doing what my parents asked of me: trying not to be late, looking fairly presentable, being prepared, and acting responsibly. By doing so—by refusing to challenge myself or the status quo—I hadn't run the risk of being rejected. "Sweetness and light" had been the way to go.

As for music theory, I knew lots of chords and scales, having learned them from my piano teachers, but I hadn't had any formal music theory training. I had assumed that all the theory courses at Oberlin had a purpose, that they were all related to one another, and that if you missed one, you wouldn't be prepared for the next one. Yet, here I was, thinking about trying to "get out of" Theory I! I wasn't really sure what Theory I was all about, even, but, like Melody said, maybe I knew most of it already. So, I went downstairs to sign up for the "Get Out of Theory I" test. When I got there, I signed up for a time slot and found that my major composition professor, Joseph Wood, would be giving it. Well, might as well give it a try.

Several minutes before my appointed time, I knocked on the door, heard a faint reply, and entered. Mr. Wood was sitting at a small desk piled high with music manuscripts, some professionally printed, most written by hand. He was short, with a pasty complexion, blue eyes that seemed to be half open most of the time, and a Lucky Strike cigarette hanging from the corner of his mouth. He definitely had what I now know is an "East Coast" attitude. (And, yes, smoking was allowed in the teachers' offices back then.)

"I'm Bob, er, Robert Ayars," I said.

He said something unintelligible.

"I'm here to take the test to get out of Theory I," I added, helpfully.

"Sit there." He nodded at a really old upright piano covered with piles of music.

I followed his direction, noting that the composition teachers didn't seem to get their first choice of the better pianos, either.

He got straight to the point with no minced words, asking a few questions about my music background and the compositions I had sent with my application. Then, he had me play some scales, mostly minor since they were the more challenging.

"All right," he said. "I want you to establish a key, then modulate up a tritone."

A tritone is a note that is six half steps above a given note. I thought I understood what he was saying and figured the easiest key to use would be the key of C. Up a tritone would put me into the key of G♭. So, I established the key of C by playing a

C chord, then I moved up a half step and played a D♭7 (a D♭ dominant seventh chord), which I knew was the dominant, or "V," chord of the key of G♭, the key I wanted to get to. This "V" chord automatically resolved to the key of G♭, the desired key.

Three chords—C, D♭7, and G♭—that's what I played. It worked for me.

Mr. Wood sat back in his chair when I finished and said, "That's it?"

"Well," I began, "I'm not sure how much you wanted me to play, but I think I did what you asked. I started in C and then modulated up to a G♭."

"Well, yes, you did, but you didn't spend any time in the first key. And when you modulated, you just jumped up to the new key. You got there, but it wasn't very pretty." Then he asked, "You play jazz, don't you?" Just like Melody had. But, I did test out of

the class.

And that was my introduction to Professor Joseph Wood, my mentor for three years. He was the perfect teacher for me, musically. He had been an arranger for some early radio shows in New York and would tell horror stories about being given fifteen minutes to produce an arrangement for violin, flute, clarinet, and accordion. He also related several truisms, in his own special East Coast style. One was an example of the importance of a conductor.

"You really don't understand the importance of a conductor," he began, "until you have to conduct in a place like

Radio City Music Hall. You stand there in the orchestra pit with your timpani and percussion on 48th street, and your bass section on 49th street. And they're all looking at you to bring them together." I didn't think I would ever actually experience that feeling in that hall, but I did.

Another Joe Wood truism was his explanation of achieving an emotional effect at the end of an original composition. "The size of the group doesn't matter: string trio or full orchestra. And it doesn't make a difference whether it's a big, loud, brassy ending, or one that just dies out. Every ending should be the kind of ending that doesn't leave a dry seat in the house!" Now, there's a vision . . .

Necessity being the mother of invention, as they say, I had finally found a way to stand out at Oberlin, other than playing after-dinner music at the dorm. I certainly wasn't the top musician; I was just another piano player in a sea of amazing freshmen pianists who were devouring great concertos, Chopin Études, and a myriad of contemporary pieces. My major wasn't piano, however; it was music composition/theory, something different. In my theory courses (beginning with Theory II), I explored the inner secrets of why music sounds the way it does; why Bach and Palestrina and Copland sound the way they do; and how to write, compose, and arrange music—the nitty-gritty of it all. And in so doing, once again I became unique, taking a different path by being a composer. I was still gaining attention by playing and performing jazz, but with music composition as my major, I was creating and controlling the music I performed, using the right combination of rhythm, melody, harmony, and form. I was happy again.

I spent the summer after my second year at Oberlin at Culvermere, a resort in upstate New Jersey near the bustling town of Branchville. To quote the brochure, "Culvermere, a gay, informal, complete vacationland, is situated on beautiful Culver Lake, nestled in the Pocono-Kittatinny Mountain area of northwestern New Jersey. All sports and excellent food await the visitor here, and Culvermere's friendly folk make vacations long-remembered for their enjoyment."

Culvermere was my alma mater of show business instruction, where, just by watching, I learned how to put on a show—whether a small duo in a wine bar or a major symphony concert in an outdoor venue. My main instructor was Dave Wilson, who, with a couple of friends, would come "up from the City" on weekends and put on shows—mostly burlesque-type—with a band overture, skits, singers, and instrumentalists. For most of us, this type or genre of music was totally new: medleys of Broadway show tunes, blackouts at the end of a skit or bit, and chasers or bow music played to cover the exiting performers. I always smile when I remember skits like *Quiet in the Library, Doctor Make-M-Better*, and *Cucamonga* ("Slowly I turned, step by step . . .").

Now, you may not recognize Dave Wilson's name, but soon after putting on weekend shows at Culvermere, he directed several *Miss America* pageants and some memorable music/variety TV shows in the '60s. From there, he went on to a twenty-year career directing *Saturday Night Live*. Looking back, I'm sure all of us in the Culvermere band felt honored to have Dave as a director, and to musically support him as he directed those Culvermere shows.

Actually, the organization of the musicians and the music at Culvermere was quite good. We were advertised as "a nine-piece resident band": two trumpets, one trombone, three saxes, piano, bass, and drums; all very fine young musicians, mostly from Ohio State University and Oberlin. Each evening's entertainment had a different theme, with the appropriate band costume. Tuesday was Foreign Night: white pants, white shirt, and a red sash around the waist. Wednesday nights were Latin Nights: the same getup as on Tuesday, but I think we added a straw hat. Thursday was Dress-up Night and the famous *Miss Culvermere Contest*. The winners of these weekly contests came back on Labor Day, the last week of the season, to vie for Miss Culvermere of the year, with the winner receiving a free week's vacation for the next season. Friday and Saturday nights were "show" nights, meaning coats and ties for the band. Since this was a weekly type of resort, guests would leave on Sunday about noon, passing the new guests just arriving. So, Sunday night was "Get Acquainted" night, and things were very informal, dress-wise. Monday was our day off. Some of the band members shared car rides into Manhattan, while others just stayed and recouped for the next week. And that's how our summer went, week after week.

There was live music from 6 p.m. to 3 a.m., and this is how we worked that out: our trombone player, Gary Potter (a good friend, still), also played bass, and the alto sax player also played piano. So, we divided the band into a quintet and a quartet, and we alternated weeks of the following schedule:

6-9 p.m. — The Quintet (trumpet, sax, piano, bass, drums) played cocktail music

9 p.m.-midnight — The Big Band played shows and dance music

Midnight-3 a.m. — The Quartet (trumpet, piano, bass, drums) finished out the evening playing dance music.

Our days were free to do whatever, i.e. practice, and check out the week's group of girls. (The odds were pretty good: about fifteen to one, girls to boys.) A couple of us participated in some of the non-musical shows, like the water show. I would do a belly flop (wearing a thick sweatshirt) from the three-meter board. I did one stint as a bottom man on a five-man waterski pyramid. Did I really do that? Yeah, but only once.

At the beginning of my second season at Culvermere in the summer of '62, one of the waiters, a rather good-looking, muscular guy from the Midwest, made a bet with some of the other waiters that he could, uh, bed each of the *Miss Culvermere Contest* winners. This was quite a challenge, in that the weekly Miss Culvermere wasn't chosen until Thursday night. This gave our resident Don Juan only two days to accomplish his task, which was unthinkable to most of us.

However, to our surprise, he won the bet, though I can't remember if anyone ever raised the question of verification. All of the contest winners did seem quite smitten with him on the Friday and Saturday of their week's stay—holding hands, stealing little kisses now and then—the type of behavior one would expect of such a pairing.

There was a slight problem, however, that no one had anticipated: the return of all the weekly contest winners for the season-ending *Miss Culvermere Pageant.* I'm not sure when our Don Juan realized his dilemma, but when the twelve winners began arriving for the Labor Day weekend festivities, our hero was seen silently slipping out of town, heading west.

And not only did his friends lose their bet, but it was also up to them to answer the questions asked twelve times: "Where is he? Where did he go?"

During my second season I also got a side job as church organist for Christ Union Chapel, a small church located on the shores of Culver Lake, a mile or two from Culvermere. I was to perform for twelve services during the summer as well as twelve Sunday evening "lakeside" sing-alongs. On the first Sunday of my job, I borrowed one of the musician's cars and drove to the church. There, I met the soloist, a local summer resident. She'd been singing at the church for several seasons and had the whole process down to a science. First, we would rehearse her selection for that first Sunday's service. Then, afterward, we'd stay and rehearse the next eleven solos for the entire summer, numbering each one. Each Sunday, I'd arrive a little early, pick out that week's solo and look it over. I'd then sit down at the organ, say "hi" to the soloist—whom I hadn't seen since the previous Sunday—and start to play the service.

It was quite surreal, playing dance music for inebriated eighteen- to twenty-two-year-olds on Saturday nights, and then playing a totally different genre, church music on an electric organ, on Sundays. Though I enjoyed playing the morning services, the fun part of my church job occurred each

Sunday evening, about 6:00 p.m. I'd arrive at the church, walk down to the dock and board a fifteen-by-twenty-foot raft (or, float, as it was called), which was several pieces of plywood strapped to several empty ten-gallon oil drums. A small railing kept people like me and the large wood box of hymnals from falling overboard. The minister, a very jovial guy, would board and then start the five-horsepower Johnson outboard motor, and away to the middle of the lake we'd putt-putt. During the short ride, I'd sit at the very small reed organ perched in the middle of the raft and just hold on. This small organ was powered by my pumping the two foot pedals that provided air flow to the reeds. The only problem was that the sound of the organ went up in the air and instantly disappeared. So, no matter how hard or how fast I pumped, it never sounded loud enough.

After we'd drop anchor, about fifteen or twenty canoes and small motorboats would pull up alongside the raft and expertly tie their crafts together, being careful not to tip anyone over. I'd hand out the hymnals to our floating congregation—families, mostly, up from the city to enjoy a week of summer fun at the lake. Everyone had a favorite hymn, and we'd sing it as loud as we could. However, as the minister pointed out, there were two hymns that probably should not be sung:

"Stand Up, Stand Up For Jesus" and "How Firm A Foundation"—for obvious reasons!

One Sunday evening, a family who'd been regulars at our evening songfests told us that the husband had been transferred to Hawaii. His two young girls weren't very happy to learn that their next Christmas would be without snow. So, the minister suggested we sing some Christmas carols to cheer them up. So we did. And, to me, "Adeste Fideles," "Silent Night," and "Joy To the World" never sounded as beautiful as they did that evening, bouncing off the waters of Lake Culver.

The good things about Culvermere were the food and, for us college guys, a plethora of women. The bad were the musician's lodgings and the money, but, all in all, with the musical knowledge I gained, it was definitely worth it to me. Oh, and everyone had a funny name. Mine was "Boo-Boo," the character from the Yogi Bear cartoon. I was simply known as "Boo-Boo the Piano Player." So, Culvermere took a serious-minded composition and theory major from Oberlin Conservatory of Music and turned him into a, well, a semi-pro musician, ready to tackle the musical world.

My Oberlin story would be incomplete without reference to my dear Jeannie Graff. Oberlin wasn't the easiest place to meet girls, what with all the classes and practicing, but I did date a little, and each girl I dated instantly seemed to be the "one" for me, but only for two or three weeks or so. Then, someone new would catch my eye, and I would move on. That was before I met and dated Jeannie Graff. A beautiful, young woman from Indiana, Pennsylvania, Jeannie was also in the Conservatory, a piano major. Unlike me, she was on the shy side, having gone to an all-girl prep school. We had a lot in common, musically, in that we both played popular-style piano. Where she learned to play by ear, I don't remember, but she was very good at it.

We fell in love our freshman year, spending virtually all of our free time together. We'd play pop duets at the dining hall, go to movies, and talk about "us." Our plan was to go to Salzburg, Austria, for our junior year, return to finish our education at Oberlin, then marry. While we didn't say so in so many words, we both knew it was going to happen. It was a plan both of our families were aware of, as they included us in family plans. I had the opportunity to spend a few days with Jeannie's family at their home in Pennsylvania. In turn, my mother honored her with a party in Terre Haute when she came for a visit during the summer between our freshman and sophomore year.

Shortly after spring break of '61, Jeannie suffered a leg bruise while attempting to mount the back of a motor scooter I was riding. We both thought that was all it was, a seemingly innocent injury. But the pain didn't go away, so Jeannie went to the college clinic to have it checked out. I was busy with classes and didn't realize she'd actually left campus to go home for some special medical examinations. A few days later, still really in the dark about what was going on, I received a call from her mother.

"It appears to be much more serious than a bump on the knee, Bob," her mother began to explain.

"I don't understand."

"We're taking her to a hospital in New York City. Sloan Kettering."

"I've never heard of it."

"It's a cancer hospital."

"You mean . . . "

"They think she has cancer. Bone cancer."

Cancer? Why Jeannie? Only older people got cancer, right? What kind of cancer? What was going to happen to her, to us? Lots of questions, and no real answers. This wasn't the kind of feeling I wanted. It was a feeling I'd never had before. Someone I really cared about was sick, very sick. And for the first time in my life, I was unable to do anything to help. The accidental fall had revealed her bone's weakness, and I, as always, had kept my emotions inside, all the while unconsciously thinking, " . . . sweetness and light . . . " The truth is, I really didn't know what to feel. I'd been hiding my emotions for so long, protecting myself from life's disappointments, that I really didn't know how to act, what to say, or how to express any of it. They say that if you put on an emotional mask to hide something, and keep it on long enough, it gets comfortable and becomes difficult to remove. That's what had happened to me. "Sweetness and light" had become my mask, and I didn't know how to take it off.

Since I was playing piano at Culvermere that summer (the summer before Jeannie and I were supposed to go to Salzburg), I was close enough to visit her in New York every Monday, my day off. She was always cheerful, and we'd laugh as if things would return to normal. But they never did. During the summer, to prevent the spread of the cancer, her left leg was amputated. I handled that situation calmly, too, not talking about it—almost pretending that it hadn't happened. I guess that in my mind, and in my dreams, we'd always be together, and if she only had one leg, it wouldn't be the end of the world. Sometimes when I wanted to visit she was too sick for visitors, and I understood that. It was difficult being with her and trying to keep an optimistic attitude, knowing that she'd never be able to go to Salzburg, and that she probably wouldn't be able to come back to Oberlin. It was difficult trying to visualize anything in the future. It was just one day at a time.

Looking back, I realize, sadly, that I was thinking less about her struggle and more about how her situation was affecting me. Her cancer was getting in the way of all of our plans, spoiling what we had. Her parents had told a fellow Oberlin music student, Gary Potter, who also played in my summer band, about Jeannie's condition. "He's someone you can talk to," they said. Even though Gary was willing, I didn't really talk to him because I didn't know what to say, or how to let out what I was really feeling.

Then, when Jeannie died in August, I went to her funeral, still keeping my emotions to myself. People there looked at me sadly, told me that things would be all right, and that I had my life ahead of me—all those clichés. I was hesitant to look at her in the open casket, not wanting to . . . I don't know, just not wanting to have the last sight of her be that one. So, I glanced at her from a distance, and saw her face, unsmiling, her arms resting on her chest. Her family was there, but I don't remember her siblings, even though the three of them were present. Her dad was crying; her mother was stoic, consoling. I guess I was shutting myself off from the pain of losing her. My emotional mask was firmly in place.

Then, about a month later, I was off to Europe, a trip I had dreamed about—we had dreamed about—but now it was only me. Whenever my classmates attempted to express their sympathy about Jeannie, I would instinctively look away, not knowing how to respond, and then softly say "thanks" before quickly changing the subject. Looking back, I realize just how hard I was working to hide my emotions. The mask had become a part of me that, for the most part, I never discarded.

I think I became more comfortable wearing that mask for my entire year in Salzburg. That and the differences in the culture, customs, and language all made the loss of Jeannie more bearable. In the first few weeks, there were times when I thought of her, the plans we'd made, all of it. But I was soon so involved with my music studies and the experience of living in a foreign city that the pain lessened.

Salzburg in '61 and '62 was delightful, a city whose musical foundation was evident everywhere. For instance, every church had excellent choirs and organists performing great music every Sunday. If you got up early enough, it was possible to catch four different masses by Bach, Beethoven, Brahms, and, of course, Mozart, all on a Sunday morning.

The Festspielhaus (Concert Hall) and the Mozarteum where we studied were probably the second and third most well-known attractions in Salzburg, the first being the birth house of Mozart. We learned to avoid the crowds visiting this historic spot on Getreidegasse, all of them carrying cameras and taking pictures of everything. Some of the American tourists were really annoying, talking loudly and complaining about the lack of space in the small, crowded streets. A few of us decided to wear lederhosen to try not to look American. It worked fairly well, until four of us went out to a nice restaurant for dinner one evening. We ordered in the best German we could and enjoyed our meal. When it came time to pay the check, the waiter presented the bill, said, "Zwei hundret, vierzig schillings," paused, and then said, "That'll be twelve bucks." Well, so much for trying to blend in.

Memories of my first year in Salzburg are many, but a few that stand out are:

1) Having Thanksgiving with a turkey (a Butterball, I think) provided by the U.S. Army Base at Berchtesgaden, Germany.

2) Playing the xylophone solo in Britten's "Young Person's Guide to the Orchestra," with the Mozarteum Orchestra—I nailed it.

3) Christmas with our adopted Austrian families, and seeing real candles on Christmas trees.

4) A car trip with classmates to sunny Spain to celebrate New Year's Eve.

5) Another car trip in the spring to visit some famous and very ornate German church organs.

6) Getting on the ship in Southampton, England, ready to cruise home for my senior year at Oberlin.

OLD WARNER HALL - OBERLIN CONSERVATORY OF MUSIC

MOZART'S BIRTHPLACE
SALZBURG, AUSTRIA

MOZARTEUM - SALZBURG, AUSTRIA

6. The Poem

I returned to Oberlin for my final year, a year that should have been full of promise. Instead, I was actually afraid of returning to the same pathways and buildings where Jeannie and I had walked and made plans. My classmates, having witnessed my "sweetness and light" attitude in Salzburg, knew I avoided any conversation about Jeannie's death. Now, back at Oberlin, their concern faded as their focus turned toward graduation and getting on with their lives. I, too, was focused on getting through my senior year and covered my emotions as usual. But there were many nights that Jeannie's smiling face appeared while I drifted off to sleep. Those were the hardest times. I tried to put her out of my mind, and felt guilty about it, but it was the only way I knew how to go on. Putting the loss of her behind me and concentrating on my music became the one sure thing in my life.

Our senior recital was to be the culmination of all we had learned in our chosen craft. My composition teacher, Joe Wood, suggested a program of several of my works: begin with a piano sonata; then a percussion piece; and end with a new, large, long work featuring a symphony orchestra, a large chorus, and a vocal soloist—quite ambitious, even for me. With his approval, I searched the library and found a fairly short poem by "anonymous." The text told a rather dramatic story, one that could easily be put to a melody. The poem was in three sections, much like the movements found in musical pieces. So, with the basic musical form in mind, I went to work, first putting a melody to the text and laying out the general form of the piece. I tried to make the words fit the melody, singing it to see if it was understandable. When I was finished with the melody, I started filling in the places where the chorus and orchestra would help embellish the vocal solo. When I was finished, I found that the entire piece was about eight minutes long. To a non-musician, eight minutes doesn't seem very long. But to a composer, it's a lifetime. I spent many hours figuring out which sections of the orchestra should play, which voices of the chorus should sing, all without covering up the vocal soloist.

Even though I had a full load of other music classes—theory, choir, history, and piano lessons—almost every day of that first semester was taken up with composing my work: orchestrating, preparing the separate parts for the orchestra players and the chorus, then copying all the parts by hand (no computers at that time). I had to get it all done in a hurry so that I could plan rehearsals for all three elements of the piece: the Oberlin College Symphony, the Oberlin College Choir, and the soloist, Ruth Stoffel. In my dorm room, I continued to copy the full score, from which I would conduct. Since ink and I didn't get along, I used IBM leaded pencils for the full score, as well as for all the parts, working late into the night. My roommate, Bill Burrows, a pre-med student, was at first simply curious:

"Are you ever going to finish that thing?" (This would become a constant query.)

I ignored him.

"Every night I see you bent over your desk, making little marks."

I continued to ignore him.

"Hey, the snack bar's still open. Let's take a break. I'll spring for coffee."

"Nah, you go ahead. I want to make sure this sounds right."

"You mean you can just look at that and hear it?" he asked.

"Yeah, well, it's a gift. And it's making me a wreck. But I've got to finish it. The recital's in January, just six weeks away, and I'm going to lose two of those weeks to Christmas break. I just gotta get this done."

"If it's that important, I'll bring back a cup."

I accepted his offer and continued to focus relentlessly on the work. After he left, I pulled out a can of shellac to spray on the score to keep the pencil from smearing, a trick I'd picked up from another composition student.

When Bill came back with the coffee, his first comment was, "Ugh! What's that smell? It's like an old test tube full of sulfur!"

"It's just shellac in a can," I said. "I'd open the window, but it's raining. Sorry. I should be through in about an hour."

"Forget it," he said, and quickly headed downstairs to the lounge, where he slept for the next several nights. I didn't care. I was on a mission to be interrupted only by a two-week holiday break.

In December, I flew to Houston to visit my parents. My dad had been transferred back by Marathon Oil. While there, I noticed that my heart would start beating rapidly, then suddenly quit for a few beats. It happened often enough for me to tell my parents, and they insisted I see a doctor. During the examination, the doctor began asking me what I thought were odd medical questions.

"Tell me about your life," he said. "Your file says that you're a student at Oberlin, right? Good school for music, I hear."

"Yes, I'm a composition major."

"And this is your final year?"

"Yes."

I went on to tell him about my senior recital, and the complications and deadlines I faced, and this led to him asking even more "non-medical" questions.

"Talk to me about your personal life. Do you have a girlfriend?" He stared intently, fingering his stethoscope as he frowned.

"Well, yes . . . yes," I stammered. "I did, anyway."

My mask was slowly giving way.

"So, it ended, recently?"

"She died. Bone cancer." The phrase itself, like the truth, was simple. But as the words left my mouth, I knew there was nothing easy about it. Yet, somehow, just saying it out loud seemed to allow me to breath more easily.

The doctor sat down on the stool by the examination table and issued a kindly smile. "I'm sorry," he said.

I had nothing more to say. So we both sat in silence for a while as he thoughtfully looked me over. Then he offered his diagnosis.

"What you have is a small heart murmur. I have to believe it's at least partly due to all the pressure you are under, but it's mostly due to grief."

I tried to stay cool, but it wasn't easy.

"The good news is, you're going to last at least until your concert. But I would suggest you take a break soon and take some time to grieve."

I knew he was right, but I still had to focus on the concert, so I couldn't give myself permission to do that, yet.

Back at Oberlin, after the break, the pressure didn't let up: more rehearsals, more recopying of parts, more shellac spraying. And I was having midterm exams in my other subjects, as well. The pressure just kept building.

About a week before the concert, the conductor of the Oberlin Orchestra called me into his office with a suggestion that added even more pressure.

"Mr. Ayars, I think it would be better if you were to conduct this work instead of me. I know you had conducting experience in Salzburg, and, if you'd like, I'd be happy to give you a few pointers. I know you can do a fine job of it."

"Well, I guess I could," I said, my mind thinking a million thoughts and my heart murmur now a constant, nagging companion. So, now, on top of everything else, I was going to conduct my own work, instead of sitting with the audience in the concert hall and listening to it. Another hurdle to jump, more pressure, more possibilities for mistakes. But I couldn't let people know how I felt, couldn't let them know that I had no idea if I actually could handle all of this: the composing, the copying, the rehearsing—plus the conducting. I couldn't let them see me sweat. The success of the concert depended on my ability, as a composer and a conductor, to enable the performers to do their best. But could I really do it all?

The answer was, simply, that I became so involved with everything that I never had time to think about whether I could or couldn't do it. Deep down, I felt that I could pull it off. I also knew I couldn't give in to the pressure or stray from my musical path.

Up at 6:00 a.m. every morning, going to classes, taking tests, rehearsing in the afternoons, tweaking and spraying parts at night, then falling into bed about 2:00 a.m.—this continued up until the night of the concert. I kept working on the composition, the melody, the text, the chorus echoing the soloist here and there, the way the orchestra supplied the proper background for telling the story. It was all coming together.

My concert was very well attended. A concert of original works by a student composer was something of an oddity, I guess. I put on my best dark suit, not having a tux, and presented myself backstage, watching the performers play my collected pieces. It seemed to go all right, but I was only half listening as I constantly scoured my score, making sure to remember to cue the winds here and the brass there. Then, Mr.

Bourne, the staff stage manager of Warner Concert Hall, explained how things would happen for my final piece:

"The orchestra will go on first, then the chorus, then your soloist. I'll hold you here until it's time for you to enter. Normally, the orchestra stands when the conductor takes the podium, but you're not at that level, yet," he smiled. "So, just walk through the violins, climb the podium, and when the coughing and shuffling has quieted down, you can start."

"Break a leg," Mr. Bourne said, pushing me on stage.

I walked through the orchestra to the podium, and the orchestra members suddenly started shuffling their feet and tapping their bows on their stands, their way of saying, "Break a leg."

I really don't remember the performance. I do remember the myriad small thoughts racing through my mind: cue the chorus here, slow the tempo there, let the soloist have more leeway at this spot. I kept looking at my score, making sure that, if it said to conduct in 4/4 time, I conducted in 4/4 and not 3/4. I know I forgot several cues for the chorus and for the soloist standing next to me, and for the different sections of the orchestra. Suddenly, I was looking at the last page of the score and it was almost over. I had chosen to end the work quietly, with a single snare drum roll, and as I did, I remembered one of Joseph Wood's performance rules about not leaving " . . . a dry seat in the house."

And then it was over. I put my arms down, suddenly realizing how tired they were. There was a moment of silence before the applause started. I took a deep breath and felt my heart, as if prompted by an unseen hand, return to normal. I smiled at all the performers, mouthing the words, "thank you." Turning to face the audience, I saw my friends and classmates all clapping. On the aisle, about halfway back, sat Jeannie's parents, having driven over from Indiana, Pennsylvania, for the event. I gave them a special nod. (My parents weren't at the recital, as we had just been together for Christmas break in Houston; in January of '63, there weren't many flights going back and forth.) I then bowed and left the podium, walking back through the first violins as the orchestra again shuffled their feet and tapped their bows.

After an encore bow, I was ushered into a reception room next to the stage for a small party, a ritual given to every senior after their final recital. I stood by the entrance, shaking hands with many of the audience members.

"So, this is what you do. I always thought you just played piano in the dining hall after dinner," laughed Sam, a philosophy major.

"Yeah, a little of this, a little of that," I replied.

"Well, old buddy, all that shellac really paid off," said my roommate.

"Yeah, well, thanks for putting up with the smell."

"You did very well, Mr. Ayars, very well, indeed. Congratulations," said the conducting professor.

REHEARSING MY SENIOR RECITAL - 1963

MY SENIOR DORM - WILDER HALL, OBERLIN COLLEGE

Then, Jeannie's mom greeted me with a hug, as she always did. "You were wonderful," she said with her firm voice. "Everything was wonderful, just wonderful."

"The whole concert was really fine, and thank you for choosing that piece to end with," her dad added, quietly. He was the calmer of the two; I had to lean in to hear him. "You made us all very proud, and I'm sure Jeannie would have liked it, too."

"I hope so," was all I could say. Confused, I didn't know how to react.

Then it was all put into perspective when one of my female classmates came up, gave me a hug, and tearfully said,

"It was beautiful, so beautiful. I honestly had trouble holding back the tears. You did a wonderful, wonderful job:

you, the orchestra, the choir, and the soloist. I found myself thinking about her during the whole piece. Jeannie would have really appreciated it, knowing you thought so much of her to choose that poem. It must have been a pure labor of love. It was so sad, but I know why you chose it. I'm sure she was with you the whole time you worked on this, wasn't she?"

And then I connected the dots. I stood there, frozen, trying to recover from the realization that the truth had been so obvious to everyone but me. In my efforts to forget the loss of Jeannie, to put it out of my mind with "sweetness and light," to cover my emotions, I'd ended up creating a musical tribute to her. As dense, as selfish, and as oblivious as it sounds, it was the first time I realized the significance of the title of the anonymous poem I'd selected.

It was "The Death of the Sweetheart."

The Second Movement:

My Leitmotif

> Always have something to get up for in the morning.
>
> —Bob Ayars, my father, upon his retirement.

7.

From Salzburg to Las Vegas Via the Army

I knew, after my last year at Oberlin, that although I appreciated the classics, my path was taking me more to the popular side of music. And with my background in both, I felt I was perfect for something like Walt Disney, an organization that blended classical and popular music in many of their productions. But, instead of rushing out to conquer the world, I applied for and received a teaching assistantship back in Salzburg, acting as an assistant theory teacher and counselor for that year's junior class. This gave me a chance to study with other teachers—Cesar Bresgen, in particular. It was also a fun opportunity to travel with a new girlfriend, a sophomore vocalist. I think, though, that I mostly was afraid to go outside my musical comfort zone and felt more secure with people and places I already knew and understood.

Cesar Bresgen was an Austrian professor of composition at the Mozarteum. Although not that well known in the United States, he was highly regarded in European musical circles, especially among composers. He had an excellent command of English and was friendly and soft-spoken during my lessons.

He smiled often and was always encouraging. I remember one time when he showed me a different way of composing:

"Think of your melody, ja? Close your eyes. Don't even look at what you're doing," he told me, smiling. "The idea is to draw a line to show your melody on a piece of paper, without using a piano. Put your pencil on the left side of the paper and, with your eyes closed, slowly draw the pencil across the paper, moving your hand up when the melody goes up and down when it goes down, ja? And then you make different movements when it's loud, like going over the line, making it darker. If you come to the end of the paper, use the next sheet, und so weiter, ja?" He paused to let it sink in.

"But, I've never composed anything without a piano. I can hear the notes in my head, but if there's no piano, I'll be lost, like driving without a steering wheel," I replied.

"Ya, I understand, but the point is, mein lieber, to let your imagination do the work in a different way, ja? When you are finished, take these lines to the piano and make them into notes, high and low, loud and soft, fast and slow. I've heard that other composers have done this with great success. This is what Bach did; this is what Mozart did; this is what Stravinsky did." It was tough to argue with that group of composers.

So, I tried it. I can remember taking the gondola or ski lift up the Gaisberg (a popular skiing destination not far from our hotel) on several spring afternoons, sitting on a bench by the gasthof café, looking out over the hills, closing my eyes, and making use of Cesar's suggestion. And it really worked! Honestly, to this day, I still use this method if I get stuck when I'm arranging a piece. I'll close my eyes and, in my mind, draw a line to mark the ebb and flow of the music.

I took several courses in Salzburg, similar to ones I'd taken at Oberlin: Fine Arts, German, Piano, Composition, and Orchestral Conducting. But I think the most important course was day-to-day living in a different culture. During this second stay in Salzburg, I expanded the things I could do with music by teaching a simple jazz course at the Mozarteum. The challenge was to teach this American form of music to a group of people from several different countries, not all of whom spoke English. I had to do the best I could, expressing my thoughts in German. There were four nuns attending the class, and talking about the trumpet playing of Bix Beiderbecke or the compositions of Duke Ellington and Billy Strayhorn while looking at the Sisters was a bit strange, but I discovered that they knew the words "jazz," "be-bop," and "baby." Yes, the language of music is universal!

Also on this second Salzburg trip, a small portion of me appeared in a movie you may have heard of, starring Julie Andrews and Christopher Plummer: *The Sound of Music.*

Here's how that happened: Several students at the Mozarteum were chosen to be extras for the movie, to portray young people in street scenes, taking walks in the country, etc. A fellow student mentioned that the film needed a timpani or kettledrum player for an orchestra scene, and asked if I was available. In music schools around the world it is common for composition majors to play the simpler instruments in the percussion section: triangle, bass drum, and timpani drum. At Oberlin, I'd played timpani in a small orchestra for a piece by Bach. At the Mozarteum, they had put me on xylophone for Britten's *Young Person's Guide to the Orchestra*, so this sounded like a natural for me. The drums being used in the movie, however, weren't timpani, but instead *pherd paukin* (German for "horse timpani"), large drums that were slung over a parading horse.

The scene had Captain von Trapp (Christopher Plummer), his wife (Julie Andrews), and his family of seven children singing "So Long, Farewell" in a folk-song contest. They were accompanied by a forty-piece orchestra composed mostly of Austrian policemen. (There's a lot of music everywhere in Austria.) The job lasted several nights, and was filmed from 10:00 p.m. until about 4:30 a.m. to have more control over the light and sound. I was told to wear a dark suit and tie and to be at my drums precisely at 9:45 p.m. The film was being shot in the Festspielhaus, a large auditorium used by many orchestras in the annual Salzburg Music Festival. Even though I had the correct sheet music on my stand, I was told that we were not actually being recorded—a procedure called "sidelining," which is used to give scenes more realism. So, it really didn't matter what kind of drums I was using, as long as I was banging on some kind of drum.

At one point in the scene, one of the judges of the folk-song contest walks down the aisle to the stage and hands the character, Uncle Max, the results. The actor portraying Uncle Max, Richard Hayden, was standing on the stage directly over and behind my position on the floor in front of the stage. The director, Robert Wise, asked the older gentleman who was portraying the judge—a local actor who was enjoying his role in this American movie—to repeat his walk several times and filmed him from different angles: from the side, from the balcony, and, lastly, from directly behind him, following him down the aisle. This last version was chosen as the shot they wanted, and they reset the scene with the camera pointed down the aisle, directly at me. In the first practice run-through, down the aisle came the judge, right up to the edge of the stage. Just before he reached the orchestra, Mr. Wise yelled out, "Have the timpani player with the glasses turn around and face the stage." So, there I am, the back of my head showing for all to see. I think I got about five dollars and a meal out of each evening's work. I didn't care. I was actually in a movie . . . or, more precisely, the back of my head was.

When I landed back in New York after my second year in Salzburg, I brought with me a new Volkswagen and, freshly equipped with everything I thought I needed to succeed, I headed for Houston to see my folks. Then, I would be off to Hollywood—perhaps Walt Disney—to start my career as a musician. But, when I got to Houston, I found a letter from dear Uncle Sam asking me to join the ranks of others who were being drafted. Damn! A brick wall between me and my career. But I had to fulfill my military obligation somehow. So, after checking around, I decided on a plan that would allow me to be in the Hollywood area and still serve. I would enter the military via the Los Angeles Army Induction Center and then hope to find a local Army Reserve or National Guard outfit in which to enlist. For me, one weekend a month and two weeks of summer camp was better than becoming a full-time soldier.

While driving west in my new VW, with lots of time to think, I started having serious thoughts about trying to start a music career. What was I going to do, just walk into a major recording studio and become, what—a composer, an arranger, a conductor, a pianist? I started thinking about the great musicians who were already working in Hollywood, all well-known and exceptional musical artists. Was I really their equal? And why should any studio hire me instead of them? I had no experience, nothing remotely similar to what they'd done. And did one actually get a studio job like that, anyway? Was I setting myself up for another embarrassing situation similar to my experience at Northwestern? I knew I couldn't go through something like that again. Should I enter the Army for two years and just forget about being a musician for a while? Wow! So many questions, and lots of self-doubt. And then the questions were answered in a little California town called Indio.

I drove at night to avoid the desert heat; just me and a few truckers on yet-to-be-completed Interstate 10. At about 7:00 in the evening, just after crossing into California, some music came into my head, a tune by Neal Hefti from the movie *How to Murder Your Wife*. It was the chord progression he used when the leading lady, Virna Lisi, first comes out of a fake cake at a bachelor party. I kept running those chords over and over in my head, trying to visualize them, but I kept missing something. It just didn't sound right, and I was determined to find that progression, so, in Indio, I stopped at a bar that advertised live music, hoping to find some kind of a piano. This was a musical problem that couldn't be solved by drawing a line on a piece of paper.

There was a small spinet piano next to a small dance floor. Three people sat at the bar, all locals, I'm sure. I asked the bartender if I could quietly use his piano for just a couple of minutes. He looked at me a full ten seconds, then said, "Yeah, sure, go ahead."

"Thanks." I sat at the old piano, trying different chord progressions, hoping to find the right combination.

"You a piano player?" one of the patrons mumbled.

I glanced his way and noticed that he looked like he'd been bolted to his barstool for the last forty years.

I said nothing and continued to search for the correct chords. I could feel the locals looking at me, which made me quite nervous. I'm sure I didn't sound like a very good player, trying out all sorts of chord possibilities. Then, suddenly, I found the exact combination, a series of ascending chords with the bass note moving in a downward motion. You hear those chords and you can almost see Virna rising from the cake!

I played the chord progression as I remembered it from the movie, slowly and softly, following Ms. Lisi out of her cake. Even the bar patron agreed and said,

"Hey, that sounds nice. Do you know that old song . . . ?"

I quickly got up, turned to the bartender and said,

"Sorry. I gotta go. Thanks again." And I was out the door.

It may sound funny, but finding those simple chords made me more certain than ever that my career was in popular music. Back in my VW, I began formulating a new plan. What if I could use my music in the military, like playing clarinet in a band or organ in a military chapel? Music was my talent, my way of getting noticed, of being someone unique. And why not in the Army? There just might be a musical opening for me. I started smiling as I headed toward San Bernardino, thinking lots of positive thoughts about my future. Thanks to those chords, I couldn't wait to get started with my musical life, civilian or military.

I arrived in Glendale, California, around 6:30 on a Sunday morning. After I had a full breakfast at a local diner called Foxy's Restaurant, I called my Aunt Carolyn. Turns out that Foxy's was her favorite local dining place, so she drove over for her Sunday breakfast before we headed to her duplex apartment. She was the registrar at Occidental College, a very fine and well-respected school in Eagle Rock, just next door to Glendale. She was talkative—even more so than I am, if that's possible—and after telling several college stories of her own, she asked to hear all about my Oberlin years, my stay in Europe, and what my plans were.

"Well, Aunt Carolyn, I'm pretty positive about going into popular music. I'm planning on following up with some contacts here in L.A., visiting several recording studios and the local Musician's Union, then seeing about that Disney contact mom told me about, the husband of one of her cousins. I think he's in the accounting department at Disney's Buena Vista office. I know it's not the music department, but it's a Disney lead. But first, I've got this military thing I've got to do, so, for a couple of months, my life's going to be on hold. Hope you don't mind me staying with you for a while."

"Well, we'll see what we can do for you for the time being, uh, Bo," she smiled. "Do you mind if I call you that? In all her letters, your mother refers to you as 'Bo.'" I didn't mind. I had never minded being called that by my parents, so why not my relatives, too?

"Sure, call me Bo," I said.

After another cup of coffee, her second, my fourteenth, I followed her back to her small, one-bedroom duplex. She took the three large couch cushions and put them on the floor, showed me where the coffee was, said a quick goodbye and was out the door on some errands, giving me some late-morning sleep time. Those cushions would be my bed for the foreseeable future.

I lay on my makeshift bed, rethinking my new plan regarding my immediate military future. I had to smile, though, because here I was, in Glendale, California, a town right next to Hollywood, California—one of the great music capitals of the country—sleeping on the floor of my aunt's duplex. Before I could do anything musical, however, a huge chunk of my life would be taken away from me, thanks to Uncle Sam. I quickly fell asleep, exhausted from driving, talking, and planning.

The next day, Monday, I went to the Army Induction Center in downtown L.A. After signing in and getting a brief physical, which included multiple shots from a sinister-looking automatic "shot" gun, I was classified as 1A: available for duty anywhere in the world the government wanted to send me. My musical career started to look further and further away.

A few days later, I was informed that I would report to Fort Polk in central Louisiana on October 12, 1964, Columbus Day. How fitting that I would begin to explore a brand new world on the day commemorating Mr. Columbus. Ironically, Houston, Texas, was just a couple of hours away. Well, at least I'd be close to home.

My assignment left me with a couple months to find an alternate military unit with a shorter active-duty period. I checked out the Army Reserve, and found that the 63rd Infantry in Maywood/Bell had a band. Bingo! I called and made an appointment. Once there, I learned that they already had a pianist, but did have an opening for a tuba player. I had played a little baritone horn in high school, and tuba fingering is about the same; the tuba just has a bigger mouthpiece. But in order to read music for the tuba, I'd have to transpose—my nemesis. Oh, well, if the army was willing to take me for a minimum of active-duty time, I was willing to transpose on the tuba. Sounded like a no-brainer, but it wasn't all that simple to Uncle Sam.

My enlistment conversation went something like this:

"Let me get this straight," I said. "You have an *opening* for a tuba player, but you don't have the slot to send a new recruit to *train* to be a tuba player?" I asked.

"That's it," the corporal deadpanned. "Your paperwork says you can type."

"Yeah, thanks to my mother," I said.

"We do have a slot for a personnel administrator," he replied.

"What's that?"

"It's a clerk/typist with added skills. According to MOS 716 (Military Occupational Specialty, but we called it the easier-to-say Method of Service), your active duty will be two months of

Basic, then two months of MOS 716 training, then you'll come back and train one weekend a month, plus two weeks in the summer every year for six years," he said, with absolutely no emotion. I nodded.

"Our duty roster shows that we currently have a tuba player, but, let's see . . . "

He paused, running his finger across a large piece of graph paper.

"Yes, it says he's mustering out in three weeks. Sign up today as an MOS 716 personnel administrator, and when you get out, you'll be our new tuba player."

I stood there, trying to hoist in what he was saying: I'd go to school to become a personnel administrator and then, without any lessons, I'd come back to the unit as a tuba player. It didn't make sense, but he kept tapping the signature line more firmly with each passing second. He continued:

"You'll be active for sixteen weeks: eight weeks Basic Training, eight weeks personnel administration school. After that, you'll be obligated for one weekend base training per month and one two-week summer drill per year, for a total of six years enlistment. Sounds like a good deal to me. How about you?" he asked, tapping more urgently on the paper.

As odd as it sounded, this plan was definitely better than 1) joining the National Guard and being called out on every natural disaster, 2) being drafted in the Regular Army for two years or, shudder to think, 3) enlisting in the Regular Army for three years. As strange as it all sounded, I could do this. At least after a couple months of Basic, I'd be doing something musical, even if it was going *um-pa, um-pa.*

"Yeah, OK," I said. "So, I sign here?"

"Yeah."

I signed my full name, Robert Needham Ayars, Jr.

"Welcome to the Army, new recruit A-yars," he said, mispronouncing my name, again, with no emotion. I didn't correct him since it was pretty clear he didn't care. Nothing like having a totally disinterested noncom to help me decide my musical future. Well, at least I had some kind of future—just not the kind I had anticipated.

My relative at Disney did, in fact, work in the accounting department. Nowadays, he'd be running the studio, but back then he couldn't help me, except to suggest I contact the creative side of the company. But to do so, I needed a personal invitation from someone in the creative department, which I didn't have. I realized that, with only a couple months of free time before starting Basic Training, I really couldn't do much work, anyway. I did join the Musician's Union, but again, with limited time, I couldn't get a steady job. So, I mostly loafed, read books, visited some piano stores to keep up my chops, and went to a few piano bars, wanting to sit in, but not sure if I'd be welcome.

When I told Aunt Carolyn about not being able to get a foot in the Disney door, she suggested I contact my mother's cousin George Arnold, whom I had met years ago in Terre Haute. "He's in show business; maybe he could introduce you to some people."

So, in August of '64, after a couple of phone calls, I drove to Palm Springs, California, George's home at the time. He had been skating in a seven-days-a-week show in Vegas and had come back to Palm Springs to recharge. He had a new show that he was auditioning at the Tropicana, and he asked me to write some duo piano parts and play the second piano. So, the day after I arrived, he and I drove to Vegas in his Thunderbird, with the top down. All I remember of that short trip was that it was hot, hotter than Bakersfield and Houston combined. George drank up the sunshine and heat while I cowered in the passenger seat, trying to cool off by putting my hand to my forehead, the only shade I could find.

When I'd met cousin George in Terre Haute as a child in the mid-'50s, I knew he was a popular ice skater, ice show producer, and costume designer who was always smiling and telling stories about his entertainer friends, his various ice shows, and the outrageous costumes he designed for them.

Knowing him as an adult, I assumed he was gay, a term that wasn't used much at the time. I'm not sure why, but it didn't bother me; I just accepted him and his male friends for their talent—with a bit of envy, since they were where I wanted to be: working in the entertainment business.

In Vegas, I met several of George's show biz friends, including his skating partner, Phil Richards. The two of them had appeared at the Mint hotel and casino downtown. They had a rather unique act that used a very small ice rink, about eight feet square. Phil—a big, tall guy—would start spinning on the ice while holding George by the arms. As the centripetal force built up, George would be lifted off the ground and would do some rather difficult acrobatic moves. Going around faster and faster, first being held by his hands, then by his feet, he would whirl around Phil so quickly that his pants would start sliding down his legs. It was truly a very funny act, and the first time I saw it, I couldn't stop laughing at the fiasco, thinking it was all an accident. The second time, I realized that the falling pants were part of the act and enjoyed watching the audience go crazy when they saw George's predicament. In later years, George used his talents to produce several very successful ice shows, one of which was called *Nudes on Ice*, a show we musicians referred to as "Boobs on Cubes." But that's another chapter.

We did lots of rehearsals for the Tropicana show, and then the big day—dress rehearsal—arrived. The other pianist (whose name I've forgotten) and I found two pianos set up on the Tropicana lounge stage when we arrived about 1:00 in the afternoon. The only problem was that one of the pianos had only its black keys, the white keys having been removed for adjustments, I guess. Since I had done most of the rehearsing, I was the one chosen to play the piano. Unfortunately, this show didn't get produced, and George and I drove back to Palm Springs, and then I drove back to Aunt Carolyn's in Glendale and waited for Basic Training to begin.

Basic Training at Fort Polk meant sixteen-hour days filled with running, push-ups, rifle training, throwing live grenades (the scariest thing I've ever done), and more running. Sleep came easily. Mornings came quickly. I devoured whatever food they handed out and yet lost weight. It wasn't a diet I'd recommend, but I must admit, I did look spiffy (my mother's word) in my dark-green uniform back home at Christmas break. It's strange how things work out: Because Fort Ord had been temporarily closed due to an outbreak of meningitis, my Basic Training had been moved to Louisiana, which made going home to Houston for the two-week Christmas break a simple, two-hour drive. The rest of my company, all from the

West Coast, had to fly home. After the holiday break, I drove back to Fort Polk, finished Basic and, lo and behold, Fort Ord was back open, and we were flown back to Monterey, California.

Personnel administrator training was the complete opposite of Basic Training: teachers who treated us like human beings, interesting conversations with like-minded privates, and, would you believe, they even asked me how I wanted my eggs cooked in the mess hall!

And then I was out, back to sleeping on the cushions at Aunt Carolyn's duplex in Glendale. Now what? I had no leads. The only thing I could think of for employment were those piano bars. So, I began my musical career in California, sitting in, trying to get hired at a couple of the local piano bars.

Playing in piano bars can be a chore: having to play "Tiny Bubbles" or "Red Roses For A Blue Lady" for the sixth time that evening because somebody put a buck in the tip jar. But for me, playing in piano bars was a great way to learn a ton of songs, and, just as importantly, it helped me learn how to accompany singers—good, bad, or otherwise.

One of the first singers with whom I worked steadily was a guy named Tony Farrell. I had gone to a local Glendale piano bar one evening, and Tony had popped in to sing. He had a nice voice and, like me, was looking for a job. Our meeting was life-changing for me for a non-musical reason: it was the first time I introduced myself as "Bo." As I said, my immediate family called me "Bo," and now my California relatives were calling me "Bo." I was used to it, so when Tony asked me what my name was, I said, without thinking, "Bo." And it's been that way ever since.

Tony and I really did sound good together, with his crooning Irish tenor voice and my full piano accompaniments. We decided to join forces and move down to Orange County, where he had a contact for some entertainment work at another piano bar. We shared an apartment in the City of Orange and began working at The Golden Hind, a workingman's bar and grill. It was owned by a gentleman named Curly who told us, " . . . go out and buy me a piano, then I'll hire you."

So we did. I found a nice, six-foot, off-brand grand piano and, with Tony playing a homemade "gut bucket" bass made of a wash tub, pole, and twine, we became the new piano bar sensation of the area and made a lot of people happy, including Curly. He said if we played the lunch hour, he'd give us dinner on the house every night. Musicians never argue when there's food involved.

In the beginning of our working relationship, I asked Tony about his background, family, music, etc. As I remember, he responded with something that confused me, telling me he used to be a backup quarterback for the Philadelphia Eagles pro football franchise. I didn't see it. He was about five feet eight and weighed less than one hundred eighty pounds. Recently, when I researched the Eagles' football history, I couldn't find any Tony Farrell on the roster, past or present—if that was indeed his real name. Nevertheless, in fairness to Tony, I did come home one day to find one of the L.A. Rams' defensive linemen, Rosey Grier, sitting on the couch in our living room. I have no idea how Tony knew Grier, but there was Rosey, sitting and drinking a glass of iced tea. Though he was past his playing days, he was still a huge presence, but not too talkative.

As I said, working in the piano bars taught me how to play a lot of songs, and how to accompany all kinds of singers, something that became an important part of my later musical life. Another thing I learned—from watching all the inebriated patrons and musicians high on who knows what—was that I didn't want addiction to alcohol or drugs, one of the biggest pitfalls in the music business, to be a part of my life. It took away my self-control, and I liked being in control. I did try pot a couple of times, but, as corny as it sounds, when I wake up in the morning, I feel great. I really don't need an outside stimulant to get through the day or night.

Speaking of drinking, all piano bar players have a favorite booze story. Here's mine:

I was working in a country-western piano bar on North Lankershim Boulevard in North Hollywood. It was right next to another famous country-western establishment, the Palomino Club, and just down the street from a large, long-haul trucking firm. I'm not a big fan of that genre of music, but it was a paying gig, and the place was always packed with truck drivers. The piano, a small spinet, was positioned behind a piece of furniture made to look like the top of a grand piano, a style I'm sure you've seen before. Since it was my first time there, to make friends with the local patrons, I accepted their offers of a drink. My favorite off-hours exotic drink at the time was Amaretto, straight, on the rocks, something I'd sip while watching TV. My first night there, I ended up with six shots all lined up on my piano. At closing, I explained to the bartender that I really wasn't a drinker but didn't want to do or say anything that would hurt his bar business. He told me not to worry, and for me to keep asking for shots of Amaretto.

So for the next several nights, that's what I did, I kept ordering Amarettos. Toward the end of the evening, there were six or seven shots sitting on my piano. However, when I did take a sip now and then, I noticed that each one was very weak, with just a hint of liquor. Obviously, the bartender was watering my drinks, but that was his department, not mine, so I kept ordering Amarettos.

Then, about the sixth evening, an older trucker, after buying me a drink, frowned as he noticed all the shots lined up on the piano.

"Hey," he said, "you can't be drinkin' all those by yourself. You'd be pie-eyed, that's for sure."

"Well," I began, "I kind of space them out over the evening and . . ."

"Here, let me help you." He took one of the shots and downed it.

The next few moments are still a blur. It started with him yelling something unprintable to the bartender. He kept yelling and cursing about watered-down drinks, and then picked up one of the shot glasses and threw it on the floor. He then turned and stomped full steam ahead, straight toward the bartender, bumping into people, chairs, and tables as he went. He was really angry, and his mood transferred to some of the other truckers in the bar. They, too, started grabbing my shot glasses and tasting them. When they realized how the drinks had been poured, they joined trucker number one and also headed for the bartender, yelling and cursing.

Arriving at the bar, the first trucker continued yelling about how he'd been robbed, had paid full price for a watered-down drink, and what kind of place was this, anyway? He was egged on by those sitting at the bar and by the other truckers who had now joined him. The noise intensified until the bartender pulled a handgun from under the bar and fired it once into the ceiling. It was a .45 and made a hell of a racket. That really got everyone's attention, and it suddenly became very quiet. Looking up at the ceiling, I noticed that there were several holes, evidence of past disturbances. I can't remember what the bartender said, but several truckers left, still upset. So, what was I doing prior to the gunshot? When that first trucker threw that first shot glass on the floor, I instantly stopped playing, ducked down behind the piano, and kept my head low. Then, as the other truckers angrily followed him, I slowly peeked over the piano's music rack. All the commotion around the bar reminded me of an old Keystone Cops movie, so without even thinking, I started playing in that genre: the sound of honky-tonk piano as cops all pile into a small car and chase the bad guys. Everything ended up all right, and no one was hurt, but that was the last night I played that club.

8.

Professional Life Lessons

Life moved quickly after Tony and I collaborated in the spring of '65. We started playing at a new venue in a strip mall in Tustin called The Boston Bull. Lots of military personnel from nearby El Toro Marine Base made it a lively place. One evening, I met a woman named Judy Boyd. She was smart, funny, and attractive. She worked for the Santa Ana Police Department as a dispatcher, fielding emergency calls and directing the officers. "I get to tell the cops where to go," she'd say. She lived in the area and had come in to hear our music while waiting for her clothes to dry in the laundromat next door. We hit it off, dated for a few months and got married in the fall of that year. It was the first marriage for both of us. In retrospect, it happened too quickly.

Tony and I continued working during the summer, until I moved in with Judy in August. On one of my trips back to the apartment that Tony and I had shared, I discovered he had left, leaving no note, no explanation, no clothes just the few bills we had split. And, to this day, I don't know what became of my musical partner. We had some good times and made a lot of people happy with our music. I wish him the best.

In the spring of 1966, about six months after our wedding, Judy and I moved from the City of Orange to Santa Monica, mostly to be closer to the music industry. I'd make my daily trip to the big white building on Vine Street that housed Musicians Local #47 in L.A. and check to see if there were any job postings. I would jabber—network, in today's parlance—with some of the other "between jobs" musicians and, hopefully, through this networking, one day get lucky.

On one visit, I found a notice for an audition that was happening that afternoon in the Union Hall. It was specifically for a Hammond organist, so I signed up, waited about forty-five minutes, went into a small rehearsal room and found Hrach Yacoubian, a popular violinist, Helena Vlahos, a well-known belly dancer, and a few other musicians. On one side of the room was a Hammond B3 organ with a Leslie speaker. It was, and still is, the king of pop organs. I figured that playing the Hammond wouldn't be that different than playing the pipe organ I'd played while subbing for our church organist in Terre Haute.

I sat down and noticed that it was already turned on, having probably been left on by others who had auditioned. I played some of the music provided, did a couple of ad libs to show my versatility and, bingo, they said yes. I was on my way to Las Vegas and the Aladdin Hotel to be part of the *Hrach*

Yacoubian and His Revue of Sexty-Sex show! I'm sure my mother would not have approved.

Even though Judy understood the need for money, she wasn't happy about being left at home. I tried to be sympathetic to her concerns, but I kept thinking about myself playing a Vegas show. So, I left her with our car in Santa Monica and got a ride from the bass player to Vegas, about a five-hour trip. We found an inexpensive motel on the strip before heading to the Aladdin for our first—and only— rehearsal. The show included the aforementioned belly dancer, Helena Vlahos; several Armenian musicians playing the *oud* and *bouzouki* (eastern European stringed instruments similar to the guitar, but smaller); a bass player whose name I've forgotten; and Hrach on the violin. The drummer was Carl O'Brien. I include Carl's name because he's probably better known as Cubby O'Brien, a former and original Mouseketeer, who later became the drummer for The Carpenters. I rounded out the band playing organ.

On the rehearsal stage were several microphones, a few music stands and, on one side, a nice-looking Hammond B3 with a Leslie speaker. I went over to it, sat down, and looked for the On/Off button. Didn't they always have one of those? But there wasn't one, there were just two toggle switches on the top left side of the upper manual: one said "Start" and the other said "Run." Ah, now we were getting somewhere. I pushed the Start switch and heard a motor inside the organ begin to spin, and then get faster and faster. After a few seconds, I took my finger off the spring-loaded switch. It returned to its original position, and the motor stopped. Nothing. I did the same with the Run switch. Even worse, no motor sound at all. The other musicians were gathering, tuning their instruments, checking their music, and here I was, all the way from L.A., and I couldn't even turn on my instrument.

I looked around, and right next to me was Cubby, setting up his drums. I leaned over and quietly asked him if he knew anything about this type of organ, and said,

"Honestly, I do know how to play it, really. I just don't know how to turn it on."

"Here," he said, sliding onto the organ bench with me, "you hold the Start switch and count to about seven or eight, then, while still holding the Start switch, you push the Run switch, hold it and count to five or six, and then let go of the Start." He did it as he was talking and, in about fifteen seconds, I put my hands on the keyboard, and it played. What a relief!

The rehearsal went well, opening night was fine, and the job lasted about three weeks. It was hot, and the hours were weird, but the pay was good. Cubby's wife, Marilyn, and my wife, Judy, joined us for a weekend. The musicians I was working with at the Aladdin said that most casinos were hiring, as were lots of lounges and piano bars. Other musicians I met all said that Vegas was the only place for musicians. The Las Vegas bug had bitten me.

Back in L.A., with no work coming up, and the lure of Vegas just 280 miles to the east, Judy and I decided to pack up and move. In the summer of '66, we arrived in Las Vegas and rented an apartment on the strip, just a few blocks down from Caesars Palace. Those apartments don't exist today, but back then they were about $125 a month, utilities included.

The weather was hot day and night, but hey, it was Vegas, the desert. My problem was bigger than the heat, though. To avoid slews of musicians coming to the city for a quick one-month job and then leaving, Local Musicians Union #369 ruled that one must live in Las Vegas for at least six months before being allowed to work a full-time gig. This meant playing only "club dates" and "casuals" (musicians' terms for a one-time job) for your first six months in town—sporadic gigs such as a country club party, wedding, church job, or subbing for someone at a piano bar or show for no more than a few nights—nothing long term. The problem with these single gigs was, they were almost nonexistent in Vegas, a city that depended on a nonstop, twenty-four-hour schedule, with the entire town's entertainment concentrated mostly in the casinos. During the '60s and '70s, the convention business was just starting to expand, and there were occasional background music or early morning breakfast gigs for one of the large corporations. Funny, I never could figure that one out: Why would anyone want to wake up with coffee and a five-piece band? I guess it was some CEO's idea of showing off. Anyway, since one-time jobs were, as I said, very few and far between, advancing my career in Las Vegas wasn't looking too promising, at least for the first six months.

But I was determined to be part of the Vegas music scene, so I began my six-month, no-steady-work period by working as a substitute pianist in small shows and by sitting in at various piano bars. When I wasn't doing that, I was at the Union Hall playing jam sessions and networking. Judy started job-hunting, and we both hunkered down and waited. Then I remembered that I did have one thing going for me.

My second cousin George Arnold was back in Vegas and had been hired to produce the first show for the opening of a new casino, Caesars Palace. It starred Andy Williams and featured Carol Doda, the well-known topless dancer from San Francisco. George asked me to write the music for Carol's production number. We agreed on a price, and I started working on it. The only challenge was that it was needed in about sixteen hours, a seemingly impossible task, but quite common in the entertainment world. I found a quiet corner in the newly opened casino, downed tons of coffee and a couple of NoDoz pills, finished the chart about fifteen hours later and collapsed. I never did hear what I'd written. Thinking back, I know it was an immature and poorly written big band chart. I can actually see and hear the musicians' negative comments. But I didn't care. I was now a working musician/arranger in Vegas, and, of course, other jobs and commissions would start pouring in any moment.

In truth, the money from that project helped sustain us. Things were definitely paycheck-to-paycheck. Then, Judy's job-hunting paid off and she got a job as a secretary at a local modeling agency. This helped monetarily, but our financial situation was putting a definite strain on our marriage. We realized the tax advantage of buying rather than renting and found a small, two-bedroom house with no down payment and mortgage payments that were less than our apartment's rent. I also secretly thought that buying a house would help fix the cracks in our marriage. Our new house was on Sunset Drive, just east of the Boulder Highway, near the Showboat Casino. We moved in late September of '66 and enjoyed the feeling of actually belonging to the Las Vegas scene, despite our meager incomes.

Actually, at one point, we were down to just one dollar, expecting a check in the mail the next day. So that night, with no food at home, we went to the Showboat Casino on Boulder Highway for their famous forty-nine cents breakfast special: bacon or sausage, two eggs any style, hash browns, toast, juice, and coffee. The only problem was, this special was served from midnight to six in the morning, and it was now just nine thirty in the evening.

We sat down at the counter and ordered coffee. Our plan was to drink coffee until midnight and the beginning of the forty-nine cents breakfast special, the coffee being included in the price. We talked about absolutely nothing for about an hour and a half, sitting there, drinking coffee. About eleven fifteen, the waitress, a seasoned veteran, took pity and offered us the breakfast special a bit earlier than usual. The sad thing was that we only had enough for the two breakfasts and tax, a total of one dollar, exactly what we had. My folks had instilled in me the ethic of being paid for work done. I felt bad, not properly tipping the waitress, so about two weeks later, having received some more work money, I swung by the Showboat after one of my evening subbing gigs, found her, and gave her the huge sum of five dollars as a delayed gratuity and to thank her for her kindness. She thanked me, probably surprised. It was one of those life lessons that make you feel good, knowing you've done the right thing.

GEORGE ARNOLD'S "NUDES ON ICE"
AT THE OLD ALADDIN

BELLY DANCER HELENA VLAHOS
EXOTIC BOTH THEN AND NOW

HRACH YACOUBIAN
IN THE ARMY IN OREGON

9.

The Aladdin

When Milton Prell reopened the old Tally-Ho Hotel as the Aladdin Hotel & Casino in April, 1966, he decided to have a show policy that was different from the other Las Vegas showrooms. At the Aladdin, instead of a headliner and an opening act, there were three very different headliner shows each night. Attendance was free in the five-hundred-seat Bagdad Theater—I guess he figured if customers saved money via free entertainment, they would spend it at the tables. The Bagdad shows began at eight o'clock and ran most of the night and into the morning. The three headliners did two shows each, with the final headliner finishing about five in the morning. Yes, there was an audience at that hour, albeit a small one: a bartender, a cocktail server, a guy vacuuming the carpet, and a couple of "working girls" comparing notes.

There seemed to be something for everyone, entertainment-wise, at the Aladdin: comedians Jackie Mason, Godfrey Cambridge, and Jackie Gayle; a small mini-play of *The Odd Couple* with Phil Foster and Joe Flynn; and several burlesque shows, one of which starred the legendary silent film actor, Ben Blue. I had met Hank Shanks, the Bagdad Theater's pianist and band leader, when I was playing the *Sexty-Sex* show. When he asked me to sub as his pianist while he conducted one of the burlesque shows, I couldn't wait. I was very happy to get this well-paying, part-time gig. The show was a typical burlesque tribute, and it reminded me of my days playing at Culvermere, with lots of intros, chasers, and blackouts, as well as a couple of topless showgirls. The show's headliner, Ben Blue, always won over the audience with his type of physical comedy, despite his advanced years.

On my first night, just as I was leaving the stage, Hank asked me to introduce and "play on" the next act, the main star that week, Godfrey Cambridge. Hank suggested I meet with Godfrey to learn what he wanted me to say. Godfrey was extremely polite and told me to simply introduce him as " . . . a man whose friends call him just plain "God," Godfrey Cambridge." So, that's what I did for the next few nights. I was no Ed McMahon, but nobody complained.

When my sub gig for Hank ended, I still went to the Aladdin's backstage area each night to watch all the various acts, hang out with them, and be part of the Las Vegas music scene. I saw the hypnotist Pat Collins and a trio of comedians including Redd Foxx, "Professor" Irwin Corey, and Jackie Vernon. There were unusual types of acts, as well: a mind reader who used my wife and me as audience participants, and a five-piece, topless, all-girl rock and roll band, The Ladybirds. These women were actually good musicians, but found that going topless got them much more work. (I enjoyed rediscovering them online, remembering their stint at the Aladdin. If all this sounds strange, check out their video on YouTube.)

10.

The DeCastro Sisters

Still unable to work full-time in Las Vegas, I heard through the grapevine that a singing group, The DeCastro Sisters, was looking for a pianist/conductor for their upcoming three-week tour. They'd had a big hit in the '50s with their rendition of "Teach Me Tonight," and they were now capitalizing on this and other songs in a show that was touring some of the country's major nightclubs. I called and arranged a meeting at the home of one of the sisters, which was located on the Stardust Golf Course. The meeting wasn't really an audition, per se, but they asked me to play some of the charts, including "Teach Me Tonight." Two of the sisters were present, Peggy and Babette. The third sister, Olgita, was not in this particular version of the group, and in her place was an American girl named Pat. She, too, was new to the group and was often referred to as the DeCastro Sisters's "cousin." Individually, Babette was the frisky one, with constantly flashing eyes. Peggy was the oldest and the funniest, often making quirky gestures and faces. Pat, being new, just smiled a lot.

Together, they liked what they heard, and I got the job. In fact, I actually stayed and began rehearsing with them that afternoon. The girls, or ladies, were well prepared, and subsequent rehearsals went well. They even asked me to write the chart for a new tune they were going to cover, the '66 hit song by The New Vaudeville Band, "Winchester Cathedral." Since they used the tried and true Andrews Sisters style, the chart was pretty straightforward. They put the show biz stamp on it with appropriate stage moves, glittering costumes, and high-styled hairdos. But underneath all that were three great performers, and that's what made them popular with their audiences.

When I got home after the rehearsal, Judy, again, didn't seem too happy with my great news.

"First, you went to Vegas for that Yacoubian job at the Aladdin. Now, we're *in* Vegas, and you're going on tour around the country, leaving me home alone even longer. I know we need the money, but how many tours are there going to be?"

To help ease this marital tension, I suggested she come to see me at one of our stops, if it wasn't too costly. She perked up a bit, but she still wasn't as thrilled as I was.

The DeCastro Sisters's first job, which was really our break-in, or rehearsal show, was in Fresno, California, north of Bakersfield, my hometown. As I recall, the club was a converted railroad roundhouse located on a still-active main line. It had a small stage with a dinky spinet piano and a barely adequate sound system. Peggy's husband, Bob, acted as our sound and light man, and we somehow provided a few nights' entertainment to rather boisterous crowds, while ignoring the sound of the trains passing just outside the front door.

Next, we flew all the way to Jacksonville, Florida, for our first real engagement and played a large motel complex west of town, on Interstate 10. Since it was the middle of January, we really enjoyed the warmer southern weather, similar to our temperatures in Vegas. Here, the Sisters were very well received, and we all had a very relaxing week, sunning ourselves by the pool every afternoon.

Our third and final stop was a one-week stay at the Hyatt Regency Hotel on Michigan Avenue in Chicago, Illinois. We opened on, I think, a Tuesday evening to a large crowd of attendees from several conventions at the Hyatt and a nearby conference hall. We performed two sets a night, at nine and eleven o' clock. The opening act was a very funny comedian, Ronnie Eastman, who was perhaps a bit too "hip" for the conventioneers. His act consisted of stories and, at the proper time, he would hit a switch to activate a tape of various spoken lines or sound effects. He was quite humorous, and his comedy reminded me of one of my early radio idols, Spike Jones.

Chicago was the closest major venue of the tour, and, per our agreement, Judy made plans to come for the last three days. Her plane was supposed to land at O'Hare Airport about noon. From there, she was going to grab a cab to the hotel and arrive about one thirty. Early that frigid January morning, however, it started to snow. At breakfast, there were about three inches on the ground. About noon, I sat in the hotel's coffee shop, waiting for her arrival. The snow kept falling and falling, and now about ten inches lay on the ground. One thirty came and went; no Judy. With no cell phones back then, I had no idea what had happened. A dutiful husband, I sat and waited, and drank way too much coffee. Finally, at about six o' clock, she struggled out of a cab, exhausted and disheveled, dragging her suitcase. Here's what happened: it had snowed so much that the Chicago airport had closed, diverting her flight to Milwaukee, Wisconsin. She'd taken a train to Chicago, which had arrived about three thirty, and then she had stood in line in the snow waiting for a cab to the hotel. She looked cold and miserable.

Since the conventioneers were using all the hotel rooms, I had been assigned to a small studio apartment two blocks from the hotel. When Judy and I got there, about seven o'clock, Judy went right to bed while I ate some soup and then hurried back to the Hyatt through the falling snow. It was packed with conventioneers who couldn't get out. And it was still snowing, now up to about twenty inches, when I walked home about midnight. In fact, it didn't stop snowing until the next afternoon, creating the biggest snowstorm in Chicago's history: twenty-three inches. I'm glad we were so close to the hotel; walking in all that snow wasn't easy.

In preparation for Judy's short stay, and to save money, I had bought some food staples, mostly bread, peanut butter, jam, and instant soups. For the next several days, we would get up, watch the news, eat, check to see how much snow had been plowed or shoveled since the last time we'd looked, change our clothes and walk to the hotel. It was strange outside: quiet, no traffic, nothing moving. Cars, buses, and trucks were abandoned all over the city. Michigan Avenue was nothing but small hills of snow where vehicles had stalled. About the only things moving were a couple of cross-country skiers making good use of the cold, fallen, white stuff.

On the entertainment side, things weren't going so well, either. The two large groups of conventioneers were still stuck in the Hyatt and, with nowhere to go, came to every one of our shows. We all became "weathered friends," greeting each other by first name every night. Sound cozy? It wasn't. The DeCastro Sisters had only enough musical material for two different shows. And, being primarily a trio, they didn't have many solo numbers. So, that's what we did, the same two shows, repeatedly, to the same captive audience of mostly men. It got ugly. With limited mobility, the conventioneers' happy hour started at about three o'clock, which meant they were pretty well lubricated by the start of the first show. They weren't mean, just very happy. During the second shows, however, the trapped throng started calling out the punch lines to the girls' jokes before the jokes were even told, yelling the name of each song before the girls announced it, and then loudly singing along.

To compound matters, the hotel asked the Sisters to continue to provide entertainment past our contracted date. Since we couldn't go anywhere, either, we stuck it out for another three days. At one of our last shows we were again playing to a captive audience. I started the intro to the big hit, "Teach Me Tonight," and at least ten guys yelled out, "Aw, shit, not that song AGAIN!" But the Sisters were troupers and kept smiling and singing though it all. My wife and I, though, couldn't wait to get back to Las Vegas, warm weather, and no snow. As it happened, just about the time we got home, my six-month mandatory waiting period was up. I started to look for some steady work. And I got some.

11.

The Stardust

"Hey, Bo, this is Guido."

"Who?"

"Guido, the piano player at The Stardust."

"Oh, yeah. Hi, Guido. What's up?" I don't remember his last name, but Guido was a character—a good-looking Latin guy I had met while doing my waiting period of "networking." He was quite the ladies' man and always had some very tall blonde, brunette, or redhead on his arm.

"I just got a great offer to play in the Caribbean for two weeks . . . "

"Great."

" . . . and I need somebody to cover for me at the Lido."

The *Lido de Paris* show, a typical Las Vegas extravaganza, played twice a night at The Stardust. Billed as "the world's greatest floor show," it had been playing there since 1958, and it was a good, steady gig.

"So, can you do it?" he asked. With this job I'd finally be getting steady money, and Guido would be getting . . . whatever . . . in the sunny climes of the Caribbean.

"Yeah, I'm available."

The night before he left, I went to The Stardust on the early side to check out the music book for the show. Since there was so much activity on stage, the band had been moved to a small alcove on the side of the stage, about twelve feet off the showroom floor. From there, the conductor could see everything, which helped him match the music to the show.

The piano was a smaller grand, in tune and easy to play. During the show I sat next to Guido, watching him play, checking the music. Nothing too difficult, I discovered—lots of chord symbol stuff, no exposed solos, just pretty straight-ahead show stuff, nothing I couldn't handle.

After the show, we went into the small band room just off the alcove. There, I saw Inga—all six feet (and more) of her—in a tall, feathered hat, four-inch heels and nothing else but a G-string. Inga spoke with a thick German accent.

"Ven vere you goink to tell me you vere leafink?"

"Uh . . . well," Guido stammered. "Bo, I want you to meet my friend, Inga."

She ignored me.

"Hi, Inga," I stuck out my hand.

She still ignored me, while glaring at Guido.

"Friend? You call me friend? Vaht I am, a dog?"

I was getting nervous, but Guido was worse.

"Uh . . . my girl. I mean, my girlfriend."

"You vill write und call every day you can. Versteht?"

"Hi," I repeated. Still, she ignored me, which is when I decided to try out my German on her.

"Ich bin in Salzburg, Österreich, fur zwei jarre gewesen," (I was in Salzburg, Austria, for two years) I said, hoping to calm things down a bit.

"Nett," (Nice) she said sarcastically, still looking at Guido and fuming.

"Jah, es est sehr kalt im winter und sehr teuer im sommer," (Yes, it is very cold in winter and expensive in summer) I added, desperate to keep our conversation going.

"Ja, das stimpt," (That's for sure) she said. Then, turning to me, "Sie waren eine musik student?" (You were a music student?)

I watched Guido head for the door, leaving me standing in front of a six-foot-three-inch, almost nude woman, speaking German, and not knowing what to say or where to look. I was almost *stumm* (tongue-tied). So, after taking a deep breath, I looked right into her two green eyes and, trying to show her that talking to nude women was something I did every day, said, "Ja, schuljahr '61-'62 und wieder '63-'64." (School year '61-'62 and again in '63-'64.) I had nothing else to say.

The next night, I got to the bandstand, sat at the piano and opened the book to check a few passages before the first show started. Nestled in our small, cramped alcove, our thirteen-piece band was barely visible to the audience. During that first show, I focused on playing, doing a good job and, hopefully, impressing the conductor so that he'd realize I was a decent sub and could be used again. During the second, midnight show, I did manage to take a few quick looks at what was happening on stage. It was the typical gaudy Las Vegas spectacular with singers, dancers, animal acts (no, Siegfried and Roy were still at the Tropicana with the Follies), and nude showgirls. Things one never got to see in Terre Haute.

The only distraction for me that night occurred after the second show, when Inga saw me in the small band room. Still wearing a feathered headdress, heels, G-string, and nothing else, she was interested to know if I'd heard anything from Guido. Wow. The guy'd been gone one day and she was already on his case. Plus, she had the notion that I spoke fluent German, which I didn't. With her high heels, my eye level was, well, about where you'd think it would be. I wasn't sure what to say in German, or where to look. I might have been the envy of a lot of guys but really I was very *stumm* as I looked either down at the floor or up at the ceiling.

My second night playing the show was uneventful. I became more relaxed at reading the book and actually enjoyed playing a couple of the charts. Then came the third night. Funny how things happen in threes.

It started out the same, at least on my part. During the first show, however, one of the big cats backstage, a tiger, had an issue with his trainer. Nothing serious, but it was decided to cut that particular number from the midnight show. It sounded simple enough, but things that sound simple in show biz rarely are.

About thirty minutes into the midnight show, things started going downhill, fast. Evidently, not all the stagehands had been informed about the lineup change, so instead of bringing the elevator up with the fake ice-skating rink for the husband-and-wife ice-skating team, up came the huge, fifteen-by-fifteen-by-ten-foot Plexiglas water tank with a live dolphin and a nude woman splashing around inside. (I never did understand the fascination with that combination, but hey, I just play piano.) The ice skaters had been doing their same bit for about four months, two shows a night, seven days a week. With that schedule, their daily routine was pretty well fixed. And that evening, the skaters either hadn't been told of the change or had forgotten. Since it was quite dark behind the curtain, they instinctively headed for the stage.

Just as the curtain opened and the lights came on for what they thought was their number, they both stepped, or rather, fell, into the huge tank of water holding the nude woman and the dolphin. The dolphin seemed to take it all in stride, but the nude woman and the skaters were thrashing around, trying to get out of the tank.

The lights were quickly killed and the curtain closed, leaving the tank with its one real and three fake aquatic creatures splashing in the dark. The elevator then took the tank back down, the stagehands removed the tank, the elevator went back up, and the stage was set for the next number, a huge Latin production piece called "The Carioca," which involved all eight nude showgirls, sixteen dancers, and two singers.

For this number, each showgirl wore a huge, almost-three-foot-tall birdcage hat that was fitted with an exposed perch. It was heavy and awkward, and required each girl to hold her cage steady with one hand. The cages, added to the girls' five-foot-ten-inch-plus height and their four-inch heels, made the girls easy to spot by the spotlight operators sitting high up in the rear of the theater. In a perfect world, the showgirls would preset themselves on marks of colored tape placed on the stage floor and stand still as the curtain opened to the dark stage. The spotlight operators would then carefully find their matching girl using a pinpoint of light from their spots, which they'd hold on the birdcage hats. On cue, they would all turn on their lights at once and, at the same time, open a small door beneath the spotlights. Out would come eight groups of four pigeons, with each group following their respective beam of light over the heads of the audience to fly to their waiting nude showgirl and land on the perch of her birdcage hat. It was involved, but quite spectacular. What could go wrong?

Well, first, the nude showgirls, not quite completely undressed, were rushed onto the dark stage, unable to see anything. The singers and dancers, normally preset on the sides of the stage, were totally out of position and began running across the stage to their assigned places. In doing so, they bumped into each other and into the nude showgirls, who were frantically looking for their tape marks while trying to balance their heavy birdcage hats. During these few minutes, the audience became restless, so the stage manager suddenly panicked and yelled into his headset, "Curtain!" Bad call.

The curtain opened on an almost dark stage filled with confused showgirls, dancers, and singers all trying to get to their assigned place. The stage manager, not being able to see much of anything and thinking all was ready, quickly yelled, "Spots!" Another bad call.

On came the eight spotlights, and that midnight audience was treated to an unscheduled show: The spot operators, accustomed to zeroing in on the same showgirl in the same place every night, suddenly saw eight nude showgirls mixed in with sixteen dancers and two singers, all running around a semi-dark stage. The operators frantically moved their spots around, trying to find *their* girl with a pin-point of light. From my perch twelve feet above and to the side, I looked over and down onto this chaos. It looked like eight large flashlights waving around at a Cub Scout sleepover.

Then, because no one had said otherwise, the pigeons were released, with each group trying valiantly to follow their respective twisting and turning beam of light. Of course, few of them did. Some ended up flying into the audience, others landed atop the curtains, and some flew into our orchestra pit and totally freaked out in the confined space. That's when they began dropping whitish "bombs" on the band members. A few of the birds were seen flying out the open doors of the backstage area, never to return. They'd evidently had enough of show biz!

But wait . . . there's more!

Just as things began to settle down, with apologies made and pauses taken, the elephants were brought out and paraded around a small semicircle runway that wound its way into and out of the audience. The elephants—a mama leading a baby who was holding mama's tail—were cute, very cute, but since there had been a change in the show's sequence, the elephants hadn't been taken out to be "drained" in the desert at their normal time. We all know that trained animals absolutely need a routine. Well, mama did all right holding it, but baby didn't and let go a rather hearty stream in the direction of the audience, hitting one couple head-on and causing others in the theater to scatter.

One of the stagehands was told to go out and quickly clean things up. He seized a mop and bucket and ran out, taking a few swipes as he went. Then, unaccustomed to the bright lights, he slipped on an unseen slick spot and went down. The band had stopped playing by this time (it's impossible to blow into an instrument while laughing). The bass player and I had stopped, since the conductor had stopped conducting, and all of us were trying to figure out what to do. The only player who continued was the percussionist, that being my friend, Leo Camera, who, with a percussionist's sense of humor, managed to accompany each spectacular visual episode with just the right amount of drum roll and cymbal crash.

Was there a show the next night? Of course, and nothing unusual happened. But, at each spot in the show where oddities had occurred the previous evening, the band just about lost it again. Ah, yes, show biz.

12.

Rusty Warren

After the temporary Stardust gig, I continued making the rounds of hotels and piano bars and hung out at the union, still networking and looking for that next gig, or perhaps an "in" with one of the house bands. One afternoon, I got a call from Hank Shanks, my bandleader friend at the Aladdin, telling me about a new addition to the talent roster: Rusty Warren. Rusty was in the middle of her Vegas run and was looking for a pianist/conductor for an upcoming Midwest tour to Detroit, Toledo, and Cincinnati. Hank thought I'd be perfect for it, and I thanked him and said I was definitely interested in doing it. I hung up, excited about this new musical opportunity. Later that day, when I told Judy, she wasn't thrilled, remembering her cold trip to Chicago and the DeCastro Sisters. To her, it meant more separation, being alone and looking at the party from the outside. But since lack of money was still an issue, she reluctantly understood. I could sense, though, that the end of the marriage was in sight.

Rusty Warren, known as the "queen" of the party records, started out as a concert pianist. She graduated from New

England Conservatory of Music and, to supplement her income, played in piano bars and clubs. This led to recordings of her original material, including the million-seller, "Knockers Up!" Her material was risqué and filled with innuendos, but not four-letter words. At the Aladdin, she enjoyed the freedom of moving around the stage and into the audience, which she could do by having someone else play the piano.

Rusty was friendly, but not overly so; she was very professional and businesslike. Her musical charts were written for a trio and a couple of horns, a departure from her solo-piano-and-drummer gigs. I enjoyed playing her show; there was lots of ad libbing, plus her famous marches "Knockers Up!" and "Bounce Your Boobies." In her own words, she'd tell the women in the audience, " . . . get your knockers up and let's show the guys we have something to give in this world today." In both these numbers, she would prance around, encouraging women in the audience to do the same. Surprisingly, most of them did, and everyone had a great time.

Conducting her show should have been simple. All I had to do was conduct—or indicate to the guys in the band—the beginning and ending of each piece. But even though these intros and endings were simple, I found I was having trouble making the guys all stop together. The problem was, I was thinking of the orchestral conducting classes I'd taken in

Salzburg, and I was being way too fancy for what was needed. After realizing that less really would be more, I cut down on my motions and things improved.

Rusty's touring show was, for its time, quite typical. We traveled with a couple of acts that were mixed into her routine: The Lost and Found, a '60s singing group, and Vega Maddux, a very funny comic opera singer who later became well known for her jewelry designs. On the music side were Don Goldie, a fine trumpet player from Florida who did a featured solo; Rusty's drummer, Pucci Franciosi; and me. We'd hire a new bass player at each venue, which was a learning experience for me: trying to work with new musicians who may or may not have played this type of show music before. I also learned to deal with stage crews, sound and light men, and theater managers.

Rusty was a pro, knowing just when to use a specific type of material, joke, or song. I never saw her get ruffled or upset on stage. She was exact in her musical requirements and asked me to write some simple arrangements for her. I was impressed that she knew exactly what worked for her, musically. She was also a very fun lady.

Her manager, Stan Zucker, had booked her into some larger theaters and sports arenas, rather than the usual comedy clubs and showrooms. I remember them very well: the

Fox Theatre in Detroit, Michigan; the Sports Arena in Toledo, Ohio; and the Shrine Auditorium in Cincinnati.

Detroit didn't have much of a crowd. I think the theater was transitioning from hosting nationally known acts to featuring more local acts, probably because, at that time, not many people came into downtown Detroit at night. Those who did, though, really enjoyed the show. But there just weren't enough of them.

The next stop was Toledo, Ohio. My parents, at the time, lived in Findlay, just south of Toledo, and I arranged for them to see the show. Up until then, my parents had only seen me play piano recitals, so this would be their first time seeing their son in a show biz setting.

The Toledo Sports Arena had presented a wide variety of shows: indoor extravaganzas, celebrities—including Elvis in '56—and some major ice-skating revues. The act prior to our one-night performance, however, had been a circus with clowns, acrobats, and innumerable animals, whose aromas lingered into our show. It turns out that the large, cavernous hall hadn't been thoroughly cleaned, so the air hung thick with a mixture of sweat, greasepaint, elephant, and popcorn.

RUSTY WARREN
(USED BY PERMISSION)

BO - RUSTY'S CONDUCTOR

Nevertheless, my parents came to the show. They weren't prudes, but I'm sure they wished I were touring with a slightly different style of entertainer. To her credit, though, Rusty gave her best "Knockers Up!" and "Bounce Your Boobies" to a smaller-than-average crowd and, before the finale, proudly introduced my parents and even highlighted them with a spotlight. As I looked at them sitting in the fourth row, I saw my normally reserved mother stand up and wave to the audience, that special "proud mother" wave. After the show, my parents told Rusty how much they enjoyed her performance. My mom used the word "interesting" to describe it. Fact is, she would use that word when she wasn't sure what to say. But, regardless of Rusty's "interesting" material, both seemed proud of their son's work. Unfortunately, due to health problems, my parents never saw me conduct Liberace, though after my mom died, my dad did see me conduct my own concert with the San Diego Symphony. I do wish that both of them could have seen more of my work, and not just my stint with Rusty.

The crowds in these larger venues weren't quite what Rusty and her manager, Stan, had hoped for. It seemed that people wanted the more casual or intimate setting of a nightclub to enjoy her type of material. After the tour, to the best of my knowledge, Rusty continued to perform, but not on such a large scale.

All this traveling, however, did finally put an end to my marriage. I was putting all of my energy into my career, which left Judy on the outside. Her job at the modeling agency wasn't fulfilling, and her unhappiness with my travel schedule drew us further apart. While I was on the road with Rusty, she found someone in Vegas who gave her the attention that I didn't. The divorce was amicable, and we stayed in contact with each other for several years. At that stage of my life, music came first, second, and third.

13.

An Invaluable Partnership

Joe Guercio was the path to my career. I'm sure he wouldn't say so, but Joe was, without his knowing, a wonderful teacher, mentor, and friend—but only on his terms. He's best known today for his work with Elvis Presley, as "The King's" musical director and conductor for most of the '70s. As Joe said in an interview, it was his wife, Corky, who suggested the idea of using the famous, six-note, *2001: A Space Odyssey* movie theme as Elvis's intro. That idea was so effective that, to this day when it's played, many people think of Elvis rather than the original movie.

Joe had been around since long before Elvis came to Vegas, as musical director and pianist for Patti Page, Georgia Gibbs, Julius La Rosa, Steve Lawrence and Eydie Gormé, Barbra Streisand, and, later, for Gladys Knight, Natalie Cole, B. B. King, and, fortunately for me, Bo Ayars.

Joe taught me the real and often harsh world of the popular music scene: in essence, what true professionals did and didn't do. After several years of producing and conducting shows for Steve and Eydie, his wife, Corky—a former "Copa Girl" from New York and a huge influence in his life—

suggested he do the same for other vocalists, i.e. find songs and "routine" them. So Joe, Corky, and their children moved to Las Vegas from the New York City area and settled into a nice, comfortable home.

Joe was just starting to make a name for himself as a producer of vocalists when we first met. One of his first clients was the husband-and-wife team of Freddie Bell and Roberta Linn. Freddie's band, Freddie Bell and the Bellboys, was a Philadelphia rock and roll group, and Roberta Linn was a "Champagne Lady" for Lawrence Welk. In January of '68 they hired Joe to produce their new act, one of several at Nero's Nook, the lounge at Caesars Palace. When I learned this through the grapevine, I got their phone number and arranged to meet them at their house just off Eastern Avenue. Since many stars and artists had homes in Vegas, meeting at someone's house was common.

A large, barking German shepherd met me in their driveway. After fending him off, a maid showed me to the music room. There, sitting and talking, were Joe Guercio and Buddy Rich, the famous drummer. It seems that Buddy and Freddie were old friends. I shook hands, not knowing what to say, and stood off to the side while Buddy, Joe, and Freddie continued to tell stories and make everyone laugh. Not wanting to be seen as an outsider, I laughed, too, although I didn't really understand many of the stories. Buddy stayed a few more minutes, said goodbye and left. Joe quickly said to me, "Hi. Grab a bench," and we got down to business.

He put some sheet music in front of me: the skeleton of their opening number from the movie and the song, *It's A Mad, Mad, Mad, Mad World.*

"Let's go," Joe said. He was all about the music.

I started playing, trying to follow the music, Freddie's and Roberta's singing, and Joe's instructions.

"Yeah, that's it," Joe yelled as his right arm began moving to the beat.

"Faster." He grabbed my arm, so I stepped up the tempo.

He was now sitting on the bench beside me, his arm on the edge of the piano, still moving to the beat. He didn't look at me. He just looked at the keys, nodding. Joe had a way of getting instantly comfortable wherever he was, especially around a piano.

After finishing one full chorus of the song, for some reason I instinctively modulated up a half step, putting the song in a slightly higher key.

"Yeah! Yeah! Good, good . . . yeah, get it on," he said, in a brisk, gravelly rasp. That was one of his favorite phrases: "Get it on!"

When we were done with the piece, I was totally exhausted. But even so, I was really happy to be in the middle of it all, creating something new and different.

"Yeah, not bad, not bad. OK, let's try the next one." Joe didn't even crack a smile as he put up the next piece of music.

That afternoon, together, we routined several more numbers. After the last one, he stood up and said,

"I need you at my place tomorrow afternoon, say about one o'clock. I got more stuff for you. Can do?"

"Sure, I'll be there," I replied.

"Here's the address. See ya." And he was out the door.

Little did I know at the time, but from then on Joe and I would be a team, forming an informal partnership that would last almost six years.

The next afternoon, I got to his house just before one and met Corrine, his wife.

"Call me Corky," she said. "Everybody does." She showed me to Joe's music room, a den with pictures of Joe with various celebrities and several entertainment mementos, including a program from a 1930s Toscanini concert.

"What's that?" I asked as Joe joined us.

"That's from a lotta years ago," he said, "but is something I'll never forget. You see, Toscanini hated the sound of people rustling their programs during his concerts, so he had the programs printed on something that didn't make any noise at all: real silk. That's one of them."

That afternoon, we did some song routines for Joanie Sommers, one of Joe's many musician friends/clients. After working up a few ideas, and setting up another work time with Joe, I went home and put all our ideas into lead sheet form: the melody, lyrics, and chord symbols. At our second work session a few days later, Joe told me that Joanie wanted us to come to Los Angeles and work with her for a few days. So, off we went. As Joe's apprentice, I paid my own plane ticket, twenty-eight dollars round trip, and my hotel room, fifty-nine dollars. It didn't bother me, though, because it was such a thrill being in the "big time," jetting off to work for a famous client. Well, it was actually a propeller plane, but it was still exciting.

Joanie was extremely friendly, relaxed and easy to work with. She enjoyed singing new songs, learning new routines and trying out new ideas as much as Joe and I, and she was definitely a super singer. On one up-tempo song, she was able to turn the phrasing around so much that I dropped a basketful of beats and was totally lost. I stopped, and looked up apologetically. She just winked, smiled and said, "Got-cha!"

I was the piano player in our partnership, while Joe came up with the routines and the clients. With me at his Baldwin Acrosonic piano, we would experiment with all kinds of songs in different styles and tempos, until something just seemed to work. For instance, he'd find a song and say, "OK, now try it as a bossa nova." We'd record it on a cheap cassette tape—which was high tech back then—and I'd take it home and transcribe it. Then, back at his house, we'd refine it by playing it in a different style, tempo, or rhythmic pattern to make it fit a particular singer or a particular part of their show. One of our biggest challenges was that so many of the popular songs of the day had no sheet music, just a recording. "Back in the day," music publishers waited until a song had gained a certain level of popularity before going to the expense of having a plate engraved and sheet music printed. So, in my little $115-a-month, utilities-included apartment, I'd put my ear next to my cassette player, listen to a wide variety of songs and make lead sheets. In college, this was called dictation and was something I used to dread. Now, I was doing the same thing, but with different composers. My Conservatory training was paying off!

For a typical client, we would get four or five songs ready, have the client come to Joe's house, and, while either the client or Joe sang, I'd play the piano. Our first clients included Julius La Rosa, Sergio Franchi, and Carol Lawrence and her husband at the time, Bob Goulet. Clients would hire Joe to revamp their current show or to add new material. Many of them would work in Las Vegas at night and come to Joe's house during the afternoon. We also traveled to New York to work with Goulet (with Bob footing the bill, thankfully), but most of the time our out-of-town work consisted of flying back and forth between Las Vegas and L.A., where we usually stayed at the Continental Hyatt House on Sunset Boulevard.

In L.A., we'd visit the artists at their homes and pitch our ideas. These artists included Barbra Streisand, Jim Nabors, Julie London, and Diahann Carroll. Normally, we'd have Bill Reddie do the arrangements, but sometimes we worked with other great Hollywood arrangers, including Billy Byers, Ben Alexander, and Allen Ferguson. In the recording studios, we worked with legendary drummer Steve Gadd, bassist Joe Mondragon, and trumpeter Marv Stamm. A typical trip to L.A. usually included meetings with the artists' managers, a few late-night work sessions, and almost always a simple dinner at a well-known Italian restaurant specializing in Beef Braciole, one of Joe's favorites. Yes, Joe was definitely a "Siciliano" Italian. He used to say that, contrary to popular belief, you didn't have to cook a good Italian sauce for hours. Half an hour, an hour, tops, was fine " . . . because, being Sicilian, you probably don't have that long before you gotta take off to avoid whoever's chasing you."

Joe was a good, solid piano player, nothing fancy or flowery, and he was definitely an idea guy with a specialty for putting two songs together in a medley. His musical concept was simple: if two songs go together lyrically, they'll go together musically, even if they're in different genres. Here's an example. He used "Today I passed you on the street / And my heart fell at your feet," the first line of Hank Williams's country ballad "I Can't Help It If I'm Still In Love With You" to lead into the main song, "The Man That Got Away," a ballad by Harold Arlen and Ira Gershwin. Then, at the end of the Arlen/Gershwin song, he used the last line of the Hank Williams song. It might not sound like much just reading about it, but I guarantee, hearing it done by a pro would rip your heart out.

Thanks to Joe's musical sense, each song was tailored to fit a particular part of an artist's show. He had a set formula for this type of main room / lounge show popular in the '60s and '70s. One of his recommendations was to have two opening songs. He explained that, during the first song, the audience really isn't listening. They're paying their tab or checking out the singer's outfit, they're not paying attention to the music. So, he'd have the artist go directly into the second song, no break, not even a "thank you." It would be a different type of song but still upbeat, like a jazz waltz. Joe felt that, during this second song, the audience truly would be listening to the singer. Then, depending on the star's ability, he would have them sing yet a third song, perhaps a slower one, but something with a positive lyric. After that song, he'd finally have the singer say "good evening" to the audience.

It worked every time, and the more seasoned performers like Bob Goulet and Connie Stevens understood this. New, up-and-coming singers sometimes questioned the idea, but in the end, they would put their trust in Joe's ability as a producer. He seemed to know exactly which song to sing in each part of the show, and he never stopped telling me how important the pianist's/conductor's job really was.

"The band falls apart, and it's up to you to cover for them," he'd say. "You get to some place where there's a bunch of lousy musicians? You let them go, and then you play the show with just the rhythm section, or, sometimes, all by yourself. You've got to be ready to do that." That only happened once in my career, but I was ready for it. More on that later.

One of our most endearing clients during this time was Diahann Carroll. I loved her style of singing: a little Broadway, a little soul. She was extremely easy to work with, and, at her request, I spent several afternoons at her home in Beverly Hills, organizing and cataloging her music. The show that Joe designed for her really accented her ability to sell a song.

After a work session on her material at his house, Joe said,

"Listen, Diahann's doing this first gig up in Tahoe, at Harrah's. How about this? I don't wanna be up there the whole time; I got Corky and the kids. You don't. So, opening night's mine, you watch me do it, then take over the rest of the gig. OK?"

"OK."

To Joe, this was probably business as usual. For me, it was something very special: my first time conducting a high-profile act in a major Nevada showroom.

"Isn't that the way to do it, anyway?" he continued. "Y'know, you get in there, you rehearse, you conduct opening night, you go to the opening night party, you get your check, then you go home!"

"Yeah, you're right. That's the way to do it."

"Great. You blow it, though, and I'll chew ya up," he said with a quick smile—though I'm sure he partly meant it.

So, up to Lake Tahoe we went. The show was great. We hired two top musicians to take with us: Bob Lanning on drums and Al McKibbon on bass. Bob was the son of the entertainer Roberta Sherwood, and, later, he took Ronnie Tutt's place playing drums for Elvis. Al was a legend in jazz circles, having worked with Thelonious Monk, Dizzy Gillespie, and James Moody. We were a mighty rhythm section, and, true to his word, Joe rehearsed the band, conducted the first night, went to the opening night party, got his check and went home—leaving me in charge. Logically, it made sense to have one of us there to make sure our material was performed correctly. Emotionally, I think I walked a little taller, knowing I was in charge of Diahann's show. In truth, this was an important development for me. The fact that Joe trusted me enough to be musically in charge of Diahann and the show made me feel as if I'd arrived as a conductor.

Joe and I worked with several well-known performers, including singers Shani Wallis and Jackie DeShannon. After we finished writing Shani's act, Joe sent me out with her to Framingham, Massachusetts, for two weeks of shows. The same thing happened with Jackie, and it became an increasingly common routine: when new material was ready, orchestrated and copied, Joe would have me go on the road with the singer to give them added support, and to make sure that Joe's musical ideas were being followed. I can't tell you what a huge learning experience this was for me, conducting all kinds and all sizes of bands and orchestras, good and bad, and, as co-producer, dealing with blasé musicians, singers' egos, meddling agents, and pushy managers. Before every outing, Joe would tell me—and sometimes warn me—about what to expect at the different venues. He had performed in many of these places and still had contacts there. I always marveled at his ability to cut through a problem and get to a solution. His knowledge and feel for show business was uncanny and always right on the mark. To me, it was all brand new and exciting.

Our reputation as music producers grew, as did our client list, which escalated to include Diana Ross, and, a short time later, Barbra Streisand, and Elvis Presley. And our "team" grew to include Bill Reddie, an outstanding arranger. Bill was the house arranger for the Dunes Hotel and churned out big band arrangements for their large, main-room floorshow "Casino de Paris," while also writing great rock charts with horns for the famous "Viva Las Vegas" lounge show featuring Bill Chase on trumpet. He also arranged several classic, big band jazz charts featuring drummer Buddy Rich. John Stroffe, the all-important music copyist, would take Bill's hand-written arrangements and transform them into music manuscript, often within a bare minimum of time. Even though we tried to stay ahead of things, John would often pull an all-nighter to get all the parts copied and to make sure everything was correctly written and legible.

Our team worked very well together. Joe would find the clients through his contacts, then he and I would meet with the artists, find them songs and routine them. I'd make the lead sheets, Joe and Bill would come up with the orchestrations, and John would copy it all. It was a fascinating business with lots of colorful characters: well-known musicians and arrangers, music producers, music jobbers (guys who pushed songs into music stores), and, of course, the artists themselves.

One of the other arrangers Joe used was Billy Byers, who was known for his big band arrangements and Broadway show charts, as well as for being a fine trombonist on many recording sessions. He was extremely bright and knowledgeable but very soft-spoken. Once, when we were passing each other on the moving walkway at the Las Vegas airport, he coming into town, I heading out, he looked at me and said, "Ah, Bo Ayars, a man not without talent." I think it was a compliment. At least I hope it was.

So, it was a wild time in "Sin City," with many shows in both the main rooms and the popular lounges. And I, as a young pianist/conductor and "semi-producer," enjoyed it all while also playing a main-room act with two shows a night, 8:00 p.m. and midnight. I was making decent money, working with talented people, meeting new celebrities weekly and honing my musical chops daily. This was my normal life. My relatives couldn't understand how I managed to get by with such a topsy-turvy lifestyle. But to me, it was just fine, thank you. Going to bed at 4:00 a.m. every day, then getting up and going for breakfast at one in the afternoon was very normal to me.

My memories of Joe are very vivid. I found him to be a tough but fair Sicilian who would say, "Wops are tops." "But," he would add, "ya gotta be Italian to say it." He was also the kind of guy who never complimented those he worked with. He'd just continue to work with you if he liked you. Our unofficial partnership lasted from 1967 through 1973. Joe taught me lots of things about conducting, little things you'd call "rules of the road." For instance, he said,

"When you're rehearsing a show, never have the singer talk to, or complain about, or make suggestions directly to the band. The singer tells you, and then you fix it. Otherwise, you come off looking like a schmuck, and the singer comes off as bossy, and nobody wins. Also, if the singer makes a mistake, talk to them in private, not in front of the band. Otherwise, the two of you look unprofessional, and you both lose respect."

Joe Guercio got the glory, and he deserved it. His ideas, his contacts, and his drive kept us working. I was the flunky, the guy he took along to play piano while he created the ideas. And I loved every bit of it: I enjoyed meeting all the celebrities, visiting their homes, tagging along to TV shows—yet never saying much, sort of like the mouse in the corner. But I often wondered what he thought of me and my small contribution to our success. I had to assume he liked working with me, since he kept calling on me, but he never actually said so in so many words. Maybe no one had ever complimented him, and that's the way he thought it should be. Funny, but after we went our separate ways, I heard he had told several people how great I was to work with. Oh well, I didn't mind, because when I was working with Joe, I was having a ball. The money, to me, was less important than the musical chops I'd use later in my career. And now, every time I stand in front of an orchestra, whether it be a symphony or a small combo; every time I try to think of an ending or an intro for an arrangement; every time I try to set the mood while accompanying singers, I feel Joe leaning over my shoulder, yelling, "Get it on! Get it on!"

Joe passed away in early 2015. The empty place in me, though, is filled with so many memories. I knew he was older and getting more frail. I really can't remember the last time we'd worked together, but I do know that, when we parted, it was always with the understanding that we'd see each other again. We were friends on Facebook, but I think one of his family members managed the account. At my wife's insistence, I had planned to make the journey to Nashville to see him one last time, but I kept putting it off, until it was too late. I really do miss my friend and wish I'd been able to see him before he passed to say, "Thanks, Joe, for all your help."

14.

The Guercio Years, Part 1

Rehearsals, work sessions, travel, lavish meals, and hot dogs; that was my daily diet during the Guercio years. We worked with a wide variety of clients, and I have fond memories of all of them. What follows are some of my favorite stories.

Diahann Carroll and Bill Cosby

Diahann Carroll was often the opening act for Bill Cosby, both in Vegas and on the road. The first few evenings of their four-week run at the Vegas Hilton, Diahann became increasingly late for her opening spot in the show. When it first happened, Cos, as he was called, came on stage in his tennis attire complete with racquet and did a ten-minute monologue. Over the next few days, when it became obvious that Diahann just couldn't be ready on time, we knew we had to do something. Bill, the comedian, only needed a mic and, perhaps, a stool. Diahann, however, being a classy singer, had a special set designed that included a large staircase that split the twenty-two-piece orchestra in two. She used the staircase as an entrance and during several of her songs.

Bill called me into his dressing room and told me his plan. It was a great idea, it involved the audience, and it would give Diahann more time to get ready. His plan was to bring a younger member of the audience on stage. Yes, we were in Vegas, where the minimum age to get into the clubs was twenty-one, but the Hilton realized there were swarms of kids who loved Bill's character, Fat Albert, from his TV show. So, in every audience, even in the midnight show, there would be several underage viewers.

Bill's plan was to invite one of these kids up on stage to help demonstrate "the power of music." Bill would ask the youngster to walk to the top of the staircase, and then, on cue, walk down the stairs and act as if he or she were slowly walking down a dark, creepy, cellar staircase. At the bottom of the stairs, the participant was told to pretend to open a squeaky door, see something frightening, and react to it.

The first kid on stage walked to the top of the stairs, half-heartedly walked back down, pretended to open a door and, with not much emotion, put his hands up and opened his mouth as if to scream.

"Not. Very. Con-vin-cing." Bill said. "Now, do it again, but this time, we'll add some musical effects."

So, the kid went back to the top of the stairs and started down again. This time, however, I gave a cue to our string players to play a low, scary-sounding tremolo, a prelude of things about to happen. At the same time, Leo Camera (again our percussionist, having made his way from the Stardust to the Hilton) started a soft timpani roll. These sounds startled the boy as he continued walking down the stairs. Now, a bit more apprehensive, he descended more slowly while the strings and the timpani increased their volume until he reached the bottom of the stairs. As he opened the pretend door, I suddenly stopped all of the players, and Leo somehow managed to produce an appropriate squeaking noise. The instant the door stopped squeaking and the kid was about to react, I gave a downbeat to the orchestra to play any note they chose as loud as they could, and hold it. I wouldn't say the kid wet his pants, but his reaction was very real.

"See? Before the music, you just went through the motions. But with the music, it suddenly became much more real, didn't it?"

The boy just nodded, still recovering from his musical "education."

"I'm sure you now understand 'the power of music,'" Bill said. Then Bill thanked him and gave him a Fat Albert hat.

Raquel Welch

Another performer I fondly remember was Raquel Welch. Joe and his team were asked to produce the music for her live stage show at the Hilton. It costarred the fantastic talents of Sid and Marty Croft and their group of puppeteers. Rehearsals for this big stage show were held in a large dance studio in Los Angeles. We would get there about 10 a.m., rehearse for several hours, take a quick lunch break, then go back to playing, singing, and dancing.

Trying to describe this show with words would be like trying to describe the taste of a lemon meringue pie—impossible. Suffice to say there were several memorable production numbers, including Raquel in her famous *One Million Years B.C.* costume trying to outwit a serpent whose tongue has a mind all its own; Raquel singing "Respect" (the Otis Redding song made famous by Aretha Franklin) with three creatures consisting only of long streams of metallic hair and moving lips; and a Raquel puppet, twirling in and out of the side curtain, only to suddenly become the real Raquel.

There were many more unforgettable scenes in her show that make me smile when I think of them: a three-foot Frankenstein "puppet" that came alive and scared the bejesus out of the audience and some band members (the "puppet" was played by Hervé Villechaize); a huge boulder that moved all around the stage by itself; and the opening number with thirty dancing-girl puppets manipulated by six puppeteers dressed in traditional mime attire, including whiteface. This was also a memorable show for me, personally, because I met my future wife, Cheryl Henry, the show's assistant choreographer and a very talented dancer who translated what producer/choreographer Joe Layton wanted into moves that Raquel could imitate. Both Cheryl and Joe were very patient with Raquel and showed her just the right way to make an entrance, and how to move and work with all the various puppets in the show.

The show opened at the Las Vegas Hilton over the Christmas holiday in 1972, ran six weeks, and then closed. It was booked into John Ascuaga's Nugget in Sparks, Nevada, in late February, and Raquel asked me to conduct for her.

"I'd love to, Raquel, but I've got a pretty full plate about that time. I'm getting married to Cheryl Henry, Joe Layton's assistant, in February, going on our honeymoon and then heading to Australia for a month's tour with Lee."

"Well, congratulations! But I guess that means you'll be busy," she said. Boy, was that an understatement!

Like Raquel's show, my marriage to Cheryl didn't last very long, however, and several months after our wedding we divorced, and I was once again a single musician.

The Ray Charles Singers

In show business, what *can* go wrong eventually *will* go wrong. An example is a show I conducted at the Hilton that included The Ray Charles Singers, a very successful group of about sixteen recording singers. They were the opening act for Red Skelton, and this was their first major nightclub show. They came in well rehearsed, sounding great, and ready to set the town on fire. Not wanting to upset or change the current show's sound gear, they rehearsed with wooden "pretend" microphones. (This was in the day before radio microphones, which give contemporary performers more freedom of movement on stage.) The group practiced their numbers, constantly moving and dancing while singing into their fake mics. It looked great: lots of energy, great dance moves, big endings.

But on opening night, they switched and used actual microphones with cords. We started the music for their first rousing number and out they came, dashing about the stage, using all the intricate dance moves they'd rehearsed. Well, about twenty seconds into this first number, one of the girls tripped over her mic cord, pulled it out of her mic and lost her vocal sound. Over the next few seconds, the same thing happened to about eight other performers who, in trying to avoid tripping over the *other* mic cords, managed to pull out their own. By the end of the number, only three singers could be heard. To their credit, the group ad libbed some silly talk for several minutes while they gathered up the fallen cords and plugged them back into their mics. But this left the sound man very confused because none of the mic cords were plugged back into the correct mics, and so the voices were totally unbalanced. The next day, the Singers re-choreographed the number and cut the group's frantic, onstage movements. For the rest of the run, they sounded great while they stood still and sang.

Gail Martin

Another delightful memory is of Gail Martin, one of Dean's older daughters. The story I remember most is about Roy Gerber, her manager, who also managed Diahann Carroll. I became friends with Roy while working with Joe and Diahann and would often stay as a guest at his office/condo in West Los Angeles. I loved listening to all the New York stories he would tell. My favorite is about when Roy, as a young talent agent in New York, roomed with another theater type, Danny Simon. Roy was extremely gregarious, outgoing, loud, and funny. Danny was just the opposite, quiet and withdrawn. Danny's brother, Neil Simon, wrote a book/stage play about these two called *The Odd Couple*. Roy lived up to his character, played by Walter Matthau.

Roy asked me to conduct Gail's show in Evansville, Indiana, in the summer of '67. There were no rehearsals prior to the engagement, so our first meeting was at her hotel in Evansville. She traveled with a nurse who took care of her ten-month-old daughter. I guess Gail had wanted to get back to work as quickly as possible following her daughter's birth.

The club we played was small and not far from the hotel. Opening night went well, and the next day, Gail was on the golf course having her picture taken by the local newspaper, the *Courier/Press*. Gail was witty, the kind of woman guys love. If you asked her a "guy" type of question about a car or sports, she'd come back with either the right answer, or something very funny. There was always a crowd of men around her, something that I guess her husband tolerated.

After the show's second night, she said she didn't feel well and went back to the hotel. The next day, she said she felt better, but did only one of the two shows that night. After that, it became a day-to-day situation: would she perform, or not? It turned out she was unable to perform for the rest of the engagement, but we were there the whole week's time. She said she felt bad about this and made sure the rest of the band was paid for the full week of work. I got the feeling, and it's just my opinion, that she really didn't want to perform at all, although I'm not sure why.

She bought me a very expensive (for 1967) Rolex watch. I still have it. The Pepsi bezel is worn, and in the latter part of 2012 the watch started to lose time. A watchmaker told me that it was " . . . a very valuable watch, worth several thousand dollars if you wanted to sell it." I paid him $1,300 to have it repaired and brought back to its original condition. I wear it proudly and smile, remembering my short week of work with the lovely and vivacious Gail Martin in Evansville, Indiana.

The Elvis Years

When Joe became the conductor for Elvis Presley, he took me with him as the organist. My job—one of the strangest I've had—was to play the low C organ pedal note from the famous opening of Kubrick's *2001: A Space Odyssey*. That note, probably the most anticipated note in the entire show, signaled Elvis's entrance. Joe would point to me, I would put my left foot on the low C pedal and mash the volume pedal down, and the show would begin. I got $600 a week, plus room and transportation, for playing one note per show! But I couldn't play that one note and then sit there for the rest of the show, so I ad libbed during the other songs, adding my own music to "Hound Dog," "Blue Suede Shoes," and "Trilogy," the famous combination of "Dixie," "All My Sorrows," and "The Battle Hymn of the Republic." In the documentary *Elvis On Tour*, I'm shown sitting at the organ wearing a purple leather vest and sporting an Afro, mustache, and goatee, and looking very serious. Years later, my two boys would freeze-frame that spot on the video and laugh hysterically.

Another Elvis memory is a bit scary. It happened during the first of two nightly shows at the Hilton, about midway through our first week of a four-week engagement. Everything was going fine, and we were right in the middle of a big Elvis hit. I'm ad libbing like crazy, the audience is screaming, and suddenly, Joe gets off his podium, walks over to me and hands me his baton.

"You take it. I don't feel so good." Then he walked off stage, holding his stomach. It was appendicitis.

I quickly took his place in front of the twenty-two-piece band directly behind Elvis's rhythm section, checked the music and started conducting. Conducting an Elvis show was not so much about technique as it was about quickness. My job was to cut off the band at the same time as Elvis either stopped singing or stopped moving, and I did so by following his karate-like moves. I don't think I ever did it correctly, but I did the best I could for about ten days until Joe recovered from his appendicitis attack.

I've also got a birthday memory of Elvis. It turned out that Elvis's pianist, Glen Hardin, and I had the same birthday. On that particular April 18, when Glen received a birthday invitation to Elvis's suite on the thirtieth floor of the Las Vegas Hilton, he brought me along, since it was my birthday, too.

We smiled as the two security guards let us into the suite. There were lots of our fellow performers there: the two vocal groups, The Sweet Inspirations and J. D. Sumner and the Stamps Quartet; Ronnie Tutt, the drummer; John Wilkinson, rhythm guitarist; Jerry Scheff, the bass player; and, of course, Charlie Hodge, Elvis's army buddy turned singing companion. In the background were several of Elvis's bodyguards, but not his manager, Colonel Tom Parker; he rarely came to these functions. Glen and I walked up to Elvis.

"Hey, Elvis," Glen said, in his West Texas accent. "This here's Bo Ayars. He's the guy who conducted you when Guercio got sick. And it's his birthday, too."

"Well," said Elvis, "Let me give you a little something for your birthday."

I was thinking of what he had given others: cars, fur coats, jewelry. I walked up to him, and he put out his hand, and I shook it. That was it, my birthday present from Elvis. I didn't think it was anything special, but perhaps to him, a handshake from the King was all one needed on one's birthday.

I hung around the penthouse, listening to insider stories I didn't understand, and toward the end of the evening, or the beginning of the morning, they all gathered around the piano and started singing gospel hymns. I really wasn't part of the Memphis Mafia, as it was called, or much into gospel, so I left. After all, I'd gotten my gift from Elvis, so my world was complete.

Here's a memory of a rather dangerous Elvis incident. Because of his popularity, Elvis only played very large venues, mostly indoor arenas with a capacity of at least 12,000. The stage was always positioned about eight feet above the arena floor to make him more visible and, more importantly, to prevent fans from climbing onto the stage. In one of these venues, however, the stage was only about four feet off the floor. For his protection, about thirty uniformed guards sat side by side with their backs to the stage, facing the audience—a very funny sight, actually.

Well, during the final number the guards—wanting to see at least a little bit of the show—suddenly got up, turned around and stood to watch Elvis sing his last song, "I Can't Help Falling In Love With You." With the guards no longer guarding, several dozen of his fans began leaping onto the stage. When Elvis saw that he was about to be mobbed, he stopped singing, hustled to my side of the stage and stood next to me while I continued playing his last song. He looked at me, fidgeting, as I looked at him.

"Wanna sit a spell?" I asked.

"What!? Are you shittin' me, man!?" he yelled. Then he took off running, heading for backstage, his limo, and freedom. Several fans surrounded various members of Elvis's band, but nobody came over to watch me play the organ. I guess what I was doing just wasn't that exciting.

The King inspired some odd behaviors, and not just in the average fan. In Denver, Colorado, we played a typically large indoor arena and, at intermission, I wandered out into the hallways beneath the bleachers. There was the standard mob of people in long lines, trying to buy souvenirs. I leaned against a wall and just watched. Then, suddenly, I saw someone I recognized. It was LaMonte McLemore of The 5th Dimension. He was standing next to a line of people, hawking programs.

"Elvis programs! Get your souvenir programs here!"

I went up to him and said that I was a big fan of his group, and asked him why he was selling programs.

"Only way I could get a seat to see Elvis," he said. "The Colonel told a couple of us that since the concert was sold out, we could sell programs and watch it for free."

Merchandising was a huge part of the Elvis phenomenon. When you went to the Las Vegas Hilton to see Elvis, you also saw several souvenir stands selling Elvis pennants, fake rings, hound dogs, banners, pins, hats, and, of course, Elvis records and cassettes. (CDs weren't around then.) The Colonel managed all these sales. For one engagement at the Hilton, he purchased about one hundred wood dowels, each six feet long, and had large Elvis banners hung from them. His idea was to mount the poles on the walls all around the casino. But when Barron Hilton heard about it, he simply said, "No." Not to waste his money, the Colonel hired an unemployed guy off the street, gave him a knife and had him whittle a point on all of the six-foot dowels. Then he painted each one a different color, slapped on an official Elvis sticker and sold them as "Elvis Presley Giant Toothpicks."

One of the Colonel's regular assistants would gather all the merchandise sales receipts from the previous twenty-four hours and take them to the Colonel's suite every morning at about 10:00 a.m. These receipts were for all the cassettes and records sold, plus all the souvenirs, including the above-mentioned toothpicks, the stuffed hound dogs, the coffee mugs, the thimbles—anything and everything you can imagine, as long as it had an Elvis sticker or Elvis's name on it.

The assistant's routine went like this: He'd knock on the Colonel's door. The Colonel would answer, usually wearing a terrycloth bathrobe. The Colonel would then go over to his desk and sit down and think, saying nothing, while the assistant stood there. After about thirty seconds, the Colonel would say a dollar amount equal to what he thought was the total amount of merchandise sold in those twenty-four hours. The assistant told me that the Colonel was never more than two dollars off! Pretty amazing, and shows that the Colonel really " . . . knew the territory."

Red Skelton

This next memory is both funny and sad. Don Ferris was the music director for the famous comedian Red Skelton. Unlike Red, Don was a very quiet guy, but he was a thoroughly professional musician and conductor. Red, with Don's help, had written at least one hundred short instrumental pieces to be used during his pantomime skits. Don's way of organizing and conducting all this music was quite simple. After being with Red for so many years, he knew there were about twenty or so of these musical "bits" used per show. Now, normally, band music was printed on 9" x 12" sheets of paper, a slightly larger size than the oft-used 8.5" x 11" letter-size paper. The larger size music sheets were more difficult to copy, a major issue in the early '70s. Don, however, had all the instrumental parts for our twenty-two-piece orchestra printed on letter-size paper. He told us to place the sheets horizontally on our music stands, with the top edge where he'd written the title of each piece pointed toward the right. This made it easy for the players to spread out the charts on their stands and still see the titles. For himself, he'd take several stiff, white, cardboard pieces, the kind found in new men's shirts, and write a single title on each with a black Sharpie pen. When a particular piece was needed, Don would simply hold up one of his white cards and show it to the orchestra. We would then pick out the corresponding title from our sideways music, turn it upright, and wait for Don's cue. If the audience had seen this, I'm sure it would have been distracting. But we were hidden behind a large curtain. Between the skits, Don would sit silently in a chair next to his music stand that held all his title cards.

Don was also Red's pianist, but since I was available, he enjoyed the freedom of just conducting. Between shows we'd chat about the business, venues where we'd worked, etc. He seemed to be happy doing his job, secure in the knowledge that his boss was in demand. About halfway through Red's four-week engagement, Don confided that he'd just put a large down payment on a fancy house near Beverly Hills. He seemed, for Don, quite excited about it.

Then came our final two shows. Everything was going fine until the end of the first show, when Red paused during his final monologue to state that after all his years of entertaining, he was quitting the business to devote all of his artistic energy to painting and just taking it easy. This was, as I discovered later, totally unexpected. One of the world's great comedians was calling it quits.

After the show, I looked for Don to see if he'd known about it. He was nowhere to be found. I honestly became a little concerned. I was just about to step in and take over the conducting when, fortunately, just before the start of the second and final show, Don came in and sat in his chair as always, waiting for Red's part of the show to start. I breathed a sigh of relief. Ah, everything was OK.

The first few selections in Red's show were always the same. Even so, Don always stood and showed us his title cards. But tonight, instead of showing them, he slowly gathered all the thirty-or-so cards together right before Red's first skit, tapped them to make sure all the sides were squared up and then threw them all up in the air like a Frisbee, right toward the orchestra. There was a slight smile on his face as he then sat down in his chair, not saying a word. None of us knew what to do. The music cue was just seconds away.

"Don," I whispered. "Don, the cue, the cue."

Nothing.

"Don," I said a bit louder, "are you going to start us off?"

Again, nothing.

Meanwhile, the members of the orchestra had gathered up the cards and handed them to me. With one hand I quickly handed them to the still-sitting Don. With the other, I gave the cue to the band to start the music. I kept looking at Don, making sure he was all right. As we played this first cue, Don looked at the cards, shuffled them, made sure the edges were straight, and, once again, threw them at the orchestra. He was totally bombed and probably had been drinking during the entire two-hour break between shows. I found out later that Red's news had also been news to Don. He had just dropped almost all of his savings on a big home, and now he was out of a job.

After his second throw of the cards, Don slowly turned and walked off stage, hidden from the audience by the curtain. I leaped up, gathered as many of the title cards as I could and continued to conduct the orchestra while reorganizing the cards and trying to listen to Red's monologue to find out what the next skit would be. I squinted to see the five-inch TV monitor and strained to hear Red's routine. Thankfully, the music was straightforward, with no pauses or tempo changes. Plus, the band had been playing the show twice a night, six nights a week, for the last month. I just wanted to get through this last show without too many clams—musicians' lingo for calamities—on my part. Finally, Red's last number was over, and I slumped down in Don's chair, exhausted. I'm not sure if Red knew what had happened, but for me, it was the defining moment of that famous phrase, "No matter what, the show must go on."

Diana Ross

Joe's fame somehow reached Diana Ross, who had just split from the Supremes. Diana was planning her first solo appearance, and her manager arranged a short work session at Joe's house. I remember thinking how small and thin she was, with darting eyes that made her seem very vulnerable. After Joe gingerly discussed a few ideas we'd come up with, she thanked him very softly and then said that she'd rather open her first solo show with a very special song that had touched her, a song that spoke to a people who had been persecuted, as had African Americans. We leaned forward, eager to hear what song this might be. I was thinking along the lines of "We Shall Overcome" or "Give Peace a Chance."

"The song is . . . " she paused, for effect, and then solemnly said, "'Hava Nagila,' the Jewish folk song."

Joe and I looked at each other, trying to cover our surprise. After a few more minutes of talk, she thanked us and said we should work on that idea and get back to her. Then, she picked up her purse and, followed by her bodyguard, left the house for her waiting limo. Joe and I just looked at each other, not knowing what to say. I do know there was a bit of laughter, though. I don't know what her first song ended up being, but I do know that Joe and I didn't produce it. We just couldn't quite see "Hava Nagila" as the very first song that Diana Ross would sing in her first solo performance after leaving the Supremes. Sometimes you win, sometimes you lose.

15.

The Guercio Years, Part 2

Besides the main room acts, Joe and I would also produce shows for lounge singers. One was Andrik, a singer from Holland. Today, he's a well-known spokesperson for several humanitarian causes. Back in 1969, he was a young, hip, blond pop singer. Joe Guercio and I "modernized" his act by writing several new arrangements and helping him with his first performance at the Riviera Lounge. The four horns and three rhythm players all stood during the performance, adding to the "hip" feel of the show. To add to the pop feel, I played organ.

The Riviera Lounge hired Andrik as an opening act for their headliner, comedian Jack Carter. On opening day, Jack was told that his conductor had a family emergency and wouldn't be able to make the engagement. So Jack asked if I would conduct his show as well as Andrik's. Logistically, it worked fine. The two shows were back-to-back: the first started at 10:00 p.m., the next at 11:00 p.m., and same pattern was repeated at 2:00 a.m. and 3:00 a.m. It worked great in another way for me, too: back-to-back shows offered a double paycheck—a no-brainer. Jack's show consisted of his pianist, me, acting as his musical "foil." I was like an Ed McMahon to his Johnny Carson. He often referred to me as a "rejected rabbinical student from Brandeis University . . . ," which was very funny to me, since I was a Presbyterian from Oberlin Conservatory of Music.

So for the next four weeks, my work schedule was set. I'd start with the first set of shows at 10:00 p.m. At midnight, I'd go to the coffee shop for a "late" dinner and return for the second set of shows beginning at 2:00 a.m. Remember, this was the "old" Vegas: non-stop, twenty-four hours a day. Jobs lasted four weeks, with shows six nights a week and Sunday nights off. The money outlook was good and the work was fun.

Then, on Thursday evening of my first week of this schedule, an artist with whom Joe and I had previously worked, Connie Stevens, opened at the Landmark Hotel, about two blocks from the Riviera. Another musical friend, Mitchell Ayres (no relation), was conducting her. He was perhaps best known for his work as Perry Como's conductor in the '50s, and for being the music director for *The Hollywood Palace* TV show in the '60s. I'd met him through Joe when we were working with Diahann Carroll on her *Hollywood Palace* appearance. Mitchell was very outgoing, and after hearing me accompany Diahann, had remarked that there were three great Ayars: Mitchell Ayres, Lew Ayres, and Bo Ayars. I had felt quite honored to be in that company. Joe, on the other hand, didn't like Mitchell. It seemed that on a previous *Hollywood Palace* show, Mitchell hadn't let Joe conduct for Steve and Eydie, Joe's main clients at the time. I'm not sure of the circumstance, but it irritated Joe quite a bit.

So, as I said, Connie's opening night was the first Thursday of the four weeks of my double-conducting job at the Riviera. Her two shows were at 8:00 p.m. and midnight. With my late-night schedule, I was able to attend her opening night eight o'clock show and stay a few minutes afterwards to congratulate her and say "hi" to Mitchell. I left them about 9:45 p.m. and quickly drove the short two blocks to the Riviera for my 10:00 p.m. show with Andrik.

The next evening, Friday, while eating my midnight dinner in the Riviera's coffee shop, I learned from some other musicians that, tragically, Mitchell and a female musician had been struck and killed by a car while walking across the busy street that separates the Landmark and the Hilton. They both were wearing their musician stage clothes, all black. They weren't in a lit crosswalk, and the car that hit them was traveling under the speed limit. It was an unfortunate accident; I was almost in shock and sort of floated through the second set of shows.

After I left the Riviera early that Saturday morning, I couldn't stop thinking about Mitchell. I'd seen him only hours before, and now he was dead. I lay in bed, thinking of all the things he had accomplished and of what he'd talked about doing in the future. It was so sad.

About 10:00 a.m. the next morning, I got a call from Connie's manager, Norton Styne, the son of Jule Styne, the composer of many great songs ("The Christmas Waltz," "Diamonds Are A Girl's Best Friend," "Just In Time," and many more) and of the great musical, *Gypsy*. Norty said that, because of Mitchell's death, Connie's shows on Saturday night had been canceled, but she wanted to continue performing her four-week engagement starting on Sunday evening. Since the Riviera Lounge was closed during the day on Sunday, he asked me to conduct her first show that night, while Si Zentner, the house bandleader, watched and learned the book. Si would then conduct the second show that night and the rest of the shows during her four-week run. I was happy to help, and it was a no-brainer since I'd conducted Connie's show many times in the past.

There was a bit of tension on that first Sunday evening show with Connie. She was most gracious, publicly thanking me for taking over after the Mitchell tragedy. When she said my name, though, I think it was the first time she realized that he and I shared a same-sounding last name. She paused, looking at me quite sadly, and continued. While I was conducting that first show, I saw Si sitting in the wings, occasionally looking at the score I'd given him, but mostly drinking coffee and talking to the stagehands. Then, about halfway through the show, I looked over, and he was gone.

For the second show, I was nervous about Si's conducting, knowing he'd skipped out on the first show. I could sense that there might be a crash, musically. So, I asked Joe Close, the pianist for the show, to let me play the piano part just in case, and to stand in the wings and be ready to take over the piano part from me if I had to take over the conducting from Si.

The show started, and, thank heavens, the orchestra of twenty-two men was totally professional, with the uncanny ability to sense what was needed, even though it wasn't always written in the music. The very first production number ended with a dramatic fermata, or musical hold. The orchestra came to the end and held the last note as was written. Si, on the other hand, seemed totally lost and continued to conduct the band, waving his arms and quickly turning the pages of the score. The musicians, now also lost, didn't know what to do. Their music said to play one note and hold it, and that was what they were doing: holding their note and waiting for a cutoff that, as I could see, wasn't going to happen. Si continued waving his arms faster and faster, probably in panic. Bottom line: Connie's opening number was in jeopardy. I quickly moved from the piano to the podium, motioned Joe Close to come on stage and take over the piano and stood next to Si.

"Mind if I take over?" I asked, quietly.

"No, please, go ahead," he said, stepping down as I cut off the orchestra and started them on their next number. I'm sure it was humiliating for Si, but, to me, there comes a time when, if you can't do something, admit it and get on with something else. I saw Si a few times afterward, but we never spoke. I can't speak for him, but I'll never forget that feeling of helplessness, watching him try to conduct an orchestra that would not follow him.

At a quick meeting the following day, Monday, it was decided that I would continue to conduct both of Connie's shows. This meant that I'd be conducting a total of six shows every night. First, I got permission from the music union to do a "triple leader" gig, i.e. conduct three different acts in one evening: Connie Stevens, Jack Carter, and Andrik. (According to the union, this had never happened before.) Then, it was just a matter of logistics. Here's how my schedule went:

8:00-9:30 p.m.Conduct Connie's first (dinner) show at the Landmark Hotel.

9:30-10:00 p.m.Go out the stage door and drive from the Landmark to the Riviera, a leisurely three-minute ride.

10:00-11:00 p.m.Conduct Andrik's first show.

11:00-11:55 p.m.Conduct Jack's first show.

11:56 p.m.Race out the front door of the "Riv" to my waiting car ($10 valet service per night, to bring it to the front, ready to go) and make the ninety-second drive back to the Landmark.

12:01 a.m.Screech to a halt in a reserved parking place next to the Landmark's stage door ($20 a week to the stage guy to keep it available at that hour).

12:02 a.m.Run, or rather, walk briskly, onto the stage. (I'd asked the pianist, Joe Close, to conduct the overture, which was done behind a large screen, so Joe was not seen. After the overture, a three-minute film of Connie's family life was shown. When the screen lifted, I was there, conducting.)

12:05-1:30 a.m.Conduct Connie's second show.

1:30-2:00 a.m.Go out the stage door and drive from the Landmark to the Riviera, a leisurely three-minute ride.

2:00-3:00 a.m.Conduct Andrik's second show.

3:00-4:00 a.m. Conduct Jack's second show.

4:01 a.m.Go home and collapse for eight solid hours.

On the following Wednesday, when I got to Joe's house to work with Julius La Rosa, the talk was about the tragic accident with Mitchell Ayres. Joe, being the Italian—emotional and passionate—still couldn't shake the "snub" Mitchell had given him years earlier. "I didn't wish him any ill will," Joe said, "but I just can't be totally sorry he's dead." I guess one doesn't forget when they're treated unfairly.

A very special memory of the later Guercio years involves Barbra Streisand and the time we were asked to add some material to her 1972 show at the Las Vegas Hilton. I never worked with Barbra when she originally appeared with Liberace at the Riviera in '63; I was busy graduating from Oberlin. But working with Joe gave me the opportunity to coproduce and accompany her for her three-week engagement at the Hilton in 1972, and we flew to L.A. for rehearsals at her home.

Her house wasn't overly lavish: a simple, large, one-story ranch in Bel Air, just a few blocks off Sunset Boulevard. It was nicely furnished and very homey, with colorful accents, family pictures, and braided carpets that all blended well together . . . nothing ostentatious. As I remember, she was recently divorced from Elliott Gould, and their son, Jason, was living with her at the time.

Back then, I had a mustache and curly hair, and several people thought I looked a bit like Elliott, one of the stars of *M*A*S*H* (the film). I didn't see the resemblance, and thankfully neither did Barbra when she sat next to me at the piano, singing and whacking me on the arm, saying, "Yeah, that's great, that's great." I distinctly recall how gracious, friendly, and funny she was as we sat at that baby grand, trying this song and that song, some fast, some slow. I would play a little, she would sing, Joe would make suggestions and ask me to do something different, like a new tempo, a new key, or a new style. Relaxed and funny, Barbra seemed to love to try standard songs a bit differently than the norm, to put her own spin on each and, in doing so, create her own unique way of interpreting it. To this day, it's very difficult for any singer to sing a Barbra Streisand song without evoking the way she performed it. They simply must admit that, " . . . when *Streisand* sings a song, that song's been sung."

As a person, Streisand was very businesslike, but friendly—not pushy, as I'd heard. It's very simple: when she gets out on the stage, she wants everything to be as perfect as it can be. Early in her career, I think, she may have gotten bad information and, because of that, didn't trust many people and their ideas. For instance, Joe and I would decide that a song might have five different types of endings: slow, fast, big, soft—that type of thing. He and I would pick the three that seemed to be the best to our ears and go to the rehearsal. Streisand would ask for what we had, and we would say,

"Well, these are the three best ways to end it out of about five that we tried."

"I want to hear all five," she would say.

We did have one idea for a great opening number combining her son Jason's favorite song at the time, "Sing," heard on *Sesame Street*, and "Make Your Own Kind Of Music," a popular, upbeat song of the '70s. As Joe conceived it, the two songs worked perfectly together, one leading right into the next, same tempo but a different feel. Barbra liked it, too, and used it as her opening song in that Hilton show, as well as on an album she recorded with Quincy Jones.

Another of Joe's creations was combining the Carole King song "Where You Lead" with the Penn and Oldham song "Sweet Inspiration," a medley that's still popular with Streisand fans. (I still have a cassette tape of our rehearsal sessions.)

When we finally rehearsed her show at the Hilton, nothing was spared on opening day; the hotel knew she would draw a good spending crowd, so we were given several extra hours of rehearsal. It went very well, as all of her shows did, with an opening night as exciting as any I'd ever seen—and the opening song, "Sing," that Joe and I arranged for her, was a blockbuster. Like a true professional, she surrounded herself with the best musicians available from L.A. and Vegas, with

Joe as her conductor. I felt quite honored to be part of a group of such talented artists.

I did get to share the spotlight with Streisand on one song, however—a silly tune about being " . . . in love with Harold Menger." It was just for singer and pianist, a cabaret piece that had me trying to follow her as she led me through a bunch of vocal antics: suddenly fast—then stopping—then singing very, very slowly—then suddenly getting faster and faster and then— suddenly just stopping, leaving me dangling and unsure of when to play the next chord. It was like trying to catch a cat that doesn't want to be caught. At the end of the number, I would give a huge, crashing chord and almost fall off the bench. And, really, I wasn't acting; it was that challenging. But I loved trying to keep up with her.

Another memorable number was a duet she sang with herself, her famous blending of "One Less Bell to Answer" and "A House Is Not a Home."

At the end of the three-week engagement, she gave me a signed note of appreciation and a copy of each of her albums. Every time I see one of her TV appearances, I return to 1972, remembering the time that I was fortunate enough to work with her.

Special Musicians: Ray Brown and James Moody

Two of the more notable individuals I could never forgive myself for failing to mention are Ray Brown and James Moody.

Ray Brown was, and still is, a jazz legend, known as the bass player's bass player. Making music with Ray was like making music with God—he was that amazing. I got a chance to play piano with him during a Diahann Carroll concert in Los Angeles. It was a benefit for something (I can't recall what), held at the Los Angeles Music Center, downtown. I was nervous as hell, knowing that Ray would be playing bass on this job, along with several other first-call L.A. musicians. There was one chart that included a rather long section of a jazz trio: piano, bass, and drums. Being the piano/conductor meant that I'd be playing my not-so-great style of jazz with the jazz world's ultimate bass player—sort of like me trying to go one-on-one with Shaquille O'Neal. During a rehearsal break, Ray came over and complimented my conducting and playing. I thanked him for the compliment and said I was a bit nervous playing with such a great group of musicians, him especially. "Ah, come on," he said. "You were great. You sounded fine. You're doing a great job." Those comments, coming from Ray Brown, meant something very special to me. I'm sure they weren't all true, but the fact that he took the time to say them is something I've always remembered.

"Moody," as James liked to be called, was one of the premiere tenor sax players of the century. His name is a legend among all musicians. He was unique: funny, accessible, and, to me, a very good friend. Our relationship was based upon friendship first, and music second. He played in the Hilton band for several years, saying that he wanted to improve his reading and his flute playing. He did both, and, while there, we became friends. We were both Aries, both very talkative, and we connected in a non-musical way.

Moody was also a great tennis player. He offered to teach me how to play racquetball, a game I thought would be fun, mainly because I'd be out of the desert heat. We got to the court, closed the door, and he proceeded to show me a few moves. Then we played a game. The high score is twenty-one. He spotted me fifteen points, then beat me twenty-one to fifteen. I didn't play much racquetball after that.

Moody was always handing out gum. He would buy it by the gross at Skaggs Drugstore. "Here," he'd say, "have a chew," and he'd thrust a stick of gum at you. He did that to all the band members, friends of friends, anyone. There was so much gum being chewed on the Hilton stage that, one night, a few wrappers found their way into the large Dancing Waters system on the Liberace show, totally "gumming up" the fountain.

JAMES MOODY AND BO

I always admired Moody's musical ability, but I think I was happier to know him as a person. I last saw him when he came to Portland, Oregon, to play in a jazz festival about five blocks from my home. He'd lost some weight, but that permanent smile was as bright as ever, and his playing was amazing as always. He was so gracious to my wife Barbara and me, asking about our activities here in the Northwest, and was genuinely a delight to be with. I've got a picture of Moody and me that was taken in Las Vegas. It's in a very prominent place in my music room.

The Third Movement:

The Crescendo

> Beware of painted pianos and thin chefs.
>
> —Liberace

> By now, I've seen my share of painted pianos and thin chefs.
>
> —Bo Ayars

16.

Lee

In late summer of '72, I met Liberace for the second time (the first being back in 1954 in Terre Haute when I was thirteen). Here's how it all happened:

I was conducting Diahann Carroll at the Hilton in Vegas. At that time, Joe Guercio was music director there, and I was the "house" piano player, one of the permanent musicians in the Hilton orchestra. Joe and I had produced Diahann's act and, as was often the case, he was having me conduct many of the shows. Diahann's last night of her four-week run was on a Monday. Liberace was opening the next night, so the rehearsal for his show was on that Monday afternoon. Liberace's conductor, Gordon Robinson (whom Lee called "Doctor," even though he never really got a degree), was using our setup to do the musical rehearsal. Since I was the house pianist, I went to the rehearsal, not sure if I would actually play in the show. I quickly discovered that Gordon's "book" did, indeed, require two pianos. Liberace's piano was, of course, center stage, so I played second piano. For the rehearsal, my piano was placed next to the Hammond organ I'd played in Diahann's show. During the rehearsal break, I went to Gordon and said,

"You know, a few of the pieces we just played might sound good with some quiet organ chords behind them. I've got the Hammond right here. Mind if I give it a try?"

"That sounds like a good idea. We've got a couple of pieces in the next section. Go ahead and try it."

So, after the break, I played some simple background chords for "Let Me Call You Sweetheart" and "It's Impossible." Lee seemed to like it, probably because it was a very different type of accompaniment. After the rehearsal, Gordon introduced me to Lee, who thanked me for the organ sounds. I was tempted to mention cousin George and our Terre Haute meeting, but decided not to; Lee was surrounded by several members of his staff, and it didn't feel like the right time or place to bring it up.

On opening night, Lee was again center stage, but now my piano and the Hammond organ were off to the side of the stage, almost hidden in the wings. After the first show, Lee stopped me backstage and said how much he liked the way I played the organ, saying, "I love the organ sounds." I was glad he liked my addition to his show.

The Hilton crowds were huge, and Lee always got a standing ovation after every show. Then, about a week into the four-week run, I got a call from Jim Nabors's manager. Jim's conductor was having some sort of personal problem and couldn't make Jim's shows at the Circle Star Theater in San Carlos, California, a theater in the round a few miles south of San Francisco. He asked if I could fill in. Financially, it made sense; the conductor's pay at the Circle Star would be more than my sideman pay at the Hilton. So, I said yes and started calling around, looking for a piano sub for the Hilton gig.

Mike Montana, a talented pianist and friend, said he was available to sub. That night I told Gordon, and he OK'd it, adding that he didn't know I conducted. Unfortunately, Mike didn't play organ and, like me several years before, had no idea how to turn it on. I told him not to worry about it, and to just play piano, since the organ had been an add-on idea and was not really required.

Evidently, during Mike's first evening subbing for me, Lee told Gordon that he missed the sound of the organ. Gordon told him about my conducting for Jim Nabors at the Circle Star, and Lee told his manager, Seymour Heller. It seemed that Lee and Gordon were looking for a replacement for Gordon, who was retiring after twenty-six years as Lee's music director. Wow! Talk about timing. So, thanks to my organ playing— which got me onto Lee's radar, so to speak—and my conducting experience, I got The Call from Seymour, as recounted in Chapter 1. The older I get, the more I totally believe in the "small world" phenomenon. And it never ceases to amaze me how one's life can change so suddenly and unexpectedly.

Lee once told me that Seymour was tough but fair, and, since Lee hated dealing with negatives in the world and resorted to his own version of "sweetness and light," the partnership worked just fine. While it's true that Lee was an extraordinary performer, it was actually Seymour who was the big "push" behind the scenes, always seeking better playing— and paying—engagements, and sifting through the hundreds of daily requests for a Liberace performance. I've heard it said that a manager is merely an agent who is tired of getting only ten percent. My bet is that Seymour earned every penny of his commission from Lee, as evidenced by the way he handled Lee on both a business and

a personal level.

Seymour once told me about a conversation that occurred almost yearly: Lee would "take a meeting" with him just after Thanksgiving, which was usually the last tour of the year. Lee would be tired, needing a rest, and not in the mood to do any more tours for a while.

"You know, Seymour," the conversation would begin, "I'd really like to cut back some next year, do fewer shows if possible. What if I worked, say, just three big performances in some large hall or theater?"

"Absolutely," Seymour would reply. "If we worked three shows at a large venue, you'd make . . . " and here, he would pause, jot something on a piece of paper, and say, " . . . about $50,000 per show."

"Oh," Lee would say. "Well, I'll need to make more than that. How about if I worked just two weeks?"

"Two weeks?" Seymour would say, again jotting something on a piece of paper. "Well, that would give you about $600,000."

This would go on for several minutes, with the amount of work and the resulting salary going up until, finally, it would end up being about thirty-two weeks and an amount well into the millions of dollars: the exact time and amount that Seymour had originally planned. Behind every great entertainer is an even greater manager.

After I agreed to be Lee's music director, it was arranged for me to go to Sparks, Nevada, home of John Ascuaga's Nugget Casino Resort. There, I was to take over Gordon's conducting duties a few numbers at a time, slowly working my way until, by the end of the engagement, I was conducting the entire show. At pre-arranged parts of the show, Gordon would walk off, and I would walk on. This gave me a chance to really perfect my conducting of Lee's show and was a really great way for Lee to introduce me as his new music director. Gordon conducted the very last number of the very last show as a sort of farewell, before which Liberace introduced me and said goodbye to Gordon. Ironically, my first, independent conducting job for Lee was at Gordon's alma mater, Loyola University, in Baton Rouge, Louisiana—a place he'd always wanted to conduct but never had.

Unlike the large showrooms and theaters in which Lee usually performed, the Nugget's Celebrity Showroom stage was about the size of a Vegas lounge stage, so it was a challenge to put on the type of show that Lee presented in the larger venues. His lavish productions included several pianos, three or four cars, several large statues, hanging chandeliers, a large orchestra with strings, and the famous Dancing Waters, a colored fountain that moved in time to the music. So, when I first saw the Nugget's small showroom stage, I knew that there was no way Lee's show—with all those props—could possibly work. I'm guessing the stage was thirty feet wide by twenty feet deep, with a stage ceiling of no more than fifteen feet. But, as Lee's Stage Manager Ray Arnett would often say, "With Lee, it's crystal ball time"—meaning that Lee assumed the small stage would just magically hold all the props required for his show. Add to this mix Lee's guest artists, a group of talented young singers known as the Mike Curb Congregation, and you had the potential for mayhem. Oh, and if that weren't enough, the Nugget had a clause in Lee's contract that said that Bertha, a six-ton, twelve-foot-tall elephant, would be the opening act for every performance. But, somehow, someway, over time, Ray made everything "magically fit."

The opening act, Bertha, must have lacked union representation, because she worked seven nights a week, fifty-two weeks a year. In her act was an "elephant girl" named Cindy, who was studying to be a veterinarian. She and Bertha really trusted each other, so when it came time for Cindy to lie down on her back on the stage floor and let Bertha slowly lean forward on her elbows with her belly on the floor, Bertha would gently do so until Cindy was literally buried beneath Bertha. But Cindy only worked six nights a week. So, on the seventh night, Bertha would go through the same motions but land quite heavily on her elbows, shaking the small stage but not caring, because she knew Cindy wasn't there. It was a sight to see. And feel.

It turned out that Bertha, like me, had a substitute, a smaller elephant named Tina, who was possibly an offspring. When Bertha's arthritis got bad in her advanced years, Tina took her place. Honestly, Tina didn't really like show business, and she would often walk off stage right in the middle of her act and head straight into the kitchen area next to the stage to see what food she could find. Trying to stop her was like, well, trying to stop a hungry elephant. It always caused a wild commotion amongst the servers and kitchen staff, as you can imagine. Ah, show biz.

I later learned that, when Lee first began working at the Nugget, he used Bertha for his entrance instead of having her perform as his opening act. This worked well because, at the time, he had just one or two pianos in his show, so the small stage wasn't a problem. He'd walk on stage with Bertha and her trainer, have Bertha pick him up in her trunk, and then greet the audience and say, "How's this for an entrance?" Back down on the stage, he'd hand Bertha a banana, a treat she really enjoyed. Then he'd say, "OK, Bertha, back on your papers," and the elephant trainer would help Bertha exit on the opposite side of the small stage and take her directly out of the building to her specially built enclosure behind the casino. This went well for the first engagement there. But, as always, Lee needed to "top" himself at subsequent engagements, usually with more costumes, props, and pianos. So, a car for his initial entrance, yet another piano, and two ten-foot-tall Grecian statues for use during the new piano's "Johann Strauss" number were added. This was a ton of gear for a very, very small stage. Oh, and of course there was still the orchestra— now slightly reduced to twenty: six brass, five saxes, five strings, drums, bass, percussion, and me—all crowded together at the back of the stage, almost hidden by the curtains.

The Nugget stage was so small that only one of Lee's many cars would fit: the small, mirrored Volkswagen convertible. His valet, Bob, attired in a formal chauffeur's uniform, would drive him onto the stage. Lee would step out of the car, and Bob would drive it about ten feet to the opposite side of the stage as the main curtain closed. It would remain parked there for the rest of the show. Then, between shows, it would be backed up to the opposite side of the stage to be ready for Lee's entrance in the second show. The statues and second piano were all kept on that same side of the stage, next to Bertha's walkway. They all had to be covered with heavy tarps so that she wouldn't brush against them.

Then, later, in the mid-'70s, the Dancing Waters fountain that Lee used in his Vegas shows—a real crowd pleaser—was brought in, which meant that there was literally no room on stage for the orchestra. So, the entire orchestra was moved to a small loading dock complete with a metal roll-up door. We were hidden with side curtains, but just barely. Crammed into this small space, it would take several minutes for all of the orchestra members to be seated. Picture the musicians, their music stands, plus a xylophone, orchestra bells, two timpani, a bass amplifier, and a drum kit, all wedged into a space about twenty feet square. And, because it was the beginning of November, we'd all be wearing coats and sweaters to guard against the cold that seeped in through the large, non-insulated, metal loading dock door. The band would sit facing the stage, cramped and cold, and try to warm up their instruments by softly blowing into them. I know the audience often heard the metal door rattling in the wind. Funny, we never played the Nugget in the summertime. It was always in the late fall or winter. Go figure.

We used six microphones to amplify the band, half of them on the strings section. I'd stand with my back to the stage, just behind the side curtains, and try to watch the show on a six-inch TV monitor. Unfortunately, the camera was located way in the back of the theater, which made Lee and his piano about an inch square on my tiny screen. To counter the huge sound of the orchestra, I'd listen for Lee's piano cues on a very small speaker placed on a stand behind my head. All of this was made even more difficult when the VW convertible was added. It was parked on the loading dock in the middle of the orchestra to be in place for Lee's entrances. And when it left our space, it would, of course, emit a nice trail of blue exhaust, which always elicited several loud coughs from the orchestra and deposited a smell that never went away.

When Lee climbed into the convertible at the beginning of each show, he would always smile and wave and joke around with members of the band. He was relaxed and cordial and seemed quite concerned with the discomfort they were all experiencing. At the end of these engagements, he would always throw a huge party for the band and their wives and girlfriends to say "thank you" for enduring all these hardships. During these parties, Lee would relax and become just another one of the musicians: joking, telling old musical "war stories," and asking band members about other acts they'd played with. These parties were among the few times I saw him being totally himself in public and not worrying about protocol or publicity. It made me realize that he really was one of us, a musician, and a very fine one.

As talented a performer as he was on stage, Lee's concept of money was a bit strange. Here's an example of what I call "Liberace Math."

One week, while working in Dallas, Texas, we, the three musicians traveling with Lee, had an afternoon off. While right downtown, we wandered over to a store nicknamed "Needless Markups," better known to the world as Neiman Marcus, the famous, high-end Dallas store. It was inexpensive fun checking out all the high-priced items: the jewelry, suits, furniture, and such. Suddenly, there was a commotion at the entrance to the store. It seems that Lee, too, had the afternoon off and had decided to do what we were doing. Of course, he had the wherewithal to actually buy these things.

A few minutes later, he saw us and called us over.

"What do you think of this?" he said, pointing to a large fish platter. It was sterling silver, about the size of a large Coho salmon, and had the imprint of a fish on it. The price? Just $700. Of course, today, it would probably be closer to $3,000.

"That's beautiful," we all said. "You should get that."

"Well," said Lee, hesitantly, "I'm not sure. Think I'll look around some more."

We all scattered for a few minutes before Lee called us over again.

"So, what do you think of this?" "This" was a very large pewter punch bowl with all the cups hanging around the edge, plus a large ladle sitting on a large pewter platter. "This" was priced at $800.

"Now, that's great, something you could really use at your parties," I said.

"Hmm," he said, "I just don't know. Think I'll look around a bit more."

We, again, left him to look around, and he, again, called us over a third time.

"Well, what do you think of this?" It was a piece of furniture with casters on the legs. The upper part was shaped like a small trunk with a roll top and was inlaid with mother-of-pearl. Inside was a Baccarat crystal decanter with six small shot glasses. The price tag said $2,500.

"That's it," I said. "*That's* what you should get."

"You're right," he agreed. "I will, and it's going to be a bargain. See, if I don't get the fish platter, that'll save me $700. And if I don't get the punch bowl, that'll save me another $800. That's a savings of $1,500, so this $2,500 piece will only cost me $1,000!" Well, it made sense to him. But the punch line is, he ended up buying all three items. So much for Liberace Math . . .

Liberace and I had a purely business relationship, and it was all about the music; I didn't hang out with him socially. When new numbers were to be added, I'd go to his house in Vegas, make a recording of him on my trusty cassette deck, go home, listen, and write the arrangements around what he had played, knowing the bands and the venues we would be working with in the future. During the recording sessions I might suggest a key change or shortening one selection or another, but nothing more. What he played on those tapes was all him, a product of the "licks" he'd learned over the years: his signature arpeggios, his chord structures or use of the left hand, and his blending of classical and popular music. That was all Liberace. So, I was really a translator: I translated what he did into an orchestral arrangement. While he did do a few new numbers—a medley of Oscar-nominated songs, for instance—most of his show consisted of his well-known selections, as mandated by his legions of fans.

The flip side to this was that Seymour often got complaints from venue owners saying that Liberace wasn't doing enough new material. Lee's solution was simple. He'd just have new costumes designed: a rhinestone-lined fur coat, or sequined hot pants. The ultimate example, to me, was a sparkling, one-piece, gold lamé jumpsuit over which he would wear four different-colored capes. To him, each cape represented a new costume. He would bow, spin and run off stage and change his cape, only to return in his "new" costume. Each time, as his conductor, I would frantically try to prolong whatever the orchestral arrangement was to accommodate his timing.

Occasionally, aspiring entertainers who worked in our shows would get caught up in "Liberace fever" and over-estimate the importance of their position or take liberties on stage or talk negatively about cast members, etc. (Only a few understood that their performances mostly just provided Lee with time for costume changes.) They'd soon learn that Lee was the boss, however. As Seymour once put it, "He," meaning Lee, "who makes the gold, makes the rules." That having been said, in my thirteen years with Lee, I never saw him act bossy or force any entertainer or act to do something they didn't feel comfortable doing. On the contrary, he would often make positive suggestions to help the act be even better than they already were. And the crowds ate it up. All the guest artists would be besieged with requests for their autographs, records, and the always-asked question, "So, what's it like working with Liberace?"

Of course, all the acts who worked with Lee were climbing a huge rung up the entertainer's success ladder and were learning something from him, too: his timing of a spoken phrase, his pacing of a show, the way he turned a challenging arena into an exciting entertainment venue with the use of simple props and lighting. Yet, with all the friendly interaction between Lee and his guest artists, no one, on or off stage, ever forgot that Liberace was the star of the show and the reason they were there. It was his show, his status, and his talent that brought in the crowds. In addition, Lee somehow managed to exert some creative influence on those with whom he performed, so that *they* felt what *he* felt—among other things, the passion and desire to give the audience a fantastic show— when performing. They all became better entertainers for it.

ON TOUR WITH LEE

WITH LEE AT RADIO CITY MUSIC HALL

AT LEE'S HOUSE IN LAKE TAHOE

Sometimes Ray, his stage manager, referred to these entertainers as "circus acts." And sometimes they seemed like just that: the talented Caribbean singer, Steve Majors, who would instantly conjure lyrics from words or themes provided by the audience; large vocal groups like The Mike Curb Congregation or Up With People; The Famous People Players, a "black light" theater troupe of socially and emotionally challenged young artists from Toronto, Canada; The Trinidad Tripoli Steel Drum Band; and Scotty Plummer, an energetic twelve-year-old banjo player from San Francisco.

Then there were the singers: young Jamie Redfern from Australia; René Simard, from Montréal; Debby Robert, a former Miss Louisiana; and Domenick Allen, a true professional singer and entertainer. Even the now-well-known Dancing Waters were given a new lease on their show business life when Lee insisted on using them as much as possible. All of these acts were eager to attach themselves to Lee; not a bad business move, actually. He loved helping them get to the next step of their entertainment career. Some, like Streisand, went on to long, successful careers. Others enjoyed their "moment in the glow" and then took a different path. Even today, Lee continues to help up-and-coming artists; the Liberace Foundation contributes millions of dollars in matching scholarships to over one hundred colleges and universities.

17.

Traveling With Lee

To be successful, show biz promoters have to weigh the cost of presenting a popular entertainer with the size of the venue and the cost of a ticket. Paying top dollar to major headliners, like Lee, was always a tricky balancing act between the known (Lee's salary) and the unknown (the potential size of the audience). Venue operators—like Buster Bonoff in Warwick, Rhode Island, and Phoenix, Arizona, and Ralph Bridges in Atlanta, Georgia—chose venues that would accommodate a large amount of people, at least 1,800-2,000 per show. This would allow them to charge a reasonable ticket price and still be able to pay the necessary expenses. Lee's manager, Seymour, knew this, and, though fair, would always try to get Lee the highest fee possible. Bottom line? A Liberace performance was a very big deal for show promoters and patrons alike.

In Florida, Lee performed in several large arenas (in Jupiter, Lakeland, and Tampa) that seated over 15,000; they were also used for hockey games, basketball games, and monster truck rallies. Lee often commented on how cold these huge arenas felt, visually. They were noisy and not as attractive as the friendly, smaller, theater-styled venues. He definitely preferred the smaller theaters, especially the ones north of the border in Canada. We would alternate our yearly tours to include first eastern Canada (Montréal, Québec, Toronto, and Hamilton) and then western Canada (Saskatoon, Edmonton, Calgary, and Vancouver). These ornate Canadian theaters held 2,500-3,000 people, and, compared to the arenas, were quite regal, with curtains, carpeted aisles, and comfortable cushioned seats.

But regardless of the venue, Lee always sold out his performances: a tent in Cohasset, Massachusetts, a nightclub in Mexico City, or a casino in Sun City, South Africa. The only somewhat unsuccessful U.S. venue I can remember in my thirteen years with him was the Eden Roc hotel in Miami Beach. For some reason, variety acts like Rich Little, Joan Rivers, or Steve and Eydie always packed the place, but not Lee. He didn't play to an empty house; it just wasn't as jam-packed as his other shows were.

The only other time Lee had audience problems was on a European tour in the early '80s. He'd finished a very successful two-week run at the Palladium in London and had been invited to tour Europe, with performances in Stockholm, Copenhagen, Oslo, Berlin, The Hague, and Munich. Lee was mostly unknown in these cities, so much so that, while the venues and supporting orchestras were first-rate, the crowds were very small—so small that promoters had to "paper" the audience, i.e. give away free tickets to fill the halls.

Besides being unknown, there was also a language problem. An example occurred in England at the Palladium: During one break in the show, Lee pointed to his rhinestone-laden shoes and asked the audience if they liked them. Of course, they roared their approval. Then he said, "They're killing me, but they match." More laughter. He then added, "I don't mind, because they make me feel horny." Nothing, just a few polite giggles. After a couple nights of this low-level response, a stage manager pointed out that the British word for "horny" is "randy." Lee changed the word in the next show, and the place almost came apart from the noise of the response.

The language problem got more severe in Europe. The English that was taught in Germany, Holland, and the Scandinavian countries was of the British variety. This meant that Lee's American jokes and funny asides received hardly any laughs, and this lack of reaction seemed to throw off his timing. At the end of most of these performances, it seemed like the audience couldn't wait to leave—not a reaction to which Lee was accustomed.

In the United States, Lee's East Coast summer shows were held in what were referred to as "the tents." In the beginning, they really were actual circus tents, perfect for a crowd of 1,200-1,800 to view their favorite stars. But as more and more of these venues extended their productions into the colder winter months, some permanent structures were built. Some still continued to use actual tents, including Ann Corio's Storrowton Music Tent in West Springfield, Massachusetts, and the South Shore Music Circus in Cohasset, Massachusetts. Even though these newer structures were built with insulated brick and mortar, they were still called "the tents": the Oakdale Theatre in Wallingford, Connecticut; the Nanuet Star Theatre near the New Jersey / New York border; and one I'll always remember, Lew Fisher's popular Melody Fair theater in the small New York town of North Tonawanda. For those unfamiliar with this area of the country, North Tonawanda (yes, there's a Tonawanda, but no South Tonawanda) lies about halfway between Buffalo and Niagara Falls and backs up to the Niagara River.

The Melody Fair was a hard-topped, theater-in-the-round building. The audience sat in a 360° circle, with Lee's piano in the middle. Sometimes, these circular stages would rotate, giving all of the audience a chance to see his piano technique. Lee usually played the Melody Fair every year in September, just after the beginning of football season. The team you had to root for in that area of the country was, of course, the Buffalo Bills. The building, which held about 1,800, was located on a grassy area with plenty of room for parking. Right next door to it was a huge, dilapidated, Wurlitzer factory with many broken windows—truly a sad-looking structure. But, somehow, it made the Melody Fair stand out a bit. The downside to this concrete theater was its lack of air conditioning. During hot and humid conditions, even with its doors and windows open, there would be only meager airflow to the audience—airflow that never reached the sunken middle area where the musicians played.

The seats were metal frames with canvas fabric; not the most comfortable, but Lee's legions of fans didn't seem to mind. The lights and sound were suspended from the strong steel girders that held up the structure. Surprisingly, the sound was quite good. There were usually four "runways" (ramps) that led from the four corners of the building to the round stage in the center. One ramp was designated the main ramp, and Lee and the acts used it for their entrances and exits, illuminated with special spotlights.

I'm sure most theater promoters had the same desire as Lew Fisher in North Tonawanda: to put on as many sold-out shows as possible. This meant adding matinée performances, usually on Saturday or Sunday afternoons, or both. But with Lew's theater, there was a challenge. He approached me one evening after our opening Friday night show:

"You know, Bo, we're sold out for the Sunday matinée," he said, twirling his waxed handlebar mustache. "That's great news for us . . . "

"Yeah," I nodded.

" . . . but we have that second show at 6:30." He paused, then added, "I know Lee's show runs about three hours, which means his 2:30 show will end about 5:30." He paused again. "The problem is . . . " (I knew what the problem was, but I let him continue.) " . . . the audience for his 6:30 show will be arriving about the same time that the first crowd starts to leave. That's 1,800 people bumping into each other. Cars, old ladies, kids, people in wheelchairs. See my problem?"

"Yeah," I nodded.

"Good. Now, why don't you go to Lee and explain this to him, and see if he'll cut some of the 2:30 show. I've tried asking Seymour, but I haven't heard back from him. I thought you, as his music director, might have some influence. Will you talk to Lee?"

Seymour and I knew that Lee would never cut his show, ever, period. In over 5,000 shows I did with him, he never cut a number and, what's most amazing, missed only one performance at the Vegas Hilton, when he had a slight case of pneumonia.

"Lew," I said, trying to sound understanding but firm, "I don't think Lee will make any cuts. I can't tell you how many times he's told me, and others, how he respects every audience he performs for and never wants to do less than a full show for them. I guess we're going to have a late start for the second show tomorrow evening. That's about all I can say."

Now, Lew was exasperated. "Well, can't you just speed up some of the numbers, make them take up less time?" As you can see, Lew wasn't a musician.

"That's not going to work, either. Lee is programmed to play each of his selections at a certain performance tempo. If I speed any of them up, it's going to ruin the show for everyone. Sorry."

We did hold the start of the second show until about 7:00 that Sunday evening, which meant overtime pay for Lew's stagehands, the sound and lighting crew, and additional personnel, but both audiences were treated to a full Liberace show. As I recall, every "double show day" presented the same problem. I always wondered why Lew didn't just start the second show a bit later. I never found out why.

One thing that was a bit comical to me concerned Lew Fisher and his use of a local tux shop. When Melody Fair first opened, he wanted it to be a respectable place, meaning that the ushers should, in his mind, wear tuxes. In the summer months, he'd hire several young high school students for these positions, and each one of them would wear a tuxedo. Lew was able to get a new set of tuxedos each week, probably for free, just by mentioning the name of the tuxedo shop. But in all the years we performed there, I never saw any usher wearing a simple black tuxedo. They were always bright orange, baby blue, flaming purple, canary yellow, pure gold, lime green, etc. And they all came with matching ruffled shirts, bow ties, and cummerbunds. With these outfits, the ushers were almost as lavishly dressed as Lee. Maybe that's what Lew had in mind all along.

Another funny memory is of a pre-show public address announcement. As in most theaters, the Melody Fair public address system was used to tell the audience to "please keep the aisles clear during the show" or "please respect your fellow theatergoers by not talking during the performance" or "will the owner of a blue Dodge station wagon please move your vehicle, it's in a no-parking zone." There were no cell phones buzzing and chirping back then, or there would have been that announcement, too. One time, though, we heard an amazing request: "Will the owner of a red Chevy Malibu please return to your car. It's not blocking traffic, and it's not parked illegally.

However, the doors are locked, and the engine is running." That brought quite a response from everyone, and Lee made a funny remark about it in his show that afternoon. It seems that, when Lee's fans came to see him, they forgot about everything except for the excitement of seeing him—including turning off their car's engine.

Every time we played North Tonawanda it was for a week's engagement, usually Tuesday through Sunday. The Sunday matinée was always sold out, and on that day, a certain group of men always attended—not the same men every time, but the same type: wearing uncomfortable suits and ties, sitting stiffly with their wives or mothers or both, arms folded across their chests, and sour looks on their faces. After learning about them from some of the local musicians, I knew the reason for their disgruntled looks, and I knew what they were thinking:

"Y'know, (female relative's name), it's Sunday, and I really don't want to be here watching this Libber-Ace guy. Come on! Don't you realize the Bills are playing one of their home games 22.3 miles from here? And I just *know* they're heading for the playoffs again this year!" The look on their faces always said, "Go on. Try. I *dare you* to make me have a good time. I just dare you."

Then out would come Lee, all smiles and in great humor, as always. And his piano playing would absolutely charm and thrill the audience—everyone, it seemed, except for these guys. At first, these unhappy football fans would only half-listen to the show while impatiently looking at their watches or checking out the people around them. But, soon, they would start watching the show, at first smiling, then laughing, and then even clapping along. As Lee played "Beer Barrel Polka," his final number, these formerly sour-faced Buffalo Bills fans would be singing the loudest, and by the end of that number, they'd be the first ones on their feet yelling, "Bravo, bravo!" I often wondered if Lee knew or sensed this scenario. To his credit, he always knew just what his audiences wanted, even if some of those in the audience didn't realize they wanted it.

With the exception of that one not-so-great European tour I mentioned, Lee only performed in English-speaking countries. Ah, but there was one other exception to the English-speaking rule, a four-night stint in Mexico City. The thing I remember about that trip was the percussion section of the orchestra. My musical arrangements were written to accommodate just one percussionist, who would play several instruments: timpani, orchestra bells, xylophone, tambourine, and shaker. The local musician did a great job reading all the percussion instrument parts in rehearsal and during the first night's show. On the second night, when I looked back to the percussion section to give a timpani cue, there were two percussionists. The next evening there were three, and on the final night we had four percussionists, all smiling, passing instruments amongst themselves, and having a great time. Whether they were relatives or just friends, I didn't know or care, as long as the music didn't suffer—and it didn't.

Another English-speaking country, South Africa, deserves a special mention in this section of memories. We performed at Sun City, a sprawling hotel-casino-showroom-shopping mall, in the early '80s. It reminded me of a Vegas-style resort and hosted several major headliners: Frank Sinatra, Elton John, Queen, Goldie Hawn, and others. The house band was excellent, and the surroundings were amazing: rhinos, monkeys, leopards—the whole Africa thing. But this was at a time when South Africa was politically blacklisted by the rest of the African continent due to racial issues.

At the end of our engagement, we were scheduled to fly back home to the United States via a rather circuitous route, due to the above-mentioned issue. Instead of flying straight north over the African continent, our airline, SAA (South African Airways)—banned from flying over any of the continent's northern section—had to fly straight west to the Atlantic Ocean and then north-west to the United States, which added a couple of hours to the flight.

We took off from Johannesburg about four o' clock in the afternoon. A few hours later, just as we were about to enjoy a lovely first-class meal, the captain announced that there was a problem with one of the 747's engines. We were dumping fuel and heading back to Johannesburg. This was going to be a very long trip. No telling when we'd finally get back home.

When we landed, all of us, including Lee, were booked on the next SAA flight destined for the United States, which was scheduled to leave in a few hours. We waited and then boarded this second 747. We started to take off but never even got into the air. As we roared down the runway, the plane struck a flight of birds, stalling two engines. The pilot instantly shut down the other two and slammed on the brakes. We heard the "pops" and smelled the burning rubber tires as they exploded from the friction.

Back at the Johannesburg airport, we sat around, not knowing what to do. Some of the group opted to spend the night in Johannesburg and take the next SAA flight to the U.S. the following evening. The airline had a limited supply of 747s and was running out of them quickly. Lee, Seymour, and I chose to change airlines and fly BOAC (British Overseas Airways Corporation, now British Airways) from Johannesburg to London, where we would change planes and head home to

Las Vegas. At the time, BOAC was exempt from the sanctions imposed on SAA, as long as it flew only to England.

So, that's what we did. Our flight north later that evening was uneventful. I slept as we flew over Egypt, Spain, France, and into London, arriving early in the morning. Lee and Seymour decided to fly back to the United States later that same day, but I chose to cash in my first-class ticket and upgrade to BOAC's supersonic jet, the Concorde, something I'd always wanted to do. It was a once-in-a-lifetime opportunity.

After a short, four-hour wait at Heathrow, I boarded the smaller, but very streamlined Concorde, along with, much to my surprise, Juan Carlos, the new king of Spain. A quiet man of about fifty, he was traveling with his wife, Queen Sophia. They really looked like a royal couple.

The Concorde held about a hundred passengers sitting two abreast and was very modern and comfortable. At the front of the cabin were two large displays showing the Mach number, Mach 1 being the speed of sound. Both read 0.0 when we boarded.

Our takeoff was nothing special, very much like a normal commercial jet. As we slowly climbed in both altitude and speed, the Mach number grew, but not very quickly. When we finally reached Mach .65, I decided to use the restroom before our "jump" over the speed of sound. I hurried to the front of the cabin to quickly do my business, very anxious not to miss the start of our supersonic flight. As I quickly exited, I banged my head on the small doorway but hurried back to my seat, strapped myself in and stared at the screen. Slowly, the numbers grew: Mach .75, Mach .85, Mach .95 . . . ah, we were almost there. Mach .98, Mach .98, Mach .98 . . . and there we stayed, not moving up or down. Then the captain came on, speaking with no emotion and a thick British accent:

"Ladies and gentlemen, this is your captain speaking. It seems we're having some injector issues with our number two engine at this time, preventing us from going supersonic. Although we do have enough fuel for our supersonic flight, were we to continue flying at this subsonic speed we would have only enough fuel to get us within approximately 750 miles this side of New York. To avoid such a mishap, we'll be returning to Heathrow Airport for repairs and, hopefully, only a three-hour delay. We're sorry for the inconvenience."

"Here we go again," I thought.

Back at Heathrow, I sat in the first-class lounge along with the king and his wife, and tried to kill time by reading magazines. This type of thing was happening more frequently than I liked, and I debated about getting back on board. However, about three hours later, when the announcement to board was made, I saw the Spanish king and queen heading for the plane and figured, if they were going, so was I.

As we boarded again, I passed their seats, nodded, and smiled a sort of "comrade-in-arms" smile. The king returned my nod but not the smile. I once again sat in my seat, strapped myself in yet again, and, without much fanfare, we took off. Again the Mach numbers increased until, with a small bump, like going over a tar strip on a street, we reached supersonic speed and the screen showed us at Mach 1.0 and increasing. That was it, like a slight bump in very light turbulence. We climbed higher and higher, and the sky grew darker—not black, but a very dark blue. A meal was served. I checked Lee's schedule for the next few months, thought about the upcoming venues, and a short time later, we landed in New York. As I left the aircraft, I once again nodded to the king and queen of Spain, knowing that our brief nodding acquaintance was over. That's as close to royalty as I've ever been, unless you count shaking Elvis's hand.

Of all the venues in which I conducted Lee, I think the Sierra Tahoe in northern Nevada was my favorite. Lee enjoyed it so much, he bought a home there.

The Sierra Tahoe Hotel and Casino didn't have the flash and glitter of Vegas. It wasn't as big and didn't offer as much variety of restaurants or entertainment, but it had a very comfortable, small-town feeling that I really liked. Everyone who worked there knew each other. It was truly a family of employees, and in some cases, literally. It was the same feeling, too, with the other Tahoe hotel-casinos: Harrah's, Harvey's, the Cal Neva on the north shore, and Caesars Palace.

The rooms weren't fancy but they were very comfortable. The food was all homemade and extremely good, and the entertainment in the showrooms was first class, with lounges that catered to the locals by presenting country acts, almost-known singers on the rise, etc.

One of our shows at the Sierra Tahoe is especially memorable to me. In this particular Liberace show, Lee played "The Old Fashioned Way," the lovely 1973 song written by Charles Aznavour. After performing it, Lee would walk over to the edge of the stage and look for a dance partner while the orchestra continued to play the song. This was always a big part of his performances: taking the entertainment directly to the audience (something that is almost a requirement nowadays). Once he'd found a partner, he would escort her to the stage and they'd dance.

This all worked very well, except for one night during the midnight show. Lee had chosen his dance partner, and they were just about to start dancing when suddenly another very nice lady—who obviously had enjoyed more than a few drinks—struggled up the stairs to the stage, walked over to Lee and his partner, and cut in. Lee, at first surprised, instantly started dancing with the second woman, leaving the first woman standing there. So, to avoid an awkward situation, I gave a signal to the band to keep playing, walked over to Lee's first partner and began dancing with her. I kept watching Lee to see what he wanted me to do. When he nodded, I gave the band the cue to finish the number. At the end, Lee and I stood there with our respective partners, and bowed. I handed the first woman back to Lee and then, at his suggestion, escorted the second woman—who was now talking quite excitedly about her dance with Liberace—back to her seat. Everything worked out fine. Lee was able to make both women feel special, and the audience loved it.

ONE OF MANY PLAYBILLS WITH
MY LAST NAME MISSPELLED

ON TOUR WITH LEE IN THE 70S

POSED ATOP RADIO CITY MUSIC HALL

UNKNOWN CITY
UNKNOWN DRESSING ROOM

18.

Memorable Vocalists

Lee enjoyed presenting up-and-coming singers in his shows—solid entertainers with whom he could collaborate. These guest artists added variety to his concerts, and they also gave him time to "change into something more spectacular" while they performed. So, any account of my time with Lee would be incomplete without the mention of these talented singers.

Debby Robert

Debby was a respected Broadway-style singer and a former Miss Louisiana (she wore the crown in 1972). She and her boyfriend/manager traveled with us. He was constantly taking pictures of her, so much so that we dubbed him "Kid Kodak." Her performances with Lee went well; she would sing several Broadway songs while he accompanied her. She was with us for only a few tours during the spring and summer of '74. Like many of the guest performers, Debby was hoping to gain more prominence through her association with Lee. Her biggest success, however, came with our tour of her home state, Louisiana.

Jamie Redfern

I had conducted Diahann Carroll in Australia in the late '60s, so the country was relatively familiar territory for me. I really liked the land and the people and returned there with Liberace in '73. One of our guest performers was Jamie Redfern. Jamie had been a winner on the Australian TV show "Young Talent Time," a program that launched the careers of a number of Australian performers. The original series ran from 1971 until 1988 and was hosted by musician Johnny Young. As I understood it, Lee heard Jamie sing while touring Australia in '71 and asked him to join his show. Jamie was still touring with Lee when I began learning Lee's show in Sparks, Nevada in November of '72, and into my first tours in '73. I was able to arrange some new material for Jamie, who was about fifteen or sixteen years old. His performance always brought the crowd to its feet.

During our tour in '73, Jamie's voice began to change. Unfortunately, someone had told him that his youthful boy-soprano voice would always be with him. When he asked me if this was true, I told him I wasn't a vocal coach, but that most male voices do change as they mature, a natural phenomenon. However, with coaching by Liberace, and some key changes, Jamie made a successful transition and continued to build a solid performing reputation in the United States and in his native Australia. I enjoyed working with Jamie and, through Facebook, our friendship continues.

René Simard

Another young singer who briefly traveled with us was the Canadian sensation René Simard. Discovered and managed by music producer Guy Cloutier, René's first albums were produced by René Angélil, who later managed—and eventually married—Céline Dion. In 1974, René Simard represented Canada at the International Festival of Song in Tokyo, where he won first prize for performance and the Frank Sinatra trophy, which was presented by Sinatra himself. René appeared frequently on U.S. TV networks with artists such as Bing Crosby, Bob Hope, Liza Minnelli, and Andy Williams. He also hosted his own CBC Television series from 1977 to 1979. It featured international celebrity guests and was produced in Vancouver, British Columbia by Alan Thicke.

René exemplified the typical Liberace act: a young singer who was very well known in a local area (eastern Canada) and who had lots of talent and personality. René later paired up with his sister and became quite a huge hit on TV in Canada, especially in the French-speaking area of Quebec. He loved the sunshine during our tour of Florida. It could have been fifty degrees outside, but as long as the sun was shining, he was in his bathing suit, soaking up the rays.

When we traveled back to Montréal with René, he and Lee were mobbed at the airport. The combination of Liberace and René attracted a huge audience, and we were totally sold out for every performance at Montréal's Place des Arts. Each night, Lee accompanied René, and the two of them brought down the house.

Shani Wallis

Shani Wallis is one of those "small world" stories. I first met Shani through Joe Guercio, who had been asked to produce a new act for her. She'd just been introduced to American audiences in the movie *Oliver,* and she was the first big name with whom I worked. She came to Las Vegas, and Joe came up with several new songs and medleys for her. I played piano, made lead sheets and helped to get the right feeling in the pieces. Since Joe was married (and had a family), and I wasn't, he suggested that I be her conductor for the first outing of this new material. That was fine with me; I loved conducting—though I hadn't done too much with this size orchestra: six brass, five saxes, three rhythm, a percussionist, and five strings. We traveled to The Meadows Supper Club in Framingham, Massachusetts, right next to Needham (which just happens to be my middle name). I felt a bit awed by the responsibility of making sure that Shani was happy with my conducting. Joe was mainly concerned that I make sure his material go well. It was also the first time I'd worked with an East Coast band—hardened musicians who thought they'd seen and played it all. Our first rehearsal, though, was a challenge: most of them hadn't seen music that was as demanding as what I'd brought. It wasn't that it was difficult; it was just of a higher caliber and called for higher notes and more intricate rhythms. To put it simply, this was some very hot big band stuff, written by Bill Readie, arranger par excellence. And I was in charge of making it happen.

Those shows in Framingham became a learning experience for me. I knew I was still gaining my conducting legs. There's nothing worse than being a fledgling conductor (no matter how good you are), standing on the podium in front of seasoned musicians, and knowing that they all know you're a beginner. And some of these veterans were, well, less tolerant than others.

I again conducted Shani at New York's Waldorf Astoria Hotel. Their showroom was beautiful but hadn't really been designed as a music venue: the solid marble everywhere made it more like an empty swimming pool, with the sound to match. But we did our best.

While in New York for this engagement, I conducted Shani on Ed Sullivan's live, coast-to-coast TV show, a definite first for me. The twenty-piece orchestra and I were placed in a glass-enclosed structure next to the performing area. For her number "As Long As He Needs Me," the technicians made a recording of just the orchestra playing the accompaniment, without Shani. Then, for the actual airing, they played the tape as she sang it live on camera. Making the recording went well, but when it came time to go on air, they asked me and the orchestra to have our music ready and to silently play along with the recording we'd made, so that we'd be ready to jump in and begin playing if something happened to the tape. I stood on the podium making small conducting motions as we all read the arrangement we were hearing. Talk about stress! Thankfully, nothing happened to the tape, and Shani did a great job.

Now, fast-forward several years, and there I was, working again with Shani and her manager/husband, Bernie. Lee had asked her to join him for several engagements in Reno and Tahoe. It was great seeing and working with her again. The reunion brought back memories of the Waldorf Astoria Hotel and *The Ed Sullivan Show*. I remembered my first job with her in Framingham and my struggles as a young orchestra conductor: missed cues, wrong tempos, and unclear arm movements. I also remembered my very heavily starched tuxedo shirt collars. I'd heard somewhere that, by asking for heavy starch in your shirts, you didn't have to have them laundered as often. That may have been true, but after several shows, my neck really hurt!

Marco Valenti

Marco Valenti was one of the Pittsburgh, Pennsylvania winners of the Metropolitan Opera Competition, an event held in various large cities across the country. Marco had a huge tenor voice and used it effectively on several well-known opera arias. I arranged some more modern selections for him: "Granada" and "Cuando Calienta el Sol." He was a big hit with all the Liberace audiences. His almost shy, humble manner on stage would suddenly change when he began to sing, his tenor voice soaring. To me, it was a magical transformation.

Marco traveled with his wife, Patty, and sometimes with their daughter, Sylvia. Patty was very protective of Marco and made sure he was always comfortable—not too cold or too hot—and not overly tired. Patty would constantly come up with new medicines to prevent Marco from catching any throat ailments, always claiming that he had to take care of his voice. But even with all these preventive measures, Marco and Patty seemed to be the only ones on tour who ever got sick. Go figure.

Lee took great delight in introducing Marco and was always very generous with his comments about him, and, indeed, about all the entertainers who appeared in his shows. While most of these entertainers revered Lee and appreciated his words of praise, a few let it go to their heads and thought that appearing in Liberace's show was all it took to be a "star." To Marco's credit, both he and Patty always respected Lee's generosity toward them and continually thanked him for giving Marco a great performing opportunity.

Since Marco and Patty were somewhat inexperienced with show business, they weren't sure how to deal with the applause, or with the adoring fans Marco soon acquired. Marco was a shy person who had been cloistered in a seminary school in his early years. However, he and Patty soon learned how to handle people's attention—mostly by smiling, nodding, and saying a meaningful "thank you." Unfortunately, during the years when Marco performed with Lee, he made some poor investments, listening to and trusting the wrong people, and so lost quite a bit of money. It was a good thing that what Marco lacked in "street smarts," he more than made up for in vocal talent.

I got a sad phone call from Marco in the early '90s. It went something like this:

"Hi, Bo. It's Marco."

"Hey, Marco! What's up?"

"I'm dying." Marco was nothing if not direct.

"Oh. Really." A slight pause, then, "I'm so sorry, Marco."

"I've got some kind of stomach cancer and I just wanted to, uh, call and apologize for all the problems I caused you: not knowing how to talk on stage, forgetting to follow you, saying all those silly things when I spoke to the audience, all of it. I'll always be very grateful for the way you helped me when I started working with Liberace. You were so nice to my family. I just wanted to tell you how much I appreciate that."

Wow. What do you say to that? For once in my life, I couldn't find any words. After a long pause, I said,

"I don't know what to say, Marco. Again, I'm so sorry. Please let me know if there's anything at all I can do for you, or Patty, or Sylvia."

Marco died not long afterward. His final phone call to me was something I'll never forget. Very touching, and very sad.

19.

Memorable Musical Acts

In addition to the talented singers mentioned in Chapter 18, Liberace also introduced other creative performers to the world of show business. What follows are my recollections of some of these memorable acts.

Scotty Plummer

Scotty Plummer was a dynamic young banjo player and one of the most crowd-pleasing acts that Lee featured. When I first met Scotty, he was about twelve years old and reminded me of Mark Twain's character Tom Sawyer: red hair, freckles, engaging, and full of talent and energy. His banjo playing was extraordinary; he played the Eddie Peabody strumming style as opposed to the bluegrass picking style. His banjo was modeled after one of Mr. Peabody's banjos, including a unique wood casing and real brass fittings. It was heavy, and as energetic as Scotty was, I often wondered how he could control his playing.

Lee and Scotty worked extremely well together. And Scotty really admired Lee: at Lee's suggestion, he had a white suit custom-made for himself and then added a sequined banjo to it as a "tip of the hat" to Lee. Scotty would become even livelier whenever Lee introduced him to an audience, and he would harness all his energy to play several up-tempo selections with the band. Then Lee—wearing an even more dazzling outfit—would re-emerge to join him for some spirited duets, numbers well known by everyone. Scotty's outfits got flashier with each tour, no doubt at Lee's suggestion. But it worked. They never got anything less than a standing ovation at each and every concert.

Scotty's energy got the best of him on one occasion, however. We were doing a week of concerts at the Front Row Theater, a theater-in-the-round just east of Cleveland, Ohio. Like so many once-glamorous venues, it's now a Home Depot, Lowe's, Office Max, or other big-box store. But in the '70s and '80s, it was *the* venue for many famous celebrities. The Front Row was modern and had really nice dressing rooms for the entertainers, as well as one large green room for the star, with a large dressing room adjacent to it. This large reception-type room had couches, tables, and a large, well-stocked, wraparound bar. The end of the bar was hinged so that one could raise and lower it to get behind the bar. The room even came with its own bartender, a very nice older gentleman who made sure everyone had something to drink, and who always stocked the bar with plenty of chips, dip, and other snacks.

The normal routine was for Lee's entourage to visit the green room after every show and enjoy a few drinks and snacks before heading back to the hotel, which was about ten miles north of the theater in Willoughby, Ohio. The green room was also used by Lee and his manager, Seymour, to entertain friends and business associates. It truly was the focal point both before and after each show.

On this particular tour, our entourage included Marvyn Roy. He and his lovely wife, Carol, had a spectacular magic act that they had presented all over the United States, Europe, South America, and the Far East. Marvyn was very clever in using electricity in his performances, and he certainly lived up to his billing as "Mr. Electric." He always worked very hard at promoting himself and performed at other venues when not working with Lee, all with Lee's blessing, of course. For this engagement, he had contacted the head of advertising at the local General Electric facility and had invited him and his wife to our Sunday afternoon matinée. Marvyn was excited about the possible extra work he might get and kept telling us about this natural connection: Mr. Electric and General Electric. It did sound like a sure thing.

So, on Sunday afternoon, just after another sellout show, the GE executive and his wife were ushered back to the green room to meet Liberace. Marvyn was just gushing over his potential new client and introduced him and his wife to everyone: Terry, Lee's dresser; Seymour and some of his friends; the theater manager and his wife; the stage manager; the sound man; Ralph Enriquez, our bass player; Chuck Hughes, our drummer; and me. He even introduced him to the bartender, with much fanfare.

Scotty and his mother, Clara, came in from the lobby, where Scotty had been meeting some of his many fans and signing several of his albums. Even after a full show and all the hoopla of meeting people in the lobby, Scotty was, as usual, very hyper that Sunday afternoon and was running around doing comedic bits with everyone while singing, talking, and laughing at the same time—typical behavior for an energized twelve-year-old. I could tell that Marvyn wasn't too happy that Scotty was distracting everyone from his all-important new GE prospect.

As the bartender poured everyone drinks, Marvyn and the GE executive moved to the hinged end of the bar, deep in conversation. The movable portion of the bar was raised, and the executive was leaning with his arm on the edge of the bar, with his fingers curving slightly over the edge. Scotty was still running around and, at one point, came running over to the bar, trying to engage anyone in conversation.

Just then someone new came into the room, another friend of Seymour's, I think, and Scotty quickly turned, flailing his arms in the air while dashing to see the new arrival. In doing so, his arm slammed into the raised portion of the bar and sent it crashing down onto the hand of the GE executive, breaking his finger. We all rushed to his aid, while someone called for emergency help. I looked at Marvyn. He was totally in shock, realizing that, in an instant, his great opportunity with GE had vanished. But other than a broken finger, the GE executive was fine. An ambulance took him to the hospital, and Marvyn accompanied him, apologizing the entire way, I'm sure. For several weeks after, Marvyn didn't speak to Scotty or his mother, even though they both had apologized many times. He finally got over the incident, however, especially when he got the good news that his initiative had paid off, and he was going to sign a multiyear contract to represent GE.

I helped Scotty make his first record, *Banjo on the Roof*, and he always delighted his audiences by autographing it for them after our shows. When he signed his albums, he would first draw a caricature of a banjo, similar to Lee's piano design. I found Scotty to be extremely enthusiastic about learning new numbers for the shows, trying different arrangements, and, in the process, never losing his focus on being an entertainer. I was very saddened to learn of his death in 1992—it was way too early for such a talented young performer. In videos on YouTube, I still enjoy watching him entertain audiences with his unique, boyish charm.

Domenick Allen

Domenick Allen and I became musical friends and still keep in touch. He was probably the most professional of Lee's guest artists: a multitalented composer, singer, and instrumentalist. Together, he and I produced several local TV jingles, one of them for the *Las Vegas Sun* newspaper. I worked with him on several of his original songs, and we collaborated on two albums. Our tours together included most of the United States, Canada, and a special tour to Sun City in South Africa. To his credit, Domenick knew exactly how this level of his career should be handled. He made the most of his time on stage with Lee, but never upstaged him. The two of them worked very well together. Domenick and Lee remained friends even after he stopped touring with us, and Domenick told me he was one of the last people to see Lee before he died.

The Mike Curb Congregation

Another of the early ensembles was The Mike Curb Congregation, about fourteen very clean-cut, energetic young singers/dancers. They had performed with other noted entertainers including Sammy Davis Jr., Steve Lawrence and Eydie Gormé, Donny and Marie Osmond, and others. They would do one or two numbers with Lee toward the end of his show and were always vibrant and entertaining.

While we were performing with The Congregation at the Nugget in Sparks, Nevada, I suffered a bit of a medical issue. While swimming underwater in the outdoor pool at the motel next to the Nugget, I ran head first into the side of the pool, breaking my nose and requiring a quick trip to the hospital. That evening, with gauze and bandages covering half my face, Lee asked me if I would be able to conduct. "Of course," I said, trying to sound calm and assured. Lee was most concerned, however, with my appearance and asked that I not do the usual bow after the overture. After seeing myself in the mirror, I agreed. I was a mess, visually, but I was still able to conduct the show. So, when it came time for Lee to introduce his conductor and the musicians, I had the band guys stand, and I waved my arm without turning around. It was, I admit, a bit awkward, but it worked.

The Young Americans

Yet another large group was The Young Americans. They were similar to The Mike Curb Congregation, with a diverse group of young singers who performed upbeat, contemporary songs. This group had several standout performers who later became well-known solo entertainers. One was Nia Peeples, a talented dancer, singer, and actor. She has appeared in several major movies, including *Fame*. For others going on to other careers, it would be a special musical time in their lives they'd never forget.

20.

Memorable Variety Acts

Lee used several different variety acts and would always include himself in these presentations. By playing piano during the act or by talking to the artist, he would help to highlight these talented performers even more.

Dieter Tasso

One of the first acts with whom I worked was Dieter Tasso, the famous comic juggler from Germany. I enjoyed watching him juggle hats and canes and then balance cups and saucers on his head—which he would place there by tossing them up in the air with his foot. During all of this, he would keep up a funny running commentary of his achievements. I also enjoyed speaking to him in German. It brought back so many memories of my time spent in Salzburg, Austria.

Russ Lewis and Brooklyn Birch

Some of my favorite variety acts involved puppets, either string or hand puppets, and ventriloquist dummies. I guess it's the ability to make an inanimate object seem real that fascinates me. As I said earlier, watching those huge puppets while conducting the Raquel Welch show was really thrilling.

Of all the ventriloquists with whom I worked, I found Russ Lewis to be just about the best. Russ and his little wooden friend, Brooklyn Birch, joined the Liberace show in the mid-'70s after compiling an impressive list of credits during the '60s, including appearances on *The Ed Sullivan Show*, *The Steve Allen Show*, *The Dean Martin Show*, *The Mike Douglas Show*, and *The Hollywood Palace*. Brooklyn, his dummy, was always the "funny man," and, one time, actually slipped in a double entendre. On this particular evening, we were performing at the Nugget in Sparks, Nevada, in the Celebrity Showroom, which had a very small stage. When Russ and Brooklyn came out for their final bit toward the end of the show, there were two large, tasteful, nude, female Grecian statues still on stage. (They were used to provide a *classic* setting for Lee's ornate Chopin piano.) Brooklyn looked up at one of the tastefully topless statues that was carrying a large urn and remarked to no one in particular, "Gee, look at the jug on that broad!" The audience and the band really enjoyed that bit of fun, although I heard later that Seymour "lightly" reprimanded Russ.

As I said, the band cracked up at this remark, which brings me to the subject of "musician humor". It's totally "inside" and is meant to be appreciated by musicians. I know, because I've told a couple of hilarious stories with musician humor to non-musicians, and they've laid a big, fat egg; zero, no reaction. A typical story that seems to be understood, kind of, by the non-musician, goes like this:

A drunk at a piano bar looks into the piano player's drink and says,

"Hey, do you know there's a fly in your drink?"

The pianist looks over to the drink, then back to the drunk, and says,

"No, but if you hum a couple bars I can fake it."

I know, I know; there are several variations of this, but you get the idea, I hope.

Barclay Shaw and Toto the Clown

And now, on to one of the most endearing puppet acts Lee featured: Barclay Shaw and his stringed puppet friend, Toto the Clown. Barclay, a very talented puppeteer, spent much of his early career in New York performing on the Catskill Mountain resort circuit with celebrities such as Danny Kaye, Sophie Tucker, and Nat King Cole. Then it was on to Miami Beach, where he performed in every major hotel showroom. Barclay spent more than fifteen years as a headliner in Las Vegas showroom revues. He also toured the Caribbean and

Australia and did TV shows in Europe and South America—but he ultimately always returned to Las Vegas. In his presentation, Barclay used several different puppets, but when Toto walked on stage (with Barclay's help), it was truly magical. To this day, I feel that it was one of the strongest segments in any of Lee's shows.

Ray Arnett (Lee's stage manager) had a special piano top constructed to fit directly over one of Lee's rhinestone pianos; it was strong enough that Barclay could actually walk on it. A set of stairs would be added toward the rear of the piano. Toto, wearing his red clown outfit with a large, white, ruffled collar, and Barclay, in a black tux, would make their entrance from the side of the stage while Lee played "Send in the Clowns." Toto was in awe of Lee as he played the piano. He'd go over to him, stand by his piano bench, lean back and look up at him, look back to the audience, and then back to Lee. Then, wanting to see more, he'd walk to the end of the piano and begin climbing the stairs. It was difficult work, and he'd pause several times to catch his breath. Then he'd get an idea. He'd pull out a balloon, blow it up and let the balloon lift him up into the air and carry him closer to Lee. The way Barclay arranged this was truly amazing. The balloon would expand as Toto huffed and puffed into it.

Once he arrived at Lee's end of the piano, Toto would lean over the music rack and watch Lee play. Satisfied that all was in order, he'd walk back across the piano, back down the stairs and head toward the side of the stage. Just before leaving, he'd turn, lift one hand and wave goodbye to Lee. And Lee would time his playing perfectly to coincide with the wave, ending the piece right as Toto disappeared off stage. The audience reaction was astounding: cheers, bravos, many tears. I looked forward to this number every show and can truly say I've never seen such a presentation or reaction since.

Marvyn Roy, "Mr. Electric"

As I mentioned earlier, we often toured with noted magician "Mr. Electric," Marvyn Roy, ably assisted by his lovely wife, Carol. And he was just that, a man who used his "highly charged" personality to actually light up light bulbs of all sizes, from the small to the huge, including an authentic lighthouse light bulb—although I'm not sure if a real lighthouse light bulb has threads on it, as Marvyn's had.

Mr. Electric's biggest challenge, surprisingly, was dealing with the many theater-in-the-round venues we would play. Here, the stage was in the middle of the audience and would often revolve. Sometimes the orchestra would be on the stage itself, and sometimes it would be placed in a pit to one side.

Most of the entertainers managed to adjust their performance to this type of revolving stage, but it was cause for great concern for Mr. Electric. While these venues were a great thing for Lee—they showed everyone in the audience his piano, his costumes, his playing style, etc.—for Mr. Electric they were nearly a disaster. In a typical showroom, almost all of Marvyn's illusions were based upon unseen movements, behind-the-curtain motions, etc. But here, with the audience seeing him from every angle, and him moving in a complete circle as he performed, Marvyn had to make some major changes. Unfortunately, he was usually not told about this type of venue until just a few days before he was to appear. But Mr. Electric, being the professional he was, would quickly drop some of the more revealing tricks and modify others. He was truly one of the more successful magicians who worked with Lee.

Famous People Players

Famous People Players was, and still is, a very talented group of mentally and emotionally challenged young adults from Toronto, Canada. Their leader, Diane Dupuy, began the group in the 1970s. They worked with us on several tours in Canada, and in Vegas and Lake Tahoe. Lee really connected with this group. Their specialty was black light theater, in which the performers wore black clothes while manipulating life-size, fluorescent-painted puppets of famous people, such as Barbra Streisand, Elvis, and, of course, Liberace. Their ability to bring these life-size puppets to life was truly amazing.

Famous People Players "auditioned" for us while we were performing in Toronto. After the performance, we all were treated to lunch. One of the performers, the group's spokesperson, made a comment I've never forgotten. She said, "All of us in the troupe have problems and handicaps. But so do you," she said, pointing to my glasses. "None of us is perfect. Everyone has some type of handicap." At the end of their tour with us, they gave me a picture of cartoon animals spelling out my name. It was cute, and each of them had signed their name as best they could on the back. I love that side the best.

Albert Lucas

I worked briefly with Albert Lucas, a very talented young juggler. He later became famous in the juggling world, holding several records for juggling various items while wearing ice skates, and for joggling—juggling while jogging. I remember Albert's parents who, at the time, insisted that Albert remain "young." He was already a talented juggler at the age of three and toured with Lee for several years, beginning when he was eight. Part of his appeal, I'm sure, came from his costume: a pair of short, dark, little boy shorts, and brightly colored suspenders. Even though Albert was twelve years old when I worked with him, he still looked like a very small boy, wearing the familiar shorts and colored suspenders. My guess is that, as soon as Albert outgrew his shorts, his parents would have an exact copy made in a slightly larger size. It's fun to watch him now on YouTube, grown up and sporting a mannish ponytail hairdo. And no shorts.

Fay McKay

I worked with Fay McKay for a short time, as well. She filled in for another act that had a scheduling conflict. I had never heard of her before, but found her to be extremely nice and friendly, a team player and a great addition to the show. Her signature routine, "Twelve Days of Christmas," was the highlight of her performance. In her version of the Christmas classic, her true love brings her drinks instead of the normal fare and, of course, she drinks each of them, getting more intoxicated as the song progresses. She continued playing many of the lounge shows in Las Vegas until her death in 2008. There are several videos online of her very funny performances.

Dancing Waters

When discussing memorable variety acts, I would be remiss if I didn't include one of the most visually exciting, the Dancing Waters, which nowadays appear every evening at the eight-acre lake in front of the Bellagio Hotel in Las Vegas. In Lee's show, however, it wasn't that large. The water tank itself was about as wide as the stage and eight feet from front to back but only about one foot deep. You'd think it would have been much deeper, seeing the amount of water pulsating ten to fifteen feet in the air, but there was only about three inches of water in the tank, just enough for the performance. Inside the tank were many feet of pipe, several multi-colored spotlights, a collection of rotating nozzles, and several very powerful water pumps. The whole unit was placed directly behind the orchestra at large venues in Las Vegas and Los Angeles, at Radio City Music Hall, at various outdoor venues, and, of all places, on that tiny stage at the Nugget Hotel and Casino in Sparks, Nevada.

I remember an audience member once asked, "How do they keep all that colored water from mixing together?" One time, as a prank, someone—who later was severely reprimanded—poured a whole box of laundry detergent into the water tank. The Dancing Waters number was canceled that evening, and the operator spent the next day blowing all the bubbles out of the pipes. Quite a sight.

21.

Memorable Shows

I once figured out that I had conducted about 5,000 Liberace shows—and that was over a period of thirteen years. Gordon Robinson, his first conductor, was with him for twenty-six years, so you can just imagine how many shows *they* did together. And Lee gave one hundred percent at every one of them. I can't remember all the stories about his shows, but a few do stand out. One of them is an early Liberace show in 1950. I always enjoyed hearing about this most memorable and career-changing performance.

Lee told me that, " . . . as corny as it sounds, Bo, it really was a dark and stormy night at San Diego's Del Coronado Hotel," a historic hotel located on a small strip of land across the bay from San Diego. Since then, a bridge has been built, but in those days the only way to cross the bay was with the Coronado Ferry, a small boat that would shuttle passengers between San Diego and the hotel. Consequently, that night the crowd was very light, " . . . probably no more than ten people," Lee said.

The hotel manager assured Lee that, with such a small crowd, he would certainly understand if Lee canceled his performance. But Lee felt that those ten people had made an effort to come to the hotel to see him, and it was his responsibility to perform for them. It just so happened that in the audience that evening was Don Fedderson, a producer for a new electronic medium called television. When Don saw how Lee thoroughly entertained such a small group of people, he knew he'd be perfect for this new visual venture. This is the sort of break every artist dreams of; Lee's performance on that dark and stormy night led to the beginning of his TV career in 1953. I've heard similar stories of how artists seem to do their best when performing under trying circumstances: very small audiences, outdoor venues, etc. These stories have taught me to always play every performance—regardless of the size of the crowd or the imperfect circumstances—as best as I can, because, as happened with Liberace, you never know who's going to be listening.

These are some of the memorable moments I either witnessed, or know about, as a result of my years with Lee.

We were performing at the Hilton in Las Vegas, two shows a night, seven nights a week. In the '70s, Lee and Elvis were the two biggest draws in the city, and the Hilton had them both. Each of their shows was absolutely packed, with tables set up in the aisles, six people seated at a table meant for two, and so on.

One such night, midway through Lee's first show, there was a commotion in the center of the audience, down front at the edge of the stage. It seemed that a woman was having some sort of a seizure. Several people were standing, calling and waving for help. But the showroom, especially toward the stage, was so filled with people and tables that no immediate help was available. The security guards and other staff just couldn't physically make it down to the woman. Lee, of course, stopped the show and asked that the house lights be turned on. He went to the edge of the stage, bent down and held the woman's hand as her friends tried to calm her. There was a quiet murmur from the audience, but Lee kept talking softly to the woman, rubbing her hand.

About a minute later, medical personnel arrived via the stage. They were able to lift the woman up with her chair and carry her off stage. Lee walked beside her, continuing to hold her hand. The group disappeared off stage for about a minute, and then Lee came back on stage. I was thinking it would be extremely difficult for an entertainer—or anyone—to recover from that situation. The entire flow of the show had been abruptly halted, the house lights had been turned on, the magic had stopped. How was he going to handle this? Would the show now be over? Should I get ready to give the band a cue to play Lee's take-a-bow music?

What Lee did was, to me, extraordinary. He came to center stage and asked that the house lights be lowered. Then, he said,

"She's going to be just fine, really. The doctors are with her, and they're taking excellent care of her. But you know, it's so funny. She's really very upset and a bit angry because she's going to miss the rest of the show!"

With that, he sat at the piano and began playing the next number. Having satisfied the audience's concern for the woman, he was able to turn it into a positive experience for them. I don't know any other entertainer who could have pulled that off quite that way. He was, indeed, "Mr. Showmanship."

Our rehearsals in the large Nevada casino showrooms always followed a routine. We enjoyed having two days to prepare. Our first rehearsal, on the day before we opened, was always very casual. Lee would be there for about an hour, checking his primary, rhinestone-covered piano, checking the various entrances and exits, and saying hello to familiar stagehands and orchestra members.

The band and I would run any new music before his arrival and go over notes, tempos, cuts, etc. If there were musical acts, Lee would usually have them perform with him, which would necessitate additional arrangements and more rehearsal time. Other types of acts, such as jugglers or ventriloquists, didn't require as much time. Often, however, their music had been written for a trio, and it would have to be enlarged to sound musically similar to the other numbers in the show. Large performing groups, such as the Mike Curb Congregation or the Famous People Players, would need much more time to check musical cues and entrance and exit logistics. Ray Arnett always seemed to come up with the right solutions to all the little challenges that would arise as we got these large groups to look professional. So, the first rehearsal would last about three hours, after which I would meet with the music copyist to go over any changes.

On opening day, the orchestra would begin rehearsing at about one o'clock in the afternoon, with the stage area usually cluttered with items for the show: several movable statue props; a hanging, lit marquee of Lee's trademark signature; the wide-but-shallow tank for the Dancing Waters; at least three cars lined up off stage, ready for their entrances; flying rigging hanging from the rafters; mic stands and special overhead lights; and the orchestra's music stands and lights. Each item, large and small, was important for the success of the show. There would be lots of last-minute hammering, sawing, yelling, and general mayhem going on, but, somehow, after about three hours, the show would take shape.

Once the stage area was secured and the spike marks (small, white strips of tape to indicate the exact location for all the pianos, cars, and statues) were all in place, the other stars of the show—Lee's pianos, on large, carpeted carts—were rolled out, one by one. In the larger venues, he always used at least two pianos, one of which was the rhinestone Baldwin with the Plexiglas top. Other pianos he used included the beautiful "Chopin," an early-twentieth-century, hand-carved and hand-painted Steinway art deco piano. Each of these "wow" pianos needed special lighting, and a lot of time was spent making adjustments to get the lighting just right. Another piano Lee sometimes used was the jeweled, upright, "rag-time" piano. I was always amazed at how easily he shifted from one piano to another, because each required a different style of playing.

Once the pianos were set, the hanging chandeliers and moveable statues were brought on, placed on their spike marks, lit, and secured. The cars were driven on stage to check for entrance and exit clearance. Finally, the orchestra was seated, and an overall sound check was done while Lee played. We, the orchestra, were squeezed in between the pianos, statues, and cars on stage, and the shooting, spraying, and swishing of the Dancing Waters behind us. Did we ever get wet? To be honest, yes. Actually, in the last few years of Lee's appearances at the Hilton, there were so many props, pianos, cars, and water effects on the stage that the orchestra was relegated to playing the show from the backstage area. We were never seen—only heard. I never felt that we played our best when we were sitting back there, but it was more comfortable, since we didn't have to wear tuxedos. And, it was a lot drier.

As you can imagine, dress rehearsal for opening night in any of the large Nevada showrooms is stressful to begin with, and even more so when a few added surprises are thrown in. I do remember one memorable opening night at the Riviera Hotel. But first, some history: Lee was the first major entertainer to open the Riviera in 1955. His salary was $50,000 a week, a huge amount of money back then . . . and today, too—equivalent to about $500,000. He appeared there again in the early '60s with Barbra Streisand as his guest artist. But for his 1980s Riviera engagement, Lee outdid himself, using three pianos, several statues and hanging chandeliers, the Riviera orchestra, two different acts, and a surprise stage effect in the final piece that was supposed to go as follows:

Lee would stand in front of the main curtain and introduce the final number, a medley of Johann Strauss waltzes. The curtain would open to reveal the aforementioned Chopin piano sitting on a cart covered in thick, purple, shag carpet. (It sounds a bit gaudy, but it really helped highlight the piano.) Lee would sit at the piano and begin playing the waltz medley.

A few minutes into the number, a second curtain would open behind him, exposing several statues and hanging chandeliers. As the medley continued, a third curtain would open to reveal the orchestra, playing along with Lee. A few minutes later, the final curtain would open to reveal the Dancing Waters, illuminated jets of water swaying in time to the music. Then, on cue, the stage manager would hit a button, and Lee and his piano would begin to slowly rotate as he'd end the medley with the beautiful Blue Danube waltz. It was a spectacular plan, and it was very, very "Liberace."

There was a slight problem at the end of the final rehearsal for opening night, however. Just as we finished, and just minutes before the audience would be arriving, someone realized that the overhead spotlight for the Chopin piano's keyboard wasn't lined up correctly. Rather than lighting just the piano keyboard, it overshot it and was shining onto the piano bench, the shag-carpeted piano cart, and part of the stage. Since time was at a premium, the stage hands, rather than getting a ladder and refocusing the light, simply lifted the piano and bench and moved them about eight inches farther out on the carpet, until the light was shining just on the piano keyboard. Perfect.

The opening night show was a huge success, with tons of fans all roaring their approval of Lee's showmanship. Then came the finale, the waltz medley. Lee stood in front of the main curtain and introduced the piece. He finished his introduction and the curtain opened to reveal the Chopin piano, with the anticipated reaction from the audience—one of the few times I've seen a piano get applause. Lee sat at the piano and began playing the first of several Strauss waltzes. A few minutes later, the second curtain opened to show the statues and the now lit and twinkling chandeliers.

Perfectly timed, the third curtain opened, and there was the orchestra, playing along with Lee. Then, a few minutes later, the final curtain opened to reveal the Dancing Waters, swaying in perfect time to the music. It really did look great.

At the musical climax, the beginning of the famous Blue Danube waltz, the stage manager hit the button for the revolving stage, and the piano . . . not Liberace . . . just the piano . . . began slowly revolving. Lee just sat there with his eyebrows raised and a slight smile on his face as he watched the piano slowly move away from him. He then looked at the audience with a rather funny expression and turned his attention back to the revolving piano that was now circling around to him. The orchestra continued to play during all this, though several of the horn players had trouble blowing their instruments while laughing at this mishap.

As the piano passed by, Lee played as many notes as he could before it revolved away from him, leaving him "pianoless" once more. The orchestra could hardly play from laughing. After another revolution, the piano was finally brought to a stop in roughly the correct playing position, and Lee finished with a huge flourish. As I recall, the orchestra and I just sat there, not sure what to do. Finally, we did play the final chord with him, and the audience went wild. It was a great, unexpected performance on a great opening night. Afterward, I told Lee that he should keep that mistake in the show. "I don't think so," he said with a smile.

The Hilton's stage was one of the largest venues in which we continually performed. It allowed many of Lee's cars to be used for his entrances, a part of his show that always delighted the audience. The vehicles included, among others, a red-white-and-blue Rolls Royce convertible, a mirrored Rolls Royce Phantom limo, and a cute, mirrored, small VW limo.

The stage at the Las Vegas Hilton was so huge, in fact, that Lee invited the Radio City Music Hall Rockettes to join him for a multi-week stint. (My ex-wife and I once invited the Rockettes to a party at our home during their engagement. Boy, did they know how to party!)

During the last years of his contract with the Hilton, Lee really made an impact at the end of his shows. He'd thank the audience, take one final bow and exit the stage and then return a few seconds later, sitting high on the back seat of the VW convertible. About a quarter of the way across the stage, he'd be lifted up at least twenty feet in the air and would soar back and forth across the stage with his mic, saying, "Mary Poppins, eat your heart out!"

I had written some "flying" music based on "I'll Be Seeing You," his theme song. As I started this music on the first night he was to fly, I watched as he was hoisted up in the air. It really was spectacular, but I noticed that his ever-constant smile was interrupted by a couple of grimaces now and then. I attributed it to a case of opening night flying jitters. Between shows, many of the celebrities in attendance came downstairs to Lee's dressing room and congratulated him on his success, especially the "flying finale." One of them, Debbie Reynolds, asked him what it felt like.

"Well," he said, "to be honest, Debbie, there was a little pain in the, uh,

hoisting area."

"Lee, I know you had Peter Foy do all the rigging. He's the best. He flew Mary Martin when she did Peter Pan, and he flew me when I did the role," Debbie said. "I know a bit about these things. Here, let me see your harness."

Lee took her into the dressing area where the costumes were kept. After a quick glance at the harness, Debbie exclaimed, "Oh, my! This is a female harness! No wonder you were in pain. Do you have a pair of scissors?"

She took the scissors and quickly made the female harness into a male harness. And during the second show that evening, I noted that Lee was, indeed, smiling all the way. But every time he flew, I couldn't help but remember his first flight.

For the opening at Radio City Music Hall we used a silent film, to which I added a live, orchestral score. Lee liked this effect so much, he insisted on using it in some of the other large venues. Sometimes this was easier said than done; most of the theaters in these larger venues (the Fox theaters in Atlanta and St. Louis, for example) had a large screen, but not the right type of projector. In order to sync live music with film, one had to use a special type of film with a click track (which required a special projector) and transmit the click track to me, the conductor, as I conducted. It sounds complicated, and it was, but that was the only technology available back then—if it was, indeed, available. So, I often ended up making a recording of myself banging on a cowbell and would use it as the click track to keep the orchestra and the film in sync.

I produced several of Liberace's recordings, beginning in 1973. He was very easygoing in the studio and played everything quite well, of course. Then came the challenge: he wanted to use these same arrangements for our upcoming tours, which didn't seem like a problem until we played our first live concert with this new material. It seemed that Lee performed differently in the recording studio than he did in front of a live audience. In the recording studio, he played all the notes pretty much as written and stayed pretty much in tempo—a little slower here, a little faster there. But in live venues, he didn't just play the piece, he performed it, playing all the notes accurately, but putting much more of himself into each song. This meant that his performing tempos were much slower than his recording tempos. A fairly consistent medium tempo in the studio would become a very slow and emotional one in front of an audience. And the opposite was also true. A nice, bright studio tempo would speed into a rapid-fire version in front of a live audience. In some cases, I had to totally rewrite the arrangements to reflect the different approaches in his performances.

In each of the two TV productions I did with Lee, he continually praised his guest artists, his musicians, and his audience. He seemed to really relax under the added pressure of filming. And you have to remember that his TV shows in the mid-50s were the first of their kind—and he did over one hundred of these half-hour shows.

Lee and his producer, Don Fedderson, realized early on that you couldn't entertain a TV audience, regardless of its size, by having Lee just sit and play the piano. Therefore, all types of visual effects were added, though they never overshadowed Lee's musical ability or personality. I wonder if Lady Gaga's flaming piano during her performance of "Speechless" at the American Music Awards was inspired by Lee's flaming piano version of "Ritual Fire Dance"? When he played "I've Been Working On The Railroad," a group of train conductors paraded past, led by his brother, George, and a model train chugged across the piano's music rack. These early TV concepts were, I'm sure, brought forward into his live shows, including the use of two beautiful Russian wolfhounds during one of his entrances. He always seemed to take whatever he was doing to the next level, thereby making everything he did truly "Liberace."

22.

Parting Ways

In the late '70s, realizing that most of my work with Lee would be in Las Vegas, my new wife, Elaine, and I decided to move there from L.A.—a similar move to the one I had made with my ex-wife, Judy, in the late '60s. I had met Elaine while conducting Lee in the Washington, D.C. area. She had come to the show with a date, a piano tuner I'd known in Vegas. She was very attractive and very musical, a perfect combination for me at that time. And though she left the show with her date, we had clicked, and over the next several months we exchanged many phone calls. This long-distance romance ended when we decided to move in together. Looking back, it was all quite romantic. She flew to Reno, then I drove her (in my new Cadillac) to the Sahara Tahoe where I was conducting Lee. We then drove to L.A., my home at the time. We lived there about a year as I continued to travel the country with Lee. Then he signed a multi-year contract with the Hilton Hotel in Las Vegas, and Elaine and I moved there to cut down on my time away from home. We bought a lovely house on the Las Vegas Country Club; quite classy. We had a swimming pool put in and proceeded to enjoy the life of a music director for a famous celebrity.

On October 3, 1981, I finished Lee's 8 p.m. show at the Hilton, rushed to Sunrise Hospital and, about an hour later, welcomed my first son, Justin—or, JJ, as we call him—into the world at 11:11 p.m. I spent as much time as I could with mommy and new son that evening, then rushed back to the Hilton with a box of blue bubblegum cigars to pass out to the band, arriving just in time to conduct Lee's midnight show. He announced JJ's birth at the end of that show.

The birth of my second son, Evan, was not as stressful but was just as exciting, and I was able to be home on September 16, 1983, since it was during a lull in my tour year with Lee. Two healthy boys, a lovely wife, and a comfortable home. Life was good.

We had a normal routine for a show biz family. I wrote arrangements during the day and conducted Lee in the evenings. About four months a year, I was on the road with him, leaving Elaine to manage the house and, with the help of a wonderful babysitter, Jenny Stewart, look after the kids. I felt a sense of security with my career and with my home.

After my work with Lee at Radio City Music Hall in '84, I got a call from Jack Eskew, one of several music directors at Walt Disney, asking me to conduct a six-week engagement at

Radio City in the summer of '85. It would be a thirty-minute live stage show called "The Magical World of Disney." Luckily, there was no conflict with any of Lee's jobs, and I was soon immersed in the company I'd dreamed about working with since my Oberlin days.

The Disney show was challenging. It featured actors and their live voices and several Disney characters with taped voices, all in sync to a silent film. Barnett Ricci was the show's producer and choreographer. Working on the show was especially fun since two friends from the past, Peter Foy and Joe Layton, were working on the show as well; Peter flew Lee at the Las Vegas Hilton, and Joe had produced and choreographed for Raquel Welch's show. Also working on the production was arranger Bruce Healey, who would later take Jack Eskew's job at Disney, and with whom I worked several years later. It's a small world in the music business.

As I said, things were going well with my life. My family had a comfortable home, and I had a great job and more possibilities on the horizon. In life and in show business, however, everything changes sooner or later, and my parting with Liberace was a change that I would characterize as unfortunate.

For the twelve or so years I worked with Lee, the scheduling process usually began with the company receiving the next year's touring itinerary, usually around Thanksgiving. This list of performance dates came from Lee's manager, Seymour, who, with Lee's agent, Roger Vorce, planned the tour year. Both Seymour and Roger knew the types of venues Lee enjoyed playing and the towns he liked to visit. They also were very much aware of the financial aspects of mounting a tour for such a large group, and they knew the salary of their high-priced star. They would put all this together and plan some very nice four- or five-week tours, plus at least twelve weeks at the Vegas Hilton.

As I said, we usually worked about thirty-two to thirty-six weeks a year and would receive the following year's tour schedule in mid-November. But in 1985, it was close to the end of November, and I and the rest of the company hadn't received any notice of the following year's schedule. Still not having heard anything in early December, I called Seymour. He said that he and Roger were still working on the tour schedule. Just after the first of the year, when I *still* hadn't heard anything, I called again, now preoccupied with financial concerns.

"As you know, Seymour, I have a family and . . . "

"Yes, yes, I know, Bo. But it looks like Lee's cutting back and only doing one East Coast tour in the spring, then a couple of weeks in Vegas at the MGM, since our contract with the

Hilton is up, and then a couple of weeks at Caesars Palace, with maybe a week or two in November at Radio City Music Hall. And that's about it."

"That's not a lot of work, Seymour, maybe six or eight weeks, tops. And you know how difficult it is to dovetail those weeks with any Las Vegas jobs I could take."

"What can I tell you? Hey, I gotta go," he replied, and hurriedly hung up.

About a month after that phone call, I received a letter confirming Lee's intentions to do a much shorter work year. It was late January, and I was looking at a maximum of only eight weeks of income for the year, down from about thirty-four—not a pleasant financial picture. Most of the musicians in town knew I was Lee's music director and, I assumed, thought I was always busy with him. So, now, having all these extra weeks available, I'd have to reconnect with my Vegas musician contacts and see what other jobs, if any, were available for a piano player. I did check around to see if I might get another conducting job with someone, but I knew it would be almost impossible, since most performers already had their piano player/conductor and weren't looking to change. Also, with so few conducting and piano jobs, musicians were very protective of their work situation, and substitutes were becoming a thing of the past. I was definitely concerned.

We did the shortened spring tour between February and early May: a week each at the Premier Center near Sterling Heights, Michigan, and the Valley Forge Music Fair in King of Prussia, Pennsylvania, and then three weeks at the Las Vegas MGM Grand Hotel. In early March, I got a call from Disney asking me to conduct a three-city Disney summer orchestra tour, featuring the Nashville, Dallas, and Washington, D.C. symphony orchestras. They asked me to think about it and get back to them ASAP. Boy, I really wanted and needed this extra work. I checked the dates and discovered, unfortunately, that the first week of the Disney rehearsals was also the second week of Lee's Caesars Palace engagement—a major conflict. What was I to do? I knew I couldn't possibly do both, and conducting another Disney production definitely appealed to me, artistically. Then there was the money aspect of the situation. Looking ahead, I realized that, after the shows at Caesars in June, there would only be two more weeks of work with Lee for the rest of the year, whereas taking the Disney job might lead to additional Disney work that would fill in my non-Liberace gaps. So, with not enough upcoming Liberace work, and with a family to consider, I really had only one choice.

When I called Seymour with my financial concerns and tried to discuss my decision to find a sub for myself at Caesars Palace, he almost yelled at me, saying I was being "disloyal" to

Lee. My response was that I had a family to support; my loyalty belonged first to my family. Seymour was upset—a response I've since concluded was due partly to his knowledge of Lee's worsening medical condition. Many of us in the show had noticed that Lee was a bit less-than-energetic in his performances at the MGM. He stayed in his dressing room with the door closed and wasn't as communicative as usual. No one knew he had AIDS, but some of us, seeing his energy level diminish, suspected it.

Seymour's first role as a manager was to support and protect his clients. His attitude was, if you didn't agree with Seymour, and, therefore, Liberace, you were shown the door. His was a world of black and white, us or them. I don't know what he told Liberace, but a few days later, in a very brief phone call, Seymour told me, "Liberace no longer requires your services."

I hung up, in shock. I had been prepared with a list of possible conductors to fill in for me that week, but that, in Seymour's mind, was out of the question. What had I done to receive such a terse, negative response? That question kept me awake that night, and for a few more, too.

It was now almost the latter part of April, 1986, and I finished the MGM engagement. After Seymour's phone call, I realized that the MGM would turn out to be the last time I conducted Liberace. I never knew if Lee was aware that I would no longer be his conductor when I said goodbye to him after the last MGM show. I do know that, no matter his condition, no matter what Seymour said or did, Lee and I parted that last evening at the MGM on good terms, communicating as we always had, as friends with a good working relationship.

Unfortunately, rumors began circulating in Vegas that I had walked out on Lee, that I was disloyal to him and, because of that, had been fired. It sounded like Seymour's words, but I never knew for sure. Of course, none of it was true. My wife and my two preteen boys were uppermost in my mind, and my decision to leave Lee was strictly financial, but I guess it came down to the old-school attitude of managers and agents:

"You're lucky to be associated with [insert star's name], and if [insert star's name] decides not to work, so be it. You find another job that interferes with [insert star's name], you're through."

Contracts and legal agreements have never been my strong suit—not a good business trait, I know. To me, it was all about the music: writing the arrangements and conducting the bands and orchestras. I never had a contract during my work with Lee; it was all done by handshake. That, and the secrecy behind Lee's shortened tour year, meant that my terminating phone call from Seymour was all I got. Legally, I was alone in the music world with no job.

On the day Lee opened his show at Caesars Palace, I tried to keep myself busy at home by preparing for my upcoming trip to L.A. and the rehearsals with Disney in the following weeks. But I kept thinking that it should be me up there, rehearsing the orchestra, making sure the intros and cut-offs were correct and the tempos were in sync, with my boss, my friend, Liberace. Human nature made me secretly hope that whomever they'd gotten to fill in would fall flat on his musical face, and they'd call me back to conduct, even if only for a week.

But, of course, no call ever came. I found a bunch of errands to run, to try to take my mind off the huge knots of frustration in my stomach. I was upset with Seymour for not understanding my predicament. I was upset with myself for not being more prepared financially for such a situation. And I was upset from hearing all the negative rumors about my split with Lee. The truth was, Seymour's loyalty was to Lee. Mine was to my family.

The following week, I immersed myself in the Disney rehearsals in Anaheim, California, wanting to forget about Lee and our thirteen years of making music together. The Disney three-city tour went very well. Conducting symphony orchestras has always been one of my biggest thrills, and doing so for such a well-known organization was huge. The tour went quickly, and I was back in Vegas with my family. And out of work.

However, as is so often the case in the entertainment industry, one thing leads to another. Conducting Lee at Radio City Music Hall in '84 and doing the Disney symphony job there in '85 led to my conducting the famous Radio City Music Hall Christmas Spectacular in the winter of '86. But this meant that, yet again, I'd be away from home for at least three months, including the holidays. To ease our financial burden and to keep the family closer together, Elaine and I sold our house in Las Vegas and moved back east to McLean, Virginia, where Elaine's parents could help with the boys while I traveled back and forth between D.C. and New York, almost on a weekly basis. It wasn't perfect, but at least the family was together.

Conducting the Christmas show at the Music Hall for the first time was a definite "wow" moment for me. It was like combining a Disney extravaganza with a Liberace show, but much more grueling: five ninety-minute shows per day for seven weeks straight. I would drop my arms at 9:30 a.m. for the downbeat of the first show and give the final cutoff for the last show at 10:00 p.m. I actually did have a relief conductor,

Don Miller, one of two pianists and also an Oberlin graduate. But my work ethic was simple: I had been hired to be the conductor of the show, and that was what I did. One time, though, Don's wife and family were coming to see one of the Sunday morning shows, and Don asked if he could conduct. I realized how important this was to him, and agreed. Shortly after, I saw him studying the scores and practicing his conducting movements in the hallway. He was really excited about it.

My normal position before every show was in the orchestra elevator area in the second basement (yes, there was a first basement), and that's where I was on the Sunday morning of the Miller family's visit. I chatted with Don, who seemed nervous as he walked around, eyes darting constantly to his scores. Hearing that the lone bass player was late in arriving wasn't helping matters.

About three minutes before show time and with no bass player in sight, I left the second basement and climbed the many flights of stairs to the sound booth on the second balcony, the perfect place to see and hear the show, something I'd actually never done before. The show started, and up came the orchestra on their elevator, with Don conducting. Listening more than watching, I felt that something was wrong with the sound. I scanned the orchestra and discovered that there was still no bass player—to me, one of the most important instruments for this type of show. (There were two seven-foot grand pianos, and two percussionists, but only one bass.) Without the sound of a bass, I felt that the show's music, and perhaps other aspects of the show, would suffer.

I quickly left my perch and rushed back down the stairs to the second basement. There, I grabbed a stagehand and asked him to bring the orchestra elevator back down during a short lull in the music. When the elevator arrived, I quickly jumped on the band cart and made my way to the bass player's chair. I knew he kept his upright bass on the cart most of the time and had seen it there before the show. Now, I'm not a bass player, but I did know the arrangements in the show, and I knew enough double bass fingerings to keep up with the orchestra. I ended up plucking the strings like a jazz bass player, instead of using the bow. After about ten minutes or so, in another lull in the show, the orchestra elevator suddenly went back down to the second basement, and a very embarrassed bass player quickly got on and took my place. When Bob Swan, the music contractor for Radio City, heard about it, he said, "In all my forty years doing this show, I've never seen a conductor do that." I know my playing was terrible, but my intentions were honorable; I just wanted to make sure the show's music went as well as it could.

Bob also provided me with a good definition of what I was: a *music* conductor.

"You see, Bo, a *musical* conductor could be a film, or stage, or TV director who happens to be musical and wants to lead the orchestra. You, on the other hand, are a *music* conductor—someone who's first and foremost a musician. Quite a difference, isn't it?" I took that as a compliment, after my bass debut in the Christmas Show.

A NOTE FROM LEE - 1984

BO, IN WASHINGTON, D.C. - 1990
PHOTO BY CHESTER SIMPSON

STARTING MY OWN MUSIC BUSINESS, MYSTRO, INC. - 1987

The Fourth Movement:

Life After Lee

The show must go on.
—Originally attributed to nineteenth-century circus folk

I can *not* play for twenty dollars, but you really should hear me *not* play for forty dollars!
—Bo Ayars

23.

The Capitol Steps

Leaving Lee brought some major changes to my life, not the least of which was a rather large void in my income. In the mind of anyone who hired music directors or conductors, I was still Lee's conductor, and to some, a person with questionable loyalties. And I found that getting decent work was just as difficult on the East Coast. I did get a job in September of '86, conducting the Chrysler Auto Show held at the Atlantic City Convention Hall in New Jersey. Somebody in the Atlantic City area remembered that I was also an arranger, and I wrote a couple of arrangements. I enjoyed working in that large hall; I was told that it takes almost a second for sound to get from one end of the hall to the other. That's a huge hall!

Later that year I once again conducted the Christmas Show at Radio City Music Hall for the holiday season, again traveling back and forth between D.C. and New York City. One time, we brought the boys up to see the show. JJ was quietly impressed, but Evan was unabashedly excited about everything. They both were really fascinated by the little people in the show, especially the character Bruce, played by David Steinberg, a talented actor. David was not quite as tall as Evan, yet was an adult (probably in his early twenties), and the boys seemed curious about his height.

"Daddy, why is he so small?" JJ asked in a rather loud voice. Before I could say anything, David, who'd overheard the question, came over and explained that it's what's on the inside of a person that's important, not just what's on the outside—a lesson I hope my sons learned.

The Christmas Show that year, 1986, was especially fun. Joel Grey, Leslie Uggams, and others made a TV special using the entire Music Hall's Christmas Show. I was filmed conducting the orchestra as Leslie sang one of my arrangements, a clip of which is on YouTube. I still watch it sometimes just to see how young I used to be. This TV special also meant extra money, something we desperately needed.

I returned home to northern Virginia in early January, 1987, not sure of what I should do, musically. I made a few phone calls, but, as I feared, all of the conductor positions with the acts I knew were already filled. I was briefly considered as a music composer for a potential Broadway musical, but it didn't pan out. I traveled quite a bit, following musical leads, but again, they were all dead ends. I started checking around the northern Virginia area for any playing gigs and made a few contacts here and there, but my income-producing ability was almost nil, something that kept nagging at me. I'm sure it was the "bottom" of the hill after being on top with Lee for thirteen years.

In February of '87, I learned of Lee's death, a tragic event that only added to my unhappiness. We were living in a small, two-bedroom apartment in McLean, Virginia. Of course, the news was all over the media, and I tried to sort out all the various "spins" on his demise, a "watermelon diet" being the most outlandish. Those closest to him were trying to protect his name, trying to keep his homosexuality and AIDS out of the press, but to little avail.

Several days after his death, I got a call from someone at *People* magazine who wanted to interview me. At the time, I thought it would be a good thing, perhaps, to get my positive impressions about "Mr. Showmanship" out to the public. So, I agreed. The interview team arrived two days later and began asking questions and taking pictures, some of me sitting at our upright piano, others of me studying some music scores. Most of the questions were about Lee's gender preference or the ever-present AIDS question: what had I known, or seen, or heard that might have indicated he was sick with the disease. I answered the questions as best as I could, honestly stating that I was unaware of his condition and really not interested in his sexual life. The team left, and I suddenly had a bad feeling about the interview. Even though I had tried to explain his tremendous ability as a pianist, how great of a showman he was, and how exciting it was to be part of his show, I sensed that they mostly had been trying to see if I knew he was gay.

A few days later, *People* sent me the article and pictures for a final review. I read the piece and found that my suspicions were correct. Almost the entire article was about his illness. It alluded to his gay lifestyle and said nothing about his accomplishments—nothing about all the people he'd entertained, nothing about the acts and other performers he'd helped promote, and barely anything about his music, the one thing that really started and maintained his career. While they didn't quote me directly, someone reading the article could easily assume that these were my thoughts. Although I'm sure the writer was doing what every other journalist would do— show the dark side to sell copies—I didn't want to be a part of it. I knew the notoriety from being in the magazine could possibly help my income, but I wasn't *that* hungry. I called the writer and said that I didn't want the article to be printed.

"Don't you realize how well known you'll be after it's published? Millions of people will read it and get to know about you," he said. "Your career will blossom. Good things will happen. You'll be . . . "

"Yes, I know that might happen," I cut in, "but I really don't want to be well known like *this*. It makes me look as if

I've sold out Lee's good name, and that's not what I want. Please don't print this."

"Well, as long as you know the exposure and notoriety you'll miss," he replied.

"I understand, but I don't want this type of notoriety."

The article was never printed, and even though I may have missed a rung or two on the career ladder, I felt good about my decision. The next issue of *People* did feature a couple of quotes from other employees and acquaintances, but my name was never mentioned. Reading that article made me very happy that I'd chosen not to have my interview printed. Lee had been a huge part of my musical life and a good musical friend, and I didn't want to ruin my memory of that.

So, I continued to look for work, following various leads and possibilities. One job I did get was a Christmas Concert with the Kansas City Symphony. Because of the cost of airfare at that time of year, I decided to drive, a two-day trip each way. The concerts went well, but being away from my family at Christmas was very hard on everyone.

I perused a list of managers of pop symphony acts and found Donna Zajonc, a talent manager in Ann Arbor, Michigan. She was very successful in placing smaller, less well-known performers with symphonies, including symphony pops conductors. I drove to Ann Arbor to see if she would take me on as a client, which she did. With her help, I began conducting my own arrangements with several symphonies, primarily the Erie Philharmonic—a wonderful group of musicians. I think my experience working the Christmas show at Radio City helped me become music director of the Philharmonic's annual Christmas pops concerts, and it became a steady Christmas job for me for several years. I would rent a van and drive the family up to Erie for a long weekend. The boys enjoyed it, and they even got to be in the concert one year, sitting at Santa's knee as he read "'Twas the night before Christmas . . . " But the job was mostly seasonal, and left me unemployed for the rest of the year.

Back home, I sought work as a cocktail pianist in a restaurant, just to bring in some money. It was occasional work, nothing steady. Then luck stepped in. The boys, now three and five, were enrolled in morning sessions at a local Montessori school. There, they met the daughter of Steve Strauss, brother of Bill Strauss, one of the three creators of the Capitol Steps, the famous Washington, D.C. political satire troupe. That, in a long sentence, is how I started working with them. I met Bill at a birthday party for his niece, Steve's daughter. The group was looking for a pianist to free up Elaina Newport, another founder, for more performing duties. The third original member, Jim Aidala, was in charge of technical operations. For those who don't know about the Capitol Steps—or just "the Steps," as they're called—they are a group of current and former Capitol Hill staffers, lawyers, secretaries, aides, and consultants who poke fun at political and social issues via song parodies. Many compare them to Mark Russell, a successful, politically inspired pianist and singer. Mark, however, wrote his own songs, whereas the Steps use well-known music and write parody lyrics to it. So, we co-existed, and goodness knows there was enough material for all.

Some of the parody titles were quite clever. They used the opening line from a popular holiday song, "Chestnuts roasting on an open fire," and poked fun at the National Rifle Association by singing, "Gun nuts boasting they could open fire." Many of the Steps were fine singers; others were great character specialists, and their delivery and performances were superb. I jumped at the job, even though I was the only Step without a direct Capitol Hill connection—though I often said that by paying taxes, I was a part (albeit a small one) of the government workforce. My very first job was playing on one of their many recordings, which can still be found on their website. [www.capsteps.com] The important things about the Steps job were 1) it was in music, 2) I was making money, and 3) I wasn't traveling.

The Steps' three initial founders, Bill, Elaina, and Jim, sifted through the daily news stories that provided most of the material for the parodies. They'd read a news story in the morning paper, such as Dan Quayle's misspelling of a popular vegetable, or a whale that got stuck in an ice floe, or a certain lady friend of a certain president who . . . well, you know . . . and they'd come up with a clever parody that always ended with a great punch line. And because there were (and are) so many "oops" moments in politics, every day there were lots of new song ideas and parodies to be created, learned, and performed. Often, and this is said with pride, a news story would break at 8 a.m. and we'd have a song about it in our show that night. On one occasion in late 1989, Bill and Elaina wrote a song about Manuel Noriega seeking sanctuary in a Catholic church in Panama. The idea was to actually use the humorous parody song "The Vatican Rag," written by the comic singer/pianist Tom Lehrer, for the Steps parody, thus making our song a unique "parody of a parody." Bill and I went to the PBS studios in Georgetown about noon to make a quick recording, hoping to air it that evening. About halfway through the recording session, we got a call from Elaina saying that Noriega had given up, and was being taken out of the church, thus making the song and all of our work on it a moot point. An idea is presented, an idea is taken away . . .

The Capitol Steps shows were always a challenge for me. Even though I knew most of the songs they used, my job as pianist was to get the right key for the singer, the correct style for the song, the right number of repeats or verses (sometimes called the routine of the song), and then come up with an intro and an ending. Because of the need for quickness, there were never any rehearsals. I'd arrive at the show, which was usually in a large hotel, get handed a set list with nothing but song titles, be advised of any last-minute adjustments, check with the singers for their keys, then go on stage and play the show. Of course, the set list titles reflected the parody, not the original song. See if you can guess the original song in the following: "Return to Center," "A Whole Newt World," "Unzippin' My Do-Dah," "Wouldn't It Be Hilary?" and "Can You Feel the Rub Tonight?"

Some titles were simple, but others were a test of my small brain. There were usually twenty-two songs in every show, each with a seemingly familiar, yet skewed, title. Some titles were obvious, but the tough part for me was remembering the "real" songs when the titles were obscure: "Ollie Would" ("Hooray for Hollywood"), "Gorby Gorbachev" ("Bad, Bad Leroy Brown"), and "Wolf Blitzer" ("Moon River").

My musical nightmare, which I still have to this day, starts with Bill and me standing in the wings of a large theater, getting ready for a big Capitol Steps show. Just before I'm about to go out with my set list, ready to play the show, Bill stops me, and hands me a sheet of paper.

"Here's a brand new list of songs, none of which you know, and none of which we've ever rehearsed. I don't know the keys or styles of any of them. Oh, and I've written a new opening number to an original song I wrote," he says, as he ushers me toward the stage. "You don't know it, but it goes something like this: dumb-dee-needle-doo."

And with that, he pushes me on stage where I sit at the piano, looking at a list of totally unknown songs in unknown keys and styles, with an opening song that's literally being composed as it's being performed. Now, please remember, this is only a dream. It never really happened. But fifteen years after leaving the Steps, it still wakes me in the middle of the night.

After about a year of accompanying the Steps, I was asked to be their booking manager as well as their lead pianist. It really wasn't difficult. The Steps were so popular and in such great demand by trade associations, political action groups, and candidate fundraisers, nationwide, that my booking job consisted of answering the phone, putting down a date for a function, getting the info, and hanging up. When I first joined the group, we performed about eighty to a hundred shows a year. When I left the Steps in 1998 we were up to more than four hundred shows, used three or more different troupes, had several pianists, multiple roadies, a bunch of sound equipment, and a fair share of CDs for sale. As I understand it today, the number of shows has increased.

At first, the shows I played were held around the D.C. area, mostly in various hotel ballrooms. Our roadie would set up the stage per our specs, including a small, curtained, changing area. This is where we'd keep all the props and costumes, and where we'd spend hurried minutes going over new material given to us by Bill Strauss. Of course, *he* knew all the words— he'd written them. I'm sure having a photographic memory helped. Most of the other Steps, however, were either handed lyric sheets at the shows or received them via their answering machines, sung by Bill or Elaina. As the world became more technologically savvy, the lyrics would be faxed. I'm sure they're now transmitted via smart phones and MP3s.

The shows were always well received. One aspect that bothered me, however, was the amount of last-minute creativity: constantly updating lyrics, changing the routine or key of a song, putting in a new song at a moment's notice. But that's the way Bill operated, and I think he actually enjoyed living on the edge, artistically.

I should state clearly, up front, that I'm not into politics. We had a mock political convention at Oberlin in 1959, and, to me, it seemed to draw mostly lawyer-types who enjoyed hearing their own voices. Yes, the game of politics plays a role in our lives, but, like water polo, it's just not my thing. That said, there are several memorable moments I do recall from when we entertained and poked fun at our elected officials. Here are a few that stand out:

One afternoon, we were asked to do a quick, twenty-minute show for some Republican senators at a small office building on Capitol Hill. We got there and learned that former president Ford would be dropping by. Bill quickly chose one of our songs, the title of which escapes me, and asked if the former president would join us in singing it. His aides agreed, so my job was to quickly teach him his part. Many of our leaders are great at politics and governing but fall short in the singing department. Ford was one of the latter. I'd sing him the line, and he'd sing it back to me in a totally different key. Of course, the aides surrounding him vocally praised his ability or smiled and laughed to keep the moment light. But he was a trouper and kept practicing the song. Then, just before he walked out and did his number, he pulled me aside, shook my hand and thanked me for trying to make a singer out of him. He was a very nice man.

As our fame grew, we were invited to more and more high-level events. One was the president's official summer lawn party for members of Congress. It was held on the South Lawn of the White House. We received an invitation from then president Reagan, which suggested the proper attire: open-neck shirts for the gentlemen, dresses for the ladies. It was August in D.C., probably the worst time to be outside in the heat and humidity. But the word had come down, so all of our female performers and the female members of Congress and the congressional wives put on dresses and tried to keep as cool as possible. It was really quite an event, with at least two hundred people in attendance. Everyone looked nice, though I'm sure they weren't as comfortable as they looked. After our picnic lunch, the president and Mrs. Reagan made their entrance. To the bewilderment of many, Nancy Reagan was wearing lightweight slacks and a blouse, looking cool and comfortable.

I'd never been in the presence of President Reagan, but I remembered Rich Little's great impersonation of him. He would imitate Reagan by saying, "Well . . . " in a breathy voice. When the president spoke to us after our presentation on the South Lawn, he began by saying, "Well . . . " in a breathy voice. I could have sworn it was Rich Little.

One other thing happened to me at this function. President Reagan, with Nancy at his side, had been speaking to us from a podium next to a set of wide stairs leading down to the grass. We Steps had just finished our presentation and were standing (I was sitting at the keyboard) at the bottom of these stairs. As he finished his remarks, he and Nancy began making their way down the stairs, walking directly toward us. Suddenly, the president was mobbed by several in the congressional group and seemed to lean a little too far to the left (nothing political), looking as if he were falling. Even though there were several Secret Service agents around him, they seemed to be more concerned with the throngs of people than with the president's falling. I quickly reached up and grabbed the president's arm just as Nancy did the same thing. We both helped him regain his balance. She looked at me quickly, smiled and said, "Thank you."

One of my more vivid recollections of our commander in chief involves President-elect George Herbert Walker Bush. It was December of 1988. Bush had been elected but not yet inaugurated. He was holding a Christmas party at the vice president's mansion on the grounds of the United States Naval Observatory on Massachusetts Avenue. When we arrived, we saw the president-elect outdoors, pitching horseshoes with some of his contingent of Secret Service agents, laughing and seeming quite down-to-earth.

Inside the mansion, a lovely Queen Anne style home, Christmas decorations were everywhere: garlands and angels and candles, oh my. It was truly spectacular. Our performance venue was a large, two-story atrium. On one side was a set of exposed stairs, a natural place for the Steps to perform. The piano, a huge Steinway concert grand, was set on the opposite side of the rotunda in a small alcove with a bay window—quite nice. There were about thirty to forty guests, all close friends of Mr. Bush.

I sat at the piano, watching Bill introduce the Steps to Vice President-elect Dan Quayle and his wife, Marilyn; Henry Kissinger; and others. The president-elect and his wife, Barbara, were actually leaning on my piano, watching and listening. On the piano was a plate of fancy Christmas cookies. During Bill's intro, President-elect Bush reached for a cookie. His wife, Barbara, saw him, reached out and slapped his hand.

"Now, George," she said with a slight smile. Evidently, the president-elect wasn't supposed to have any cookies. I thought it was great "first family" humor.

The Steps began their performance on the stairs, with me playing the Steinway in the small alcove. As the show progressed, I looked up from the keys and saw the president-elect's arm sneaking around behind Barbara's back, going for the cookies. My first thought was that the president-elect shouldn't have any cookies. On impulse, I reached out and lightly slapped the president's hand. He recoiled a bit, with a surprised look on his face. I have no idea what made me do it. Perhaps it was from having close contact with such important and well-known figures in that relaxed atmosphere. I'm not sure. I didn't think about Secret Service agents drawing their weapons, or that I was striking the president of the United States. All I knew at the time was, "George shouldn't have any cookies."

After the performance, I instantly went up to the president-elect and said, "Sir, I'm so sorry I slapped your hand. Please forgive me."

"Oh, don't think anything about it, Bo," he said. "Barbara's been telling me to watch what I eat over the holidays. It sure is difficult with all these cookies everywhere." He paused, then said,

"So, what would you like to drink?"

There I was, a humble piano player standing in the vice president's mansion, being asked what I'd like to drink by the president-elect of the United States, soon to be the most powerful man in the world. I could have had any top-shelf liquor I wanted, Dom Pérignon Champagne, single malt Scotch, expensive wine, anything. So, what did

I tell him?

"Oh, a Diet Coke, thanks, Mr. President, uh, elect." Boy, I really blew it that time!

I was with the Steps for almost thirteen very happy years. It was challenging, though, since their fearless leaders and chief writers, Bill and Elaina, were forever coming up with masses of parody lines that Bill, with his remarkable memory, could rattle off with no problem. Most of the Steps kept up with all the lyrics, though I'm sure a lot of it was just short-term memory. Whatever it took, though, the Steps always proved themselves on stage, with marvelous acting and singing. If you have a chance to see them, please do. And do, please, keep voting. It gives them lots of new material.

Bill Strauss and I collaborated on several fun projects outside of the Steps. The first was his reworking of the entire Gilbert and Sullivan operetta "The Mikado," which he made into "The MaKiddo." He wrote it to be performed at high schools. He literally took each song and wrote a parody lyric for it, following modern-day high school students through their teenage educational journey. It was performed by several schools and even had an off-off-Broadway backer's audition in New York. We took some of the drama and music students from Chantilly High School—one of many fine high schools in northern Virginia—drove them to New York in a bus, put on the audition and drove them back home. It was quite an experience for them, and for me, too. And, as another "small world" example, my younger son, Evan, is now the choral music director at Chantilly High.

Another similar project, "StopScandal.com," was loosely based on the movie *Mr. Smith Goes To Washington*. In this case, Mr. Smith is a high school student who discovers that politics isn't always fair. We had a backer's audition in New York for this production, too, and used some extremely talented professional singers. It got a lukewarm reception, though, probably because it, too, seemed to be aimed at the high school market. But even though these musicals weren't produced, I thoroughly enjoyed creating new songs and orchestrations for them.

24. More Disney

In the spring of 1993, while still working for the Steps, I got a call from Bruce Healey, my Disney friend from several years before, asking me to conduct another set of Symphonic Spectacular summer concerts. It would be my third time with the Disney organization, a company with which I had hoped to work since my Oberlin days. This time, instead of just three symphony orchestras, there would be about twenty, located all around the country—so many, in fact, that two conductors would be needed. Since my last Disney job had caused such a bad feeling with Seymour and the Liberace organization, I immediately called the Steps to see if I could take about two months off during the summer to conduct the concerts. I knew that summer was typically slow for Steps shows. I also knew there were several backup pianists available since, at that time, the Steps had several regular piano players for their two or three separate performance troupes. These players included Emmy Award-winner Lenny Williams and noted music director/pianist Emily Bell Spitz. The Steps understood my request and actually looked forward to attending one of the performances at the Merriweather Post Pavilion near Baltimore. My boys were now older and were also looking forward to seeing their dad conduct. So, I packed my bags, kissed my family goodbye and flew to California for yet another set of rehearsals at Disneyland.

The Symphonic Spectacular concerts were very well organized, both musically and logistically. About halfway through the rehearsals, I was flown to Disney World in Florida to run through the music and make sure all the notes were correct. There, an excellent youth orchestra was performing nightly, and I worked with them during the day on these "note-checking" rehearsals.

Then it was back to Disneyland in California for several more weeks of rehearsing with the soloists and the chorus, the wonderful Azusa Pacific University Choir. We rehearsed in the middle of Disneyland in a very large, metal building that was surrounded by trees and not visible to the park guests. Our rehearsals lasted until about eleven o'clock each night, with a fifteen-minute break at precisely 9:00 p.m. for the park's fireworks display. They exploded directly over our building, and we would all go out and watch the spectacular show. To this day, when I see any fireworks, I'm taken back to those fifteen-minute breaks.

My part of the Symphonic Spectacular tour included conducting symphonies at the Hollywood Bowl in the Anaheim and Long Beach areas, and then on to several outdoor venues in Seattle, Kansas City, Indiana, Milwaukee, Toronto, Boston,

Long Island, Baltimore, and Atlanta. One of the biggest musical moments for me was conducting the American Symphony Orchestra at Lincoln Center's Opera House. There, I had to act like Leopold Stokowski, famous conductor of the original Disney animated feature, *Fantasia*. In front of three thousand people, I had to sternly point to Goofy and tell him, in pantomime, to get off the stage. Why? Because his conducting of the William Tell Overture was, well, goofy.

Our two-week run at Lincoln Center started just a few days after the Fourth of July, so several of us went to Central Park on that national holiday to see the New York Philharmonic. It was an amazing experience—not just because I was hearing a world-class orchestra, but because of a particular piece they performed. The concert was held at Central Park's SummerStage, a large bandshell with an immense open area with a seating capacity of tens of thousands of people. We sat on the ground with over five hundred thousand (that's right, half a million) others. I'm not kidding. Many were leaning on trees, sitting in trees or sitting on barricades, all watching the bandshell at the far end of the park, which was the length of about three or four football fields away. The sound was good, considering the size of the area and the number of people. The magical moment for me was when Maestro Kurt Masur, the orchestra's music director, went to the microphone, paused, and in German-accented English, said,

"The orchestra will now play what many of you and, indeed, members of the orchestra, consider to be their theme song. It is so much their song that I am not needed to conduct. So, please enjoy." And with that, he left the stage.

The concertmaster (the first violinist) stood, looked at the orchestra, and, though I couldn't hear it, probably counted "one, two, three," and the entire orchestra began playing the first blaring notes of the opening theme of the overture to West Side Story, the famous musical written by the orchestra's former conductor, Leonard Bernstein. After the first few bars, the music suddenly quiets to a jazz figure played by a solo alto saxophone. In the show, and in the movie as well, this is when one of the street gangs walks in, snapping their fingers. And that's exactly what over half a million New Yorkers started doing, snapping their fingers in time to the music. Imagine, that many people snapping their fingers in unison, all essentially saying, "Hey! Don't mess with me. I'm a New Yorker." It was amazing!

The Lincoln Center engagement was exciting to me in so many ways. Besides getting to "act" on stage, I was given Metropolitan Opera Music Director James Levine's dressing room, a hallowed piece of ground to me. Also, at every one of our shows, a different guest celebrity—including Cathy Lee Gifford, Regis Philbin, NBC weatherman Al Roker, and Willard Scott—would come on stage and pose with some of the characters. Every audience was great, the orchestra played superbly, the hotel accommodations were fine, and life, as a music director, was never better.

Over the course of this national tour, some of the other orchestra venues presented more of a challenge. Many were outside, hot and humid, and featured the occasional thunderstorm. Each symphony orchestra, however, more than met these, and other, challenges—including fireworks being ignited all around the stage area. But it was so much fun to watch and hear the audiences' reactions when Mickey, Minnie, Donald, Goofy, and all the other cartoon characters came on stage. Aladdin, Snow White and the Seven Dwarfs, Chip and Dale, Beauty and the Beast, Cinderella, Ariel, the Little Mermaid—all were showcased with a dozen dancers, an amazing sixty-voice chorus, and a seventy-member, local symphony orchestra. It gave me a nice feeling, being part of such a positive entertainment experience.

However, the best moments for me happened at the Merriweather Post Pavilion. Members of the Capitol Steps who attended said, "Wow, you really *are* a symphony conductor." But the proudest moment of all was when my son, JJ, about eleven years old, came over to me, smiled and just hugged me. I'll always remember that.

25.

Moving On

After my summer job conducting with Disney, I returned to the Steps in the fall of '93 and realized that I wanted to do more than play piano for singing lawyers. My summer experience conducting large ensembles, including a charity event with the Steps and the Seattle Symphony, made me miss that more creative part of the music business even more.

In the late 1990s, the boys were finishing high school and starting to go to college: JJ to William & Mary in Williamsburg, Virginia, and Evan to James Madison University in Harrisonburg, Virginia. I was finding the Steps to be financially rewarding but no longer musically fulfilling, and I started writing arrangements and conducting pops symphony concerts. With these arrangements, I created a pops program called "An Evening with the Stars," which was made up of arrangements and stories of my musical life with Elvis, Streisand, Liberace, John Denver, and John Raitt, as well as my movie experience with *The Sound of Music*. I had some success with this program with symphonies in San Antonio, Phoenix, San Diego, and Tallahassee.

The drawback with this new direction was that I became, once again, totally consumed with my music and seemed to care little for anything or anyone else. I was trying to balance my music with my family and, like before, the music eventually won. Elaine and I separated and then divorced. It was my third failed marriage; not a very good batting average. The boys, older now, seemed to understand, and were off with their own new lives in college. I decided to sever my ties with the Steps but remained friends with Bill Strauss and his family and with several other Steps. I was sorry to learn of Bill's passing several years ago. He had a superb grasp of politics, a keen mind, and a thirst for knowledge. He was also a good husband, father, and friend. I sometimes think he's up there, rewriting some of the angels' lyrics.

After the divorce, I moved to an apartment in Alexandria, Virginia, and continued to write symphonic arrangements. I conducted a couple of pop symphony concerts in Ohio and Connecticut and subbed for a few local pianists. One, Gaynor Trammer, played cocktail piano at the lovely and expensive Ritz-Carlton hotel in Georgetown. At the Ritz, the staff didn't just point you in the direction of the rest rooms, they walked you to them. But, no, they didn't stay until you were finished.

The piano we played at the Ritz was in a large, marble hallway with high ceilings and lots of echo. Even though it was a small baby grand, it made quite a big sound in that hallway. I tried to play softly to minimize the sound but, even with the soft pedal held down, it was still loud and "boomy."

One late afternoon as I was playing, a man came up and said, "My company's having a meeting in one of these conference rooms, and if you promise not to play for about an hour, I'll pay you twenty dollars." This was a first: someone was offering me money *not* to play!

Being a musician, I wanted to tell him, with a smile, that I could *not* play for twenty dollars, but he really should hear me *not* play for forty dollars! Well, I didn't say that, but I did take the money, and I went outside for a break. I wonder if he had asked me that because of the loudness or because of my pianist ability. I hope it was the former and not the latter.

As I came to work a few weeks later, I passed Gaynor in the hallway, and she stopped me and said,

"I've mentioned that I play on the train, the American Orient Express, traveling around the country, stopping in different towns, then busing passengers to different sight-seeing places? Well, I've got a trip back to L.A. next week, so I want you to cover my playing days here. Say, have you ever thought about playing on a train?"

"A train? You mean like between here and New York City?" I replied, remembering my train trips to Radio City Music Hall.

"No, a bit farther than that: Seattle, Phoenix, New Orleans, Savannah . . . "

"I love trains, but I've never thought about playing on them. I didn't even know they had pianists on board," I said.

"I know the train people are always looking for pianists, and I think with your ability, you'd be perfect. You know lots of songs, and you're the right age, if you know what I mean," she said, glancing at my white hair. "Why don't you come down to the train at Union Station next Tuesday, if you're free, and I'll show you around."

"Sounds good. I can meet you but I won't be able to stay long. I've got an afternoon gig in Bethesda at two o'clock."

We met the following Tuesday morning at 10:30, a half hour before the train was to depart, and Gaynor explained more about the train and showed me her very small, private cabin. No, it wasn't small; it was tiny—so tiny that you had to go out into the hallway to change your mind. She told me about the work hours, the food, the travel perks, etc. Each of her work trips lasted three to four weeks during the year, and she felt sure that when I returned to D.C., I could work again at the Ritz. It all sounded good to me. It would mean money, travel, and somewhat of a new musical start in the D.C. area. More importantly, what I had told her was totally true. I'd been in love with trains since first riding the *Santa Fe* from Bakersfield over the Tehachapi Loop to Glendale to visit relatives when I was was about six.

Gaynor next introduced me to several staff members, then had me try out the two different small baby grand pianos in two different rail cars; one played for cocktails, the other for after-dinner entertainment and sing-a-longs. They were real pianos, not digital keyboards, which had not yet been perfected.

"The biggest problem you'll have is keeping them in tune. I've got a tuning hammer, but I have to use it every day."

I sat down and started to play something. It was a little out of tune but definitely playable. Then, all of a sudden, there was a violent lurch and the train started moving. It was starting its next trip to California, and I wasn't supposed to be on it!

"Wait! Wait! Stop the train! Stop the train!" Gaynor yelled to no one, since we were all alone in the club car. We both started running from the middle of the car to the end, where we luckily found a conductor, talking into a radio.

"You have to stop the train," Gaynor said. "My friend and I lost track of time. He's not scheduled to be on, so you've got to stop and let him off!"

"Sorry, can't do that. Our next stop is Richmond, Virginia. Nothing before then," she said, turning back to her radio, looking peeved.

"But I don't live in Richmond, I live here," I said. "And I've got a gig in Bethesda this afternoon!"

"Well, the next station is Alexandria, Virginia. Let me radio to see if we can get permission to drop you there. This is a very busy and regulated stretch of track, so I doubt that control will let us. Sorry. That's the best I can do," she said.

Thankfully, she did get permission for the train to stop in Alexandria, but my other concern was that my car was back at Union Station. But, at least Alexandria was closer to Bethesda than Richmond, about ninety miles south. After about ten minutes of train travel through the southern part of D.C. and over the Potomac River, we slowed and stopped at the Alexandria station, which, luckily, was located right next to a Metro subway stop. I hurriedly thanked Gaynor, jumped off and waved goodbye to the train, which was now heading for Richmond, New Orleans, El Paso, and on to Los Angeles. I ran down the steps in the train station and ran up the steps to the Metro and took the first subway headed back to Union Station. I got there about twenty minutes later, claimed my car and drove to my afternoon engagement. That was a first for me and, as I heard later, a first for the train.

As it turns out, that short train ride was my first of many on the American Orient Express. My first full trip was from D.C. to New Orleans—the same route as the train from a few months before. Playing on the train was an unexpected dream come true and the gateway to my next gig and a new wife.

I made many trips on the AOE, as we called it: D.C. to New Orleans and back; Denver to Salt Lake City; Salt Lake City to Seattle; Seattle to Salt Lake City; Salt Lake City to Phoenix; and back to Salt Lake City. Two of these trips were life changing.

The first was a Salt Lake City to Phoenix trip. In Vegas, in the early '70s, I had dated Barbara Gephart, a very fine singer and musician. We dated for a couple of years but then broke up. We remained friends, however, and I ended up playing her wedding in the late '70s. We kept in contact for a while but slowly drifted apart; she had a new daughter, and I had a new wife and two sons. In the spring of 2001, she found me via email and told me that she was divorced and now living north of Phoenix in Lake Montezuma, Arizona. I told her that I, too, had just gotten divorced, had two sons, had just gotten a job playing on the trains, and would be in Phoenix on June 29th. We arranged to have lunch at the Phoenix Hyatt to catch up with each other. Of course, the train was late getting in, and since the Phoenix train station—nothing but a series of empty buildings—received just a couple of trains a week, there were no cabs. So, I had to drag my luggage about nine blocks to our rendezvous point on that sweltering Phoenix summer day.

Hot, sweaty, and looking like death warmed over, I struggled into the hotel and stowed my luggage with the bellman. I cleaned up as best I could in the men's room and found a centrally located booth in the dining area. About five iced teas later, in came Barbara Laven, née Gephart, looking just about the way she'd looked the last time I'd seen her, twenty-six or so years before. Oh, sure, we both had a few wrinkles, earned by parenthood and life's little bumps, but, to me, she looked the same.

We had lunch, talked, then had dinner, talked, then had breakfast, talked, and promised to see each other when possible. She drove me to Williams, Arizona, about three hours north, to board the train. I said goodbye, not wanting to end this brief renewal of our friendship. It was like a movie: the train slowly pulling away from the station as two people wave goodbye.

Over the next several months, we would often meet in Williams. She would drive me down to Phoenix for lunch, dinner, breakfast, and then back up to the train.

In September, we arranged for her to fly to D.C. for a visit. The plan was that she and I would drive my car back to Phoenix, where I was to start my next train trip. She arrived in

D.C. on Saturday evening. On Sunday and Monday, we talked a lot and went sightseeing, something she loved to do. Early Tuesday morning, as I checked my email, I heard and felt a loud boom. It didn't sound close, but it did sound big. I switched on the TV and, with Barbara now wide awake after the explosion, we watched the events of 9/11 unfold, including the second plane. The screen then switched to a view of the Pentagon, about a mile directly north of us in Arlington. The gaping hole in the side of the building told the story and answered all our questions about that loud boom.

We began our five-day drive to Arizona the following Thursday, avoiding most of the D.C. traffic, which was still snarled after that fateful day. The weather was beautiful: warm, dry, and with no clouds in the sky. It suddenly occurred to us that there were no contrails from high-flying jets. Of course. They had all been grounded. We also saw people lined up on all the overpasses, holding homemade signs that said, "WE ♥ THE USA." It was surreal, but seeing those signs really boosted our morale. We arrived in Lake Montezuma, and I stayed at Barbara's for a few days before I had to be in Denver, the alternate location for the start of the train's tour, necessitated by 9/11. I rented a car, waved goodbye to Barbara once again, and drove to Denver.

So, Barbara and I met in 1973, broke up in 1975, got back together in 2001 and, you guessed it, got married in 2004, partially as a result of my playing piano on a train.

The second life-changing experience happened on one of my train trips from Salt Lake City to Seattle, via the badlands of southern Wyoming. There, one morning at about 5:00 a.m., we derailed on a very bad stretch of track. We weren't going more than five miles an hour, luckily, so it was more of a shake-up than a crash. We were stuck there about eight hours before buses arrived to transport passengers to their next destination. About four hours after the derailment, a woman arrived from the home office of Oregon Rail Corporation, the parent company of the train. She was their trouble-shooter and problem-solver, Candy Westfall. After I helped get passengers onto the coaches, she and I struck up a conversation.

"So, you're the piano player I've heard about. Phil, the train's operating manager, told me about you. Sounds as if the passengers like what you do."

"Well, since most of them have the same white hair as I do, we probably feel a bit of a kinship."

"Yes, I guess so," she laughed. "Let me ask you a question. Have you ever worked on a boat, a cruise ship?"

"No, but I've been to Europe several times on them."

"Well," she said, "our company owns the *Queen of the West*, a paddle boat based in Portland, Oregon. We're in need of an assistant cruise director, someone with musical talent and good people skills. I think you'd be perfect. But I don't want you to commit until you've had a chance to see what the boat's like. It's a totally different lifestyle: small quarters, helping passengers, and lots of hours riding buses. If you can, I'd like you to visit our head office in Seattle and, hopefully, see the boat in Portland." Here was another musical challenge. It would be similar to what I'd been doing on the train, only this time, it would be on water.

26.

The Queen

Back at Barbara's place in Lake Montezuma, we talked about Candy's offer, and I decided to accept it and drive to Seattle to discuss it in greater detail. I hopped into my trusty Honda Accord and drove from Lake Montezuma to Seattle. Remember, I still had my Alexandria apartment, filled with all my furniture, clothes, books, computer, etc. During the drive, I made plans about what I should do if the job were to come through.

I arrived in Seattle on Tuesday night and met with Candy and her boss, Gary Sorrels, the next afternoon. The meeting went well, and I liked the idea of yet another challenge, but Candy thought that I should see the boat before making a decision. So, on Thursday morning, I drove south to Longview, Washington, to meet the *Queen*. I followed the directions and found the small parking lot by the river filled with three large coaches, the biggest I'd ever seen. In need of a restroom, and not seeing anything but the buses, I went over to one where a woman was standing on a small stepladder, using a squeegee to clean the coach's large front windows.

"Hi," I said.

"Hello, there. Waiting for the *Queen*?" she asked.

"Yes, I'm supposed to check it out to see if, well, if the *Queen* and I fit. Would you mind if I used the facilities on your coach?"

"No problem," she said, still washing windows. That was my first meeting with the lead bus driver, Jody Fritz, soon to be a very good friend.

Back outside the coach, I explained who I was and my possible assistant cruise director job when, suddenly, there was a long, loud whistle. We turned toward the river, and there was the *Queen of the West,* all two hundred and fifty feet of her, slowly pulling into the pier.

I stood back as about 140 passengers disembarked, boarded the coaches and drove off. A tall gentleman with streaks of gray hair came over and introduced himself as Chris Corbett, the cruise director. He was friendly, down-to-earth and very informative. I introduced myself, and told him I was hoping to be the new assistant cruise director. He said he was expecting me and gave me a thorough tour of the ship, including having me try out the digital piano, a Yamaha; it was very, very nice. I was hooked, even after he showed me my bunk in the three-man cabin. If you can believe it, this cabin was half the size of my room on the train, but with no windows, and with a shared bathroom. Ah, another challenge. But I loved it.

I thanked Chris for all his help and told him I would definitely be seeing him again. I drove back to a Longview fast food place, ate a burger and called Barbara, telling her as much as I could remember about the boat and the job details. After I hung up, I got back into the Honda and drove about 3,000 miles to Washington, D.C., arriving Sunday evening. The drive was never dull or boring, what with all the things going on in my head, the least of which was: where was I going to live?

Back in D.C., I quickly prepared for my cross-country move. Barbara and I had decided to move in together, with our first home being hers in Lake Montezuma. I sold my trusty Honda Accord, hired a truck, said farewell to my boys (now both in college), then headed west. Driving is something I enjoy. It gives me time to think, plan, and dream. And, yes, there was a bit of trepidation as well: What was I getting myself into? In what direction would my music go? At sixty, was I too old to start over? What I did have, though, was years of experience playing, producing, and arranging music— something I could never lose.

After settling into my new Arizona home, I flew to Portland, Oregon for my inaugural cruise on the *Queen*. When I first boarded, I felt quite a bit of pride, knowing that I would be the assistant cruise director of this lovely paddlewheeler. Since the boat was being readied for the next cruise, I was given a room at the DoubleTree hotel overlooking the river and my new home on the water.

Later that evening, I went on board for a meeting with some of the other staff. Candy took me aside as I entered the dining room.

"There's been a slight change in plans. Hope you don't mind, but we'd like you to be cruise director. It's a long story, but here's the deal. You and your assistant, Steve Sand, will be training with Linda Brown, the present cruise director, for one week. Then she'll leave and you'll take over as cruise director with Steve as your assistant cruise director. And the pay will be a bit more than we discussed."

Even though I'm the kind of person who likes to know as much as possible about what to expect, I've had to quickly adjust to changes or hurdles many times in my musical past. It's just part of the business. I always expected some glitch or mistake in a performance when conducting Lee's shows. If it happened, I was better prepared. If everything went well, then so much the better. I was to find out very quickly that this way of anticipating and coping with life's "alterations" would definitely come in handy

in my new job.

Once on board and ready to sail, I stowed my gear in my tiny bunk area and then met Steve, my assistant. He was a multi-talented musician with a talented mother, Margie, who also played on the boat and had for several years. Everyone on board thought of Margie as a surrogate mother. Linda Brown, the present cruise director, was very good at her position and a good singer, as well. That's one thing the company insisted upon: all cruise directors and assistants had to be able to entertain. Soon, the passengers boarded, and Steve and I began learning more about our new jobs.

The captain, Bob Wrangle, was an experienced riverboat pilot with a naval background. He was friendly, but had a strong work ethic; he wanted things done his way—the right way—or else. I learned this from watching him in the pilothouse. To me, he was similar to an agent or manager who only wants the best for his client—in this case, the passengers.

Things went fairly smoothly during our week of on-the-job training with Linda, and I fell into what I called "boat mode": up at 6:00 a.m., escorting passengers to various trips, making announcements, counting passengers as they re-board the coaches, and learning about the Columbia River and the towns that call it home. Linda was very helpful and showed me the ropes of being a cruise director.

Then it was the end of the first week. Linda left, and I was on my own as the new cruise director. There was a slight glitch, however. We were docked at the DoubleTree hotel and had just finished getting all 124 passengers and their luggage safely off the vessel, when the power on the boat suddenly went out. Instantly, the emergency power came on, and, about fifteen minutes later, the staff was told to meet in the dining room for some important information. As I entered, there was Candy, the company's trouble-shooter. This couldn't be good. She and Captain Wrangle pulled me aside.

"We've got some serious electrical issues with the boat," she said. "It's not so serious that it can't be fixed, but since there are no repair docks upriver, we'll have to do a reverse of our itinerary to keep the boat at this end of the river. This means you'll have to contact the bus drivers and let them know about the schedule change. Then contact all the excursion venues and attractions we visit to see if we can bring our passengers on a different day of the week. Oh, and you'll have a new captain," she added, introducing an older gentleman, "Gaylon Ford. He's a good guy and will help you if he can." Gaylon just nodded. "Oh, and if you've forgotten, please remember that this coming Tuesday is Christmas day. We'll be in Hood River with 110 passengers wanting something to do on that day, and I've got a feeling nothing will be open."

Gaylon chimed in, "Looks like you've got a busy first week as cruise director."

They both stood there, half-smiling, waiting for me to break down, I imagine. But, hey, this was just like conducting a symphony. There was a glitch, but the show must go on.

"I'm on it," I said, sitting at one of the empty tables with the itinerary.

I took out the company cell phone and started making calls. And, somehow, it all came together. The one exception was Christmas day in Hood River. Candy was right; nothing was open. Captain Ford came to the rescue, however, noting that the world's largest carousel museum was in Hood River. A quick phone call later, and we were informed that the museum would be happy to open for our passengers on Christmas day. They even offered one of their volunteers as Santa Claus, since there were several children with us on the cruise.

So, my first week as cruise director, although hectic, went well, and turned into eight years on the river boats. I became both cruise director and band leader with the launching of the *Empress of the North* in 2003 and sailed several times to Alaska. I had some very good assistants, on both the Columbia River and the Alaska tours, many of whom are good friends to this day.

Our Columbia River cruises on the *Queen of the West* had a weekly routine. We would leave Portland on Saturday, cruise upriver for three days and arrive at Lewiston, Idaho, on Tuesday, then turn around and cruise downriver and arrive in Astoria, Oregon, on Friday, before sailing back to Portland early Saturday morning. We'd then clean and restock the boat, board another group of passengers and do the whole trip again. Our passenger counts were high, usually 140 or so. We would stop at different ports and meet our coaches, who would pick up the passengers and take them to various scenic and historic destinations: the Pendleton Roundup, a jet boat trip in Hell's Canyon, up to Washington to view Mount St. Helens, several historic Lewis and Clark sites, etc. In the evening, different entertainers would come on board. We called them "step-ons": a seven-piece big band, a female vocal trio, various individual singers, a country-western duo, and even a juggler. We also offered dancing to a resident four-piece quartet, with me on piano, as well as lectures by various on-board historians, and, of course, lots of food.

The *Queen* was a real paddlewheeler, and so relied strictly on its paddle wheel for propulsion. If the wheel wasn't turning, we weren't moving. Our one-week trip covered about a thousand miles on the river, and this constant traveling took its toll on our vessel, meaning breakdowns. There were times when I had to muster my best face and quickly come up with an alternate plan: handling a surprise bawdy joke during our passenger talent show, or discovering that a promised tourist activity was closed and finding another activity in just a few minutes. And there were sad times, too. Our passengers averaged seventy-two years old and often developed medical problems while on board. We would quickly call for medical assistance, often pulling over to the shore to meet an ambulance. Of course, everyone would be upset when that happened, and my job was to acknowledge the incident and carry on, always a difficult thing to do. One time, I had to report the death of one of our bandmates who died of an aneurism while on board. The remaining musicians, still in shock, just couldn't play under the circumstances, so I became a one-man band, playing for all of our step-on entertainers for the week. It was yet another challenge, but not one I enjoyed having to meet.

In November of 2008, the company that owned all three of our vessels, plus the three famous paddlewheelers on the Mississippi, went bankrupt, leaving all of us high and dry—literally. One of the pianists on board, Reece Marshburn, had left the boat and taken a job at a Portland supper club. He invited Barbara and I there on one of my times off the boat, and we met Tony Starlight, the club's owner and chief entertainer. Tony is a remarkable man: extremely talented, and a club owner with a conscience, something rare in this business. Oh, and he's also an Aries, like me. I had agreed to do a couple arrangements for him while still working on the boat, and when the boat job came to an end, I began working at his club, playing and arranging various shows, including a duo that Barbara and I do.

I've been with Tony ever since and do shows with Barbara's group, Signatures, all over the great northwest; I also have some arranging gigs with the Tacoma Symphony and other orchestras.

My present schedule has me up at about 5:30 a.m., feeding and watering the cats, then heading to the music room to create musical arrangements: trio charts for the AX2 (Ayars Times Two) Vocal Workshops taught by Barbara; charts for Barbara's female quartet; eight-piece arrangements for Tony Starlight's shows; seventy-piece symphony arrangements for Signatures; and jotting down memories of the past seventy-four years. Looking back, it's always been about the music: something that has come naturally to me, and something that has made my life what it is.

BO, AS CRUISE DIRECTOR

ON THE . . .

QUEEN OF THE WEST

DAVE DUTHIE AND BO ENTERTAINING
ON THE *QUEEN OF THE WEST*

Postlude:

A Closing Piece of Music, Especially for the Organ

Living and working in Vegas, it really was tempting to get caught up in the glitter and glamour, and in wanting to be noticed, admired, and talked about. And, I think in the beginning, I was like that and let my ego get in my way.

A few years after I began living and working in Vegas, as I watched people try to be someone they weren't and do things they'd never do back in their home towns, I unconsciously adopted the following attitudes:

1) You can never be perfect, so

2) Always try to do your best at whatever you're doing, and

3) If you think you're so great that you've got it made, you're at your lowest.

I believe these are the right attitudes for me, and now, at seventy-four, I'm comfortable with being a fairly successful musician. I'm not perfect, but I've always tried to do my best and, as far as I know, have never thought I've "got it made."

I look around at young musicians and smile as they go through the same musical frustrations that I went through. But some of their frustrations aren't the same. There have been major changes in musical styles and perceptions. The volume of the music is almost more important than its melody, rhythm, and harmony. Modern technology allows for more people to be musicians and singers, but not always of the best quality. Music venues, both in Portland and Las Vegas, have entertainers and musicians perform for little or no money, telling them that "exposure" is payment enough.

Yet it *is* more about the money than ever before. I was in Vegas when Howard Hughes took over several casino-hotels, put the more unsavory owners out of work and put an end to the famous Vegas experience of almost-free food, drink, and entertainment. Even though it was called "Sin City," it was always fun. As my wife, Barbara, points out, everyone dressed up every night and showed style. Las Vegas has definitely changed since I first worked at the Aladdin Hotel in 1966. It's lost its charm, its freewheeling, twenty-four-hour excitement. I'd like Barbara to comment on her perspective of these changes:

In May of 2011, Bo and I went to Las Vegas for a vacation and to meet with the head of the Liberace Foundation. The trip gave us a chance to connect with old friends and to visit our old haunts of so many years before. Our visit was an emotional journey, to say the least. So much has changed since the salad days of the Rat Pack, Liberace, Steve and Eydie, Bobby Vinton, the Folies Bergere, and the Lido de Paris. The enclosed, luxuriously dark lounges featuring such acts as Don Rickles, Shecky Greene, B.B. King, Little Anthony and the Imperials, and A Bare Touch of Vegas have been replaced by open areas with a band stuck in the corner—if at all—and drowned out by the sound of the constantly dinging slot machines, the screaming, T-shirt-clad penny slot winners, and the loud conversations of families milling around the casino floor.

Las Vegas is not the only shock to the system. In researching the venues of that era, I've found that the theaters-in-the-round have evolved, too. Warwick's lovely tent theater run by Buster and Barbara Bonoff (who also had the Star Theater in Phoenix) is now a Lowe's, and Melody Fair in North Tonawanda is a Walmart. Oakdale Theatre in Wallingford, Connecticut is still running, but is a permanent proscenium structure—not the intimate showplace of the past.

I think half the fun of these places was being crammed in on a hot summer night in New England, sweating to your favorite performer, close enough to touch him or her, and loving every minute of the sweltering experience. When I was a backup singer for Bobby Vinton, I remember changing after the performances and having to pick off the sequins that had attached themselves to me during the two-hour show. These were true love-fests between performer and audience. Those six-week tours in the summer were a highlight of the performing life. We'd charter a bus and stay a week in each city—something unheard of now in this era of one-night stands.

So, what happened to change things so drastically? To begin with, Las Vegas hotel-casinos transitioned from being individually owned (yes, by the mafia) to being corporate run. They're managed more by accountants and less by people who know and care about entertainment and understand its important contribution to the success of the whole operation. The lounges were originally run not as moneymaking entities, but as comfortable, entertaining places designed to provide respite to weary gamblers: they could regroup, see a top-notch show, have a few drinks and then return to the casino floor, ready to spend more money. Makes sense, doesn't it? People would stay in one casino instead of hopping from one to the next, or aimlessly walking the Strip. Enter the concept that every facet of every hotel-casino must make a profit, must pull its weight financially, and exit the classic Las Vegas scene.

Gigs in Las Vegas lounges used to be the primo jobs, the goal of every traveling band. The Vegas lounges paid the most and offered the most exposure, as well as access to the stars who appeared in the showrooms. The lounges now pay less than most clubs in cities around the country and often offer only duos and trios instead of full bands. If a production show is offered, the music is recorded, replacing musicians who would have been paid for their performances. It is a bare-bones operation at best and provides no incentive for customers to stay in the casino.

The showrooms are another story. One of the rooms Bo and I both worked was the Versailles Room at the Riviera Hotel. It was a beautiful venue with bluish-purple booths and lush carpeting, a pleasure in every respect. During our visit, we slipped through the door leading to the showroom floor and *were* floored, indeed. The room was closed, the booths were not arranged, dust was the common finish on all the furniture, and sadness was the emotion of the day. A security guard came in to check on us, and we struck up a conversation, thinking it might be the best way to avoid being taken out in handcuffs.

The current state of the music industry seems to mirror our entire economy. There are the wildly successful, and the struggling-to-make-a-living musicians/performers. The middle ground is sparsely populated, meaning it is very difficult to make a living and feed a family as a musician. The Musicians Union has little power, except in the symphony realm, but symphonies are bleeding across the country, and salaries are being reduced. Even our sacred Broadway has felt the slings and arrows of the assault on live music. One player with a synthesizer/keyboard can artificially duplicate the sound of an entire orchestra. This is appealing to the money people, who don't discriminate between the digital, sterile sound of a keyboard and the warm richness of a real orchestra. They just see one salary versus twenty-five to thirty. Who wins? Musicians certainly don't, nor do performers, who become energized by the lush sound of a live orchestra. The audience? Many don't notice a difference, but many do. It's the equivalent of "dumbing down," but for purely financial reasons.

Thanks, Zel. (My nickname for Barbara is Zelda.)

So, that's my story, up until now. Looking back, it seems like a lot: all the practicing; the need for acceptance and the fear of rejection; helping to raise two boys; hanging with celebrities and politicians; being in a movie and on TV specials; making and producing records; and, oh, yes, slapping the president-elect's hand. Lots of funny and painful experiences, but mostly what's kept me going is the fun of music. I'm so glad

I've had such wonderful people touch my life: my parents who believed in me; my teachers who showed me a better way; my close friends who always supported me; Judy, Cheryl, and Elaine; and my wife, Barbara, who keeps reminding me of the importance of honesty and hard work. Yes, I've had hurdles, some of which I created myself. But, for the most part, I've enjoyed those hurdles, those challenges.

And my hope is that interesting challenges keep coming my way for at least one more lifetime, to allow me to, again, pick up my baton, a number 2 pencil, sit at a piano with 88 keys and work, musically, with a showman like Liberace. It's a nice thought . . .

ALWAYS SOMETHING TO DO, MUSICALLY

SONS EVAN AND JJ (JUSTIN) AYARS

BO, GIVING THE "JOE GUERCIO" LOOK

BO AND BARBARA

CPSIA information can be obtained at www.ICGtesting.com
Printed in the USA
BVOW08s0954010616

450161BV00015B/12/P